21 YESTERDAYS

by Joseph E. Pluta

Produced by:

FriesenPress
Suite 300 – 852 Fort Street
Victoria, BC, Canada V8W 1H8

www.friesenpress.com

Distributed to the trade by The Ingram Book Company

Contents

For my Grandchildren and for Theirs

Author's Note

This is a work of historical fiction. Names of such people as politicians, inventors, entertainers, and other well-known individuals are real. Names of several towns, universities, business establishments, and public places such as rivers and lakes are real.

Other characters, communities, and incidents are the product of the author's imagination or are used fictitiously. In these cases, any resemblance to actual persons, living or dead, is entirely coincidental.

'03 Three Oaks

After passing through the small community of Galien, the west-bound Michigan Central locomotive spewed hot ash from its coal fired boiler as it resumed full speed. Inside, the train's conductor opened the door to the last of its four passenger cars and quickly closed it behind him.

"Three Oaks!" he yelled in a loud compelling voice. "Next stop, Three Oaks!"

Almira Lawson, a spinster in her early sixties and teacher at the local school, reached for the small bag of books she had purchased in Detroit. It had been an exhausting and bittersweet Christmas trip but one she felt the need to make. Her mother, now in failing health, was unlikely to visit southwestern Michigan again.

With frequent stops to load and unload passengers as well as to stock up on coal and water, the 200 mile haul had taken over five hours.

As she disembarked, Almira noticed her dear friend, Josephine Meister, waiting in her heavy winter coat and scarf.

"Hello, Jo!" she proclaimed as she hugged the only slightly younger woman. "It's great to see you and good to be back home."

"How's your mother?" Jo asked.

"Not that well," came the reply. "But she's managing. How was the holiday here?"

"Quiet and nice."

As the door to the baggage car closed, Almira handed the books to her friend and secured her suitcase. With their full length dresses nearly touching the ground, the ladies then walked past the stores on Elm Street.

A horse and open buggy briskly drove past as the methodical "clop clop" sound of the horse's hoofs could be heard loud and clear. The couple seated under a blanket waved. With the ground frozen solid, pedestrians did not have to shield their faces from the dust. The smell of horse manure, however, was still strong since the streets were cleaned less frequently in winter.

Two men, puffing on cigars, tipped their hats as they walked past the ladies and addressed them by their first names. With cigars now in hand, each took their turn spitting in the direction of the cuspidor positioned outside the general store. One scored a direct hit while the second missed badly before shrugging his shoulders while glancing at his companion.

Downtown Three Oaks in 1903 was little more than a handful of small shops plus the Warren Featherbone factory. Ten minutes after leaving the train station, the twosome arrived at Almira's house on Maple Street.

"Come on in," the traveler offered. "I'll make some hot coffee."

Jo lived alone a block away on Cherry Street. Her husband had died three years earlier. Since that time, she had worked at Featherbone helping to make products ranging from women's corsets to buggy whips. She also wrote instruction booklets called the *Featherbone Magazinette* for distribution to dressmakers and retailers. When asked, she composed company ads for the *Ladies Home Journal* and other magazines.

Jo put some birch logs and paper into the potbelly stove while Almira began to unpack her baggage. After setting aside the lace kerchiefs she had bought for Jo, she filled an iron coffee pot with water. Since the hand pump had not been used in a few days, it took some extra arm strokes to get it primed. When the pot was full, the overflow fell into the metal pan that sat on the stand next to the pump. There was no sink or any other type of indoor plumbing fixture.

Almira then inserted several spoonfuls of coffee grounds and placed the pot on top of the stove. Within minutes, the ladies sat comfortably at the pine kitchen table and began sipping their black coffee.

"Shall I make a fire in the fireplace so we can rest on the sofa in the front room?" Almira asked.

"Only if you'll need it for later," Jo replied. "I'm fine here. I probably shouldn't stay that long. You must be tired."

"Very much so," Almira affirmed. "But I don't need a nap. It'll be nice to catch up on what has happened in town over the past few days."

"Not a great deal," Jo said with a laugh. "I did feed your horses every day. And made sure the door to the barn stayed shut. I can assure you they both were warm. It wasn't that nasty out anyway. It was colder the week before you left."

"Thank you for helping me out," Almira said with a warm smile. "Were you able to leave town at all?"

"On Christmas day," Jo began before clearing her throat, "I hitched up my horse and rode to New Buffalo. Had dinner at the home of George and Martha Holtz. It was a lot of fun."

"How are things in the booming town on the lake?" Almira asked. "It's been months since I've gotten over there."

"The Holtz's said two new families bought farms out on Germany Road," Jo answered. "Both are immigrants from just outside Berlin but they've lived in Michigan for the past ten years. Right in town, there's a new pickle factory and a new glass factory. George and Martha also took me for a ride on the path along the water. Some cottages are being built there. The owners are expecting yet more tourists once summer gets here."

She paused for a moment before resuming her description.

"We even saw three different horseless carriages," she added with a look of disdain. "Those contraptions are so noisy, they scared our horses. The smoke they make smells awful. We spoke to one of the families. They drove all the way from Chicago. Why would anyone do that when the train goes directly from Chicago to New Buffalo?"

"Beats me," Almira assured. "Rich people need their toys even if they are a nuisance to the rest of us."

"I'll never get in one of those," Jo stated confidently. "I read somewhere that, when people are exposed to that kind of speed for too long, it can cause body parts to come off and even death."

"Now Jo," Almira questioned. "I just went faster on the MC than any horseless carriage can go. And I'm just fine."

"That's different," Jo replied. "Maybe because you were inside. And the rails make the ride a lot smoother than those bumpy paths. Trains don't get stuck in the mud."

"You're right about the last point," Almira conceded. "Horseless carriages were everywhere in Detroit. I saw horses throw their riders they were so spooked by the weird noises. And, unlike horses, that machine's always breaking down. If you don't know how to fix it, you're stranded wherever it leaves you. There are a lot of back streets in Detroit where I'd never want to be stranded. Life is so much better here in Three Oaks."

"That's for sure," Jo said while nodding. "So what else did you see in that dirty, awful city?"

"They did have a pretty good sized bookstore. Much nicer than the one over in Michigan City. I brought back five or six books that I hope to read before school starts up. And I'm happy to share them with you."

"Exciting. Tell me about them."

Almira reached into her bag and pulled out each book one at a time.

"This one is called *The Wonderful Wizard of Oz*, a delightful children's story by a man named Lyman Frank Baum. He's already written a lot of different things. Let's see. *The Awakening* is about life in Louisiana, especially New Orleans. The author is Kate Chopin. Don't know that much about her. I thought I'd read *The School and Society*. This fellow John Dewey has some fascinating ideas about the future of education. Charlotte Perkins Gilman is an interesting writer. Her book *Women and Economics* talks about how women have been placed in an inferior position to men, especially when it comes to employment. As a hard working woman in a factory, you might relate to it. I've always wanted to read *The Time Machine* by H. G. Wells. And finally, here it is. The most interesting book I bought is called *The Theory of the Leisure Class* by some young economist named Thorstein Veblen. I don't think he's ever written anything before but it's a hot seller. It's hard to read but he is witty and a master at satire. His style reminds me of Joseph Conrad."

"Wow!" was all Jo could say as her big eyes glanced at the whole pile. "Which one can I borrow?"

"I'm reading the books by Dewey, Gilman, and Veblen first," Almira answered. "After that, take your pick."

"I think I might like to start with *The Time Machine*, if that's okay," Jo declared.

"Here it is," Almira said as she handed the book to her friend. "Enjoy it. But don't tell me how it ends."

"Anything else about Detroit that you'd like to share with me?" Jo asked.

"There is," Almira replied. "I read something very strange buried way in the back of the Detroit newspaper. The story said that, a couple of weeks ago, two brothers down in North Carolina were the first ever to operate a flying machine. Their name was something like Wrightman or Wrightberg. I can't remember exactly."

"That's not right," Jo stated. "Everybody around here knows that guy up in St. Joe flew his flying machine, what, four years ago?"

"Guess they hadn't heard about that in Detroit," Almira offered. "I remember it pretty well. The man's name is Augustus Herring and he flew twice in October of '99. There was a story in our very own *Three Oaks Press*."

"I know a flying machine is not that big of a deal," Jo injected, accurately reflecting the attitude of the time. "But hey, Herring did it first. He should get the credit. How come he doesn't?"

"I have a couple of ideas," the always thoughtful Almira observed. "I don't think anybody took a photo of the machine when it was off the ground up in St. Joe. The Detroit paper said photos of what happened in North Carolina do exist. In this day and age of having to verify something, a picture sure helps."

"Yeah, I guess so," Jo agreed. "What I remember is that Herring didn't brag that much about what he had done. Sometimes you have to toot your own horn a little bit to get people to notice you."

"Maybe," Almira noted, still in deep thought. "The Detroit paper said something about other attempts having been made. But the machines didn't stay up as long as the one on the Atlantic Ocean beach. I think the article also said something about being able to steer it better than what earlier flyers had done."

"That seems like a rather minor point," Jo stated. "Do you think that's really why the big city papers are ignoring what was done in a small town just 25 miles from here? Is flying close to the ocean a bigger deal than flying near our own Lake Michigan?"

"I have another idea why Augustus Herring isn't getting the credit," Almira said reflectively. "At the time he flew, something more important was going on around here."

"Of course!" Jo exclaimed as if a light bulb had instantly gone off in her head. "That was the same week President McKinley was in town."

"Exactly," Almira confirmed with a smile as if one of her students had just given her a correct answer to one of her questions.

"I remember that day well," Jo continued. "My Harry was still alive. He was so proud he actually got to see a president of the United States. We don't know what any of the other presidents even looked like. This one we saw in person. What a glorious day."

"I can still see McKinley stepping off the train that Tuesday evening, waving to everyone, shaking hands with Mayor Warren, giving his speech." Almira paused before continuing her recollection. "There must have been five or even six hundred people in the crowd from all over southwestern Michigan and northern Indiana."

"Everyone in town was filled with a patriotic spirit," Jo added. "Of all the towns in the whole country, we raised more money for the Spanish American War cannon than any of them."

"Actually," Almira corrected politely, "it was more money *per capita*. No matter. The cannon captured by Admiral Dewey in Cuba will always be right here in Three Oaks. What a tribute to the men of this entire area who fought there."

"That's exactly what my Harry said," Jo added. "It was a proud moment for all of us native Oakers. I wonder how long it will take for another president to come here. Bill McKinley was one of a kind. I curse that damn Pollock who murdered him in New York."

"Jo Meister!" Almira scolded. "You and I have many friends in town who are of Polish descent. They are all fine, hard-working people. Leon Czolgosz was an anarchist and a bit out of his mind. He is anything but typical of the Poles here in Three Oaks or anywhere else in this country."

"Yeah, I know that," Jo confessed. "I just get so upset such a good man was killed so senselessly. I know this Teddy Roosevelt was a war hero but I still worry if he'll be a good president."

"Time will tell on that," Almira offered. "Anyway, my point in bringing all this up is that all the out of town newspaper reporters were more interested in what was going on here than in St. Joseph. Don't you think Augustus Herring would have had a picture taken of him in his flying machine if all in the press weren't more excited about the president coming to our town?"

"You always have such an interesting take on things," Jo acknowledged respectfully.

"Would you like more coffee?" Almira offered.

"Yes, I would, if you're going to have some," Jo said without hesitation. "This conversation is so stimulating. I really missed sharing thoughts with you. You must be a great teacher. I always learn something whenever we visit. I can't wait to get started on the H. G. Wells book."

"Tell me more about the last few days," Almira requested.

"Work at the factory has been hectic," Jo answered. "Old Edward Warren keeps us hopping. That's okay. I'm getting a raise. Pretty soon I'll be making $4 a week."

"Now that *is* good news," Almira acknowledged with a huge grin. "He recognizes talent. Congratulations!"

"There's a lot of other stuff going on, though," Jo stated with a look of concern. "The clothing tastes of women are changing. The new styles don't need featherbone. So Mr. Warren wants to start making other items like ribbon, braid, and maybe even elastic."

"He's pretty good at identifying fashion changes," Almira reassured. "I'm sure the business will adjust to the times just fine."

"We are starting to make more of the featherbone attachment for sewing machines," Jo admitted. "He got the patent for it eight years ago and it's finally starting to sell."

"Don't worry," Almira reiterated. "Did you do anything else while I was gone?"

"I rode out to Forest Lawn cemetery to visit Harry's grave," Jo stated with a frown. "I sure do miss him."

"I'm certain you do," Almira sympathized. "He was a good man. He worked hard and he always went to church."

"At the service last Sunday," Jo now recalled, "the minister asked about getting some volunteers to help him do some painting. If Harry were here, he'd be the first one in line. Living so close to the church on the corner of Elm and Sycamore made it hard for him to turn down any request for help. In his younger days, Harry wanted to be a Methodist minister but he never got the chance to get much schooling."

Jo stopped abruptly.

"I'm sorry," she added. "I know I'm running at the mouth. Forgive me."

"Don't apologize," Almira stated reassuringly. "Everyone in town misses your husband. If there were more men like him around, I might've even gotten married myself."

"You always know what to say," Jo mumbled softly as she wiped away a tear. "I should probably get home. I need to feed my own horse."

"Thanks again for meeting me at the station," Almira said with a smile. "Oh, I almost forgot. I brought something for you."

She then exited the kitchen area before returning with the kerchiefs.

"These are for you. For taking care of my horses."

"They're so beautiful," Jo acknowledged.

The ladies hugged once more and Jo ventured out into the brisk late afternoon.

After little more than a minute, Almira heard a knock at her front door. It was Jo.

"Forget something?" Almira asked.

"Did I ever," came the flustered sounding reply. "I don't know what I was thinking. You must be starving. I intended to have you stop by for some supper. Out in my shed, I have some half frozen salami, Polish sausage, cheese, and bread. I got the smoked meat at Drier's Smoke House day before yesterday. How about if I cook it up and you come by in an hour or so?"

"Well…," Almira hesitated. "I am a little hungry. Alot actually. I was just going to look in on the horses, see what food's in my storage shed, visit the outhouse, and get cleaned up for bed. I'll probably fall asleep by 8 o'clock."

"Perfect," Jo answered convincingly. "If it's okay, I'll bring the food and cook it on your stove. Back in an hour?"

"You're a good friend," Almira said appreciatively. "Just come in the front door when you get here. You know I never lock it anyway."

Almira put her coat back on and reacquainted herself with her horses who seemed glad to see her. She took both for a brief walk before pouring them some grain and seeing to it they were set for the night.

Back inside her house, she heated some water on the stove and took it into her bedroom. There she began to peel off the several layers of clothing she had worn on the trip home. She poured the water into a basin and washed herself with bars of soap and a wash-cloth. The warm water felt soothing.

After dressing in her floor length winter sleeping gown with heavy stockings and slippers, she lit the oil lamp and took it from the living room into the kitchen. Jo was already there frying the Polish sausage in a skillet and warming the bread on a flat tin pan.

"See," Almira felt compelled to say, "here's yet another reason we should all appreciate Polish people. What would we all do without their magnificent sausage? Especially during winters when we have no vegetables."

As they ate after giving thanks, their thoughtful conversation resumed.

"So what other books did you consider buying?" Jo began.

"Half the volumes in the store," Almira replied without hesitation. "I really wanted to read *Resurrection* by Leo Tolstoy, *Three Sisters* by Anton Chekov, *The Call of the Wild* by Jack London, *Rebecca of Sunnybrook Farm* by Kate Douglas Wiggin, and *Up From Slavery* by Booker T. Washington."

"You're amazing," was all Jo could say. Almira was just getting started.

"I also wanted to get something new by Mark Twain," she blurted out. "A sign in the store said he was awarded an honorary doctorate of literature degree from the University of Missouri last year. What a writer!"

"And I so admire Jane Addams," she continued. "She has a book out with a title something like *Democracy and Social Ethics*. Some day I want to visit Hull House in Chicago."

"You must be the smartest person in Berrien County," Jo stated with admiration. "You are certainly one of the few women in the county to go to college."

"I only spent a year at Michigan State," Almira recalled. "Then my parents' money ran out. I read everything I could there. And I've never stopped. Now I'm the one who's rambling. Sorry."

"What do you think the next twenty years or so will be like?" Jo asked without even thinking her friend was running on. Instead, she wanted to tap her brain before Almira tired physically.

"Well, I'd tell you but you'd think I was crazy," Almira admitted humbly.

"Oh no," Jo pleaded. "I asked. And I'm all ears. What's going to happen?"

"Of course," Almira began, "nobody can predict the future. Not even H. G. Wells. But here's where I've been thinking we *might* be headed."

"So many new inventions are coming along. Some day these horseless carriages will be perfected once someone gets all the bugs out. Somebody somewhere may even figure out how to make them go faster and be more affordable so more people can have them. And those flying machines? Just imagine if people could get from one place to another by flying through the air. One of those new gadgets they call a telephone is in our train station. People think they're kind of silly but, if I had one in my house and you had one in your house, we could talk to each other without walking over. Imagine if someone in, say, Washington could talk to someone in California. And that Thomas Edison fellow is a genius. No telling what he might invent next. Some hotels in Detroit are lit up by electricity. What if all houses are some day? Sound can be recorded and played back. What if we could listen to music over and over again without having to hear a band play it? Edison, I'm told, has come up with a way to take pictures that move just like we do. What do you think of that? And you know what? There is still more stuff that no one has invented. Who knows what the limit is? So, do you think I'm crazy yet? A lot of people would if I dared to say anything like this to someone besides you."

Jo just sat speechless with a distant puzzled look on her face as if she was incapable of grasping what was being said.

"At least that's a view from little old Three Oaks," Almira concluded. "And no one in the big cities cares what anybody here thinks."

The Iowa Trip

The last week in January was brutally cold in Ironwood, geographically the most western town in Michigan. On a Saturday night, Carlo and his friends celebrated his twentieth birthday, the most significant event in all their lives since graduation barely eight months earlier. Some of the guys were feeling antsy to take a road trip, just to get away. They knew that, wherever they went, it would be impossible to escape the weather entirely, if at all. But a change of scenery was clearly on their minds.

A few of their former classmates were off at assorted colleges either instate, in bordering Wisconsin, or in nearby Minnesota. Carlo and his two closest friends, Mort and Dom, occasionally talked about one day taking courses at Gogebic Community College. For now, all three worked locally during the day and practiced their instruments most evenings. Forming a band was presumably high on their list of priorities as was chasing high school girls who were impressed with their freedom and their cars, if not their looks.

By any measure, the three were underachievers who possessed more fun loving capacity than drive. If, in their present state in life, they were less than thoroughly happy, they were certainly content. Mostly, they plugged along as if they were waiting for some magical event to occur, something that would change their lives and transport them to….whatever. The initiative for making something positive happen on their own, however, was sorely lacking.

"Interested in drivin' over ta Escanaba next weekend?" Mort asked as the three of them sipped beers. "There's supposed to be some new bands playin' on Friday night", he added.

"I dunno," Dom offered. "I saw the ad and, honestly, I never heard of any of 'em. They get much better groups there durin' the summer."

"I hear ya'", Carlo pitched in. "But remember, we don't just go there for the music."

"The girls are no better than here," Mort snapped. "We already struck out over der a couple a times. It's just not the happy huntin' ground it used to be."

"You talk like an old man," Dom injected. "What else we got ta do? The malt shop on Suffolk Street is pretty slow on Friday nights."

"We need ta plan somethin' special as a birthday present for Carlo," Mort suggested.

"Like what?" Dom stated almost defiantly.

"Well," Mort answered, "if you could go anywhere you want, Mr. 'No Longer a Teenager' Carlo, where would it be?"

"You mean like Hawaii?" came the response.

"I'm serious," Mort egged on. "We could all take a few days off, maybe even a week, and drive somewhere different. Minneapolis? Milwaukee? Canada?"

"Been ta all those places way too much already," Dom offered, although he actually had not. "Even they are quieter than usual this time a year. It's the ski lodges up near Marquette that're jumpin'."

"None of us can ski worth a damn," Carlo countered. "We'd probably just break a leg or somethin'. No thanks to that idea."

Undeterred, Dom was ready to try a second plan. "We could drive down ta Illinois where my brother and his wife live," he mentioned casually. "We'd have a place ta stay for free. And there's more ta do in their town than here."

"Where do they live?" Carlo asked. "And what's to do there?"

"Peoria. There are some decent nightspots and some of 'em even have bands durin' the week. Did I mention girls?"

"It sounds pretty far," Carlo replied. "We wouldn't be able to make it in one day in this weather. Are you sure it's worth it?"

"If we got an early start, we could do it," Dom insisted. "My parents drive there in one day all the time."

Mort had a plan of his own. "My sister lives in Ohio," he said. "She goes ta college in Youngstown. Got an apartment off campus with one other girl. We could go der."

"That's *really* far," Dom answered. "It would take forever and all they have there is a bunch a steel mills. If we wanted dirty air, Gary, Indiana is a lot closer."

"My cousin, Cal, lives in Clear Lake, Iowa" Carlo added. "You guys remember him. The town is in a neat little resort area on a lake. It's pretty cool for a smaller town."

"Your cousin's not that much fun," Mort objected. "All he talks about is gettin' his pilot's license."

"Just 'cause he's more focused than we are doesn't make Cal a bad guy," Carlo retorted. "He wants to do what his Dad's been doin' for years. It must be neat to jump in a plane whenever you want. Hey, we used to have lots a fun when we were kids. Go badmouth someone in your family. Cal's okay."

"How about this?" Dom suggested. "Let's nix Mort's sister in Ohio. But maybe we can combine stops in Peoria and Clear Lake. They can't be more than a couple hundred miles apart. Two days or so in each place. Whaduya think?"

"Can both of you get a week or so off work?" Carlo asked, addressing the most practical aspect of the plan.

The others nodded before Mort added: "This time a year should be no problem."

On Wednesday morning, January 28, the three adventurers began the long trek to points south. At first, it was cold but clear and the roads looked passable since it had snowed only lightly in the last few days. There was certainly no traffic. Since the car radio did not work, the guys had few distractions. Whichever two were not driving served as willing, and mostly capable, copilots.

After the first hour, they encountered some icy spots on the lonely two lane thoroughfare that wound through heavily wooded areas. When the car skid a couple of times, all agreed it was wise to reduce speed. By early afternoon, the temperature dropped to nearly twenty below. Thanks to a perfectly functioning heater, the group remained confident but cautious, as most who had been raised in the U P were. They knew there was no point in taking unnecessary chances.

The hilly Wisconsin countryside looked like a winter wonderland postcard. While site seeing was not their main objective, all three passengers admitted to each other on more than one occasion that they were enjoying the scenery. Each small town had its own charming features, most of which the guys appreciated only a little. When hungry, they stopped for a sandwich and asked how far it was to the Illinois state line.

It seemed to get flatter the farther south they went. It certainly did not get any warmer. Rolling pastures with trees interspersed at irregular intervals were now replaced by silos and the remnants of cornfields. An occasional freight train broke the monotony of Illinois prairies that were more functional in warm weather than scenic in winter.

Despite having to travel at slower than average speeds, the group arrived in Peoria by early evening just in time to catch some night spots after checking in with Dom's brother. The youthful married couple even accompanied the younger trio on their less than exciting evening out. There was music to hear at a handful of places that were different from those in the U P or in northern Wisconsin. There were even occasional female dancing partners, none of whom would ever be mistaken for a potential love of anyone's life.

The guys agreed to stay a second night more out of respect for Dom's family than any promise of a soon to be realized earth shattering experience. After the locals both went to work in the morning, the Michigan crew checked out some of the more unusual places that were recommended to them. Historic old buildings and the Bradley University campus were fun to look at for a few minutes but were not exactly their cup of tea. They told each other they were on vacation and to enjoy whatever they could see that was not available in Ironwood.

The music was better the second night but the social encounters were about the same. When they got back long before midnight, the group agreed it was time to head for Clear Lake the next day.

This leg of the journey began in mid morning. After passing through Rock Island, they entered Iowa. The bridge across the Mississippi River was impressive but the mere sight of the water below sent a shiver through the otherwise warm passengers in the car.

After being on the road awhile, they decided to stop at the first restaurant they found. It was not that far to Clear Lake, they reasoned, so there was no need to make time on the highway. When they arrived in the town of Tipton, a small place called Al's Meet and Eat Restaurant on Cedar Street looked most inviting.

A rickety old bus passed by as the threesome stepped out into the cold.

The guys dashed inside as quickly as they could and sat in a booth near the front window. Middle-aged men and women, who were probably local, filled two small tables and the lunch counter. A waitress named Ester was friendly as she took everyone's order. Three burgers and fries were about to get consumed along with two cokes and a 7-up.

As everyone took their last bite, six frozen looking young men walked in faster than Carlo and his friends had entered a half hour or so earlier. All in the larger group kept blowing into their hands as they looked for a place to sit where they could remain reasonably close together.

Suddenly, Carlo nearly spilled his drink.

"Oh my God!" he said softly, trying not to draw attention. "Do you realize who those guys are?"

Mort looked up slowly and was the next to speak.

"That's definitely Ritchie Valens and Dion," he affirmed in a slightly louder voice than Carlo had used.

"The big guy is the Big Bopper," Dom quickly added as if it was now a contest to identify the new restaurant patrons. "I don't know about the tall one," he continued.

Many fans still did not know who Tommy Allsup was. Or Waylon Jennings. But they were the new lead and base guitarists who backed Buddy Holly now that the original Crickets were not with him.

"I recognize the guy with the dark greased back hair," Carlo observed. "That's Carlo Mastrangelo of the Belmonts."

"It figures you'd know the guy with your name," Mort quipped.

The three Michiganders continued to glance across at the tables where the musicians were seated as Ester took everyone's order. After turning it in to the cook, she approached Carlo, Mort, and Dom.

"Anything else for you guys?" she asked, "Or are you ready for the check?"

Still in a daze, Mort finally answered. "Oh…yeah…sure," he said nearly stuttering all three single syllable words. "You can bring the check whenever you like. But, if it's okay, we might sit here awhile. Do you know who those guys are?"

"Sure thing, honey," came the reply. "I'll have your check in a second. You mean that big bunch over there? No, I just know they're not from around here. Just another two tables of customers. They're all real friendly and polite, though. Friends of yours?" she asked as she turned away indicating no particular interest in learning anyone's identity.

Moments later, Ritchie Valens stood up and walked over to the jukebox. Looking at Ester, he said softly: "Would you like to hear the song I made famous?"

Still not knowing who he was and thinking he was merely pulling her leg, she agreed with minimal expectation.

Except for Carlo and his two friends, no one else in the place seemed impressed. At the other tables, conversations simply resumed until the music began and Ritchie sang along as if he were over-dubbing his own voice.

"Oh Donna, oh Donna. I had a girl, Donna was her name……"

Ester and her co-worker named Betty were the first to take notice. Soon thereafter, all of the previously disinterested locals began to watch the celebrity in their midst. The kid did have quite a voice, they must have thought. And he did sound just like the voice on the jukebox. A number of them nodded as if they recognized the song. When Ritchie finished, there was a round of applause.

Carlo, Mort, and Dom could sit still no longer. They jumped to their feet and walked toward the singers.

"That was terrific, Ritchie," Carlo blurted out as if he had known the singer for years. "What are you guys doin' here in this little town?"

"We're on tour and the heater in our bus went out," Ritchie replied as he extended his hand. "These are my friends: Jape, Dion, Carlo, Tommy, and Waylon."

"Where you from?" Dion asked.

"Ironwood, Michigan," Dom responded.

"Ironwood?" J. P. howled in a deep voice that sounded like he was about to say "Hellooo Baby." "Is that anywhere near Duluth? We're all gonna be up there shortly, if the bus makes it."

"Yeah," Mort answered. "Pretty close. Only about 90 miles away. I had no idea you were gonna be der. Maybe we shoulda stayed home and gone ta see ya."

"We'll be in Fort Dodge tonight," Waylon stated calmly. "Are y'all headed that way?"

"Naw," Carlo replied, outwardly showing his disappointment. "Only goin' as far as Clear Lake before we head back home."

All of the entertainers grinned as they looked at each other before Ritchie spoke.

"Clear Lake must be where it's at," he said. "We just found out we'll be playing there on Monday night. A place called the Surf Ballroom. Monday was supposed to be an open date on the tour but we got booked at the last minute."

"Are you staying there 'till Monday?" Tommy Allsup asked.

"We might now!" Dom stated with a gleam in his eye, "if Carlo's cousin lets us bed down at his place that long."

"Where's Buddy Holly?" Carlo felt compelled to inquire, realizing that this must be the Winter Dance Party tour he had heard about back at home.

"Last we saw him, he was with the rest of the guys across the alley at the car dealer where they're trying to fix the bus heater," Dion offered. "He seemed to be pretty excited about the new Edsels on display there."

All the other singers laughed. They knew Buddy loved cars but was unlikely to make an Edsel his next choice.

"Or they may be checking out winter coats over at a department store," Dion added. "We just came from there. Ritchie and these guys from Texas aren't used to this kind of cold. Hey, it's a lot colder here than it ever gets in the Bronx."

Carlo, Mort, and Dom felt it was time to excuse themselves and started to step away.

"Well…" Mort began as he tried to initiate a graceful exit while hiding the fact that he and his star struck friends did not know what else to say.

"Hope to see you in Clear Lake," Ritchie said as if he could sense the near embarrassment of their admirers.

"Sure thing," Carlo answered forcefully. The three then walked back to their table and paid the bill. As they stepped toward the front door, they waved to the singers. Ritchie and Waylon waved back as they began to eat their sandwiches.

Back in the car, everyone was initially speechless.

"Did that really just happen?" Carlo finally asked. No one replied or spoke for the next ten minutes.

The remainder of the drive that day was far less exciting. All seemed hesitant to say very much about their chance encounter back at the lunch stop. Mostly they discussed whether they could stay a little longer in Clear Lake than they originally had planned.

After an hour, Dom finally asked: "Should we have gone into that car dealer showroom and introduced ourselves to Buddy Holly?"

"What would we have said?" Carlo replied. "That Ritchie Valens sent us?"

All three snickered but also wondered if they had passed up a rare opportunity. They knew it was highly unlikely they would ever again have a chance to talk one on one with Buddy Holly.

"Too late now," Mort contributed. "It might've been, you know, maybe a little awkward."

Before long, the sign on the highway showed that Mason City was to the right while Clear Lake was to the left. Within minutes from that fork in the road, the guys were at the home of Cal's parents. After unloading their gear, they gathered around the living room fireplace while Carlo's aunt made hot chocolate for everyone. The conversation quickly turned to the Monday night concert.

"Have you heard who's coming to town this Monday?" Cal began.

"Yeah," Carlo replied while trying to be coy. "Some guys over in Tipton told us."

"Who told you?" Cal asked wondering what the three of them were even doing in tiny Tipton, of all places.

At first, Cal did not believe the story he was hearing. He repeatedly asked for descriptions of how all the entertainers looked and dressed. Mostly, he wanted to know what they said and what they were like. A half hour later, the detailed descriptions seemed too specific and sincere to have been made up.

After checking with Cal's mother if it was okay to stay until Tuesday, the four guys headed out the door to buy tickets. They paid $1.25 each, which was higher than the usual admission price of 75¢, but well worth it in their minds.

Carlo called his mother to tell her they would be getting home on Tuesday, a day or two later than previously announced. While he did not say whom he had met, he did identify the artists they were waiting to see on Monday night. More "with it" than most early postwar parents, she recognized the names of all the rock stars Carlo mentioned.

"Be careful driving back," she said at the end of their conversation. "And tell Buddy Holly and Ritchie Valens I said hello," she concluded with a chuckle that implied she did not expect her son to actually meet either.

Over the course of the weekend, the foursome hung out at Callahan's Pool Hall on Main Street and the Corner Drug Store. The first of these seemed to have an almost exclusively male clientele while the second sported girls aplenty, many of whom were anxious to meet out-of-towners. On Saturday night, all four guys even took dates roller skating.

Cal went to work on Monday while the others drove to Mason City to check out what was going on there. It was pretty quiet. On the road both ways, no one even noticed the small Mason City airport. The guys returned to Cal's house by four o'clock to find Cal waiting for them.

"On our way to the show tonight," Cal suggested, "let's grab a bite to eat at Witke's on North Shore Drive. It's right by the Surf."

When they arrived just before six, the crowd was sparse. About 6:15, six people entered the restaurant. The three young men visited with the owner near the front door while the others started to walk past the table where Carlo's gang was seated. Cal instantly recognized the man leading the way.

"Hello, Mr. Anderson," he stated.

"Hi there, Cal," came the warm response. Mrs. Anderson and their eight-year-old son also smiled.

"This is my cousin, Carlo, and his friends, Mort and Dom," Cal announced. "This is Mr. Anderson, who manages the Surf Ballroom, and his family."

"Are all of you coming to the show tonight?" Lucille Anderson asked.

"Wouldn't miss it," Carlo replied. "We drove all the way from Michigan."

"Really?" Carroll Anderson said. "Where abouts?"

"Right on the Wisconsin border," Carlo indicated. "A town called Ironwood."

No one noticed the other members of the troupe approaching but the three new arrivals caught the end of the chatter at the table.

"Ironwood? We just left our drummer at the hospital up there. Carl got frostbite after the heater went out in our bus and he stepped in some snow."

The man speaking was Buddy Holly.

"Really?" Mort asked. "Grand View Hospital? All of you were in Ironwood?"

"We sure were," Buddy replied. "Two nights ago. I think the name of the place we stayed is called the St. James Hotel. Our bus broke down, one of many times, after we passed Hurley, Wisconsin on our way to Appleton. We had to cancel that show. The cops said they were taking Carl to the hospital in Ironwood. So we spent the night in town to be close to him. Poor guy. He's just a kid, you know."

"I work the desk at the St. James!" Carlo stated with an astonished look on his face. "But I took off to come down here. I had no idea you'd be staying there."

"Neither did we," Buddy said with a sigh. "No offense, but we would have preferred to have made it to Appleton as scheduled."

"The old hotel is starting to get a little run down," Carlo offered. "It's not what it used to be."

"Oh no," Buddy injected. "It had a nice warm bed that was great. I just meant we froze in the stalled bus out on the highway before someone stopped to help us."

"All of you sure look familiar," intoned a fairly high voice that belonged to Ritchie Valens. "Didn't we meet you a few days back on the tour?"

"Good memory. You did," Dom noted, "in a restaurant in Tipton where you were having trouble with your bus."

"It's getting easier to remember people we met on this trip than the number of times our bus failed us," Ritchie offered.

"That's for sure," the Big Bopper added while Buddy rolled his eyes in agreement.

"I thought your drummer was Jerry Allison," Carlo asked.

"Not on this tour," Buddy replied. "Tommy and Waylon, back-stage across the street, are my new band. The original Crickets are back in Lubbock. Any of you play drums?"

"I do," Mort stated nervously. "Why?"

"I think we'll be okay backing each other up tonight," Buddy answered. "But if we get into trouble, who knows? We might ask you to step on stage and fill in. Let me get your names. How about writing them down for us?"

The three raw musicians felt a little strange signing their names for three stars. When they finished, they asked the singers on tour if they could get autographs from them. All three obliged.

"Carlo, Mort, and Dom," Ritchie stated as he read from the signed napkin. "What about you?" he asked looking at Cal.

"I'm not a musician," Cal answered. "I live here in Clear Lake. I'm training to be an airplane pilot."

He stopped abruptly thinking he was beginning to ramble.

"So am I," Buddy injected. "Maybe some day we can fly together. In fact…" He stopped quickly before mumbling to the family standing next to him: "I'll bet all that's been taken care of, huh?" Carroll Anderson nodded affirmatively indicating they already had a licensed pilot for later in the evening.

"We'll be looking for all of you tonight," Ritchie offered in his customary polite manner. "Come talk to us afterwards, if you like."

"Guess there's no need for me to introduce you," Carroll Anderson said with a smile as his group left for a table on the other side of the room.

When they walked outside after eating, Cal and his Michigan guests glanced across the street and saw that Clear Lake was frozen solid. Once inside the music venue, they made their way as close to the stage as they could.

Cal's little sister arrived only moments before the show was scheduled to begin. She instinctively ran up to Cal and his friends.

"Have you heard?" she asked.

"Heard what?" Cal replied almost rudely, the way an older brother is prone to talk to his younger sister.

"The man from Dwyer's Flying Services in Mason City phoned," she began. "He said Mr. Anderson called him to rent a plane for Buddy Holly and two other guys. Mr. Dwyer asked if Dad wanted to fly the three of them to Fargo for their next show."

"What did Dad say?" Cal inquired, now recognizing his sister had something important to contribute.

"He said no. It was too late at night for him plus he thought the weather might be bad for flying. He also made some wise crack that he might've done it if the passengers were Lawrence Welk and Bing Crosby. Can you believe it? Our Dad had a chance to meet Buddy Holly and turned it down. He's really out of it. More than square."

Cal's sister rejoined her friends just as he glanced over at his.

"Imagine actually meeting Buddy Holly," he said looking Carlo straight in the eye.

Within a few short minutes, an air of excitement quickly followed a brief hush as a young man onstage approached the microphone. It was Bob Hale, a local radio DJ. He welcomed everyone and introduced Frankie Sardo who began the show singing "Fake Out." The Big Bopper followed with a number of gut busting one-liners plus a couple of wild and crazy songs most in the audience had never heard before. He was an obviously talented showman who enjoyed being funny and sometimes even borderline goofy.

Now perspiring noticeably, he exited momentarily, briefly buried his head in a towel, grabbed a dry coat, and returned with his telephone prop to do "Chantilly Lace". At this point, most in the crowd genuinely started to get into the music. Few if any realized the performer had a bad case of the flu and likely a fever.

Ritchie Valens received a huge ovation even before he strummed his first chord. As he stood in front of the microphone, he looked poised, relaxed, happy, and far more mature than someone who was only seventeen. His opening song was "Come On Let's Go". The crowd went wild.

He then slowed things down with "Donna" and "To Know Him Is To Love Him." During both, everyone was so mesmerized you could have heard a pin drop. He then concluded with "La Bamba" just before all the performers took a break. No one seemed to notice Ritchie had a cold as well.

"Can you believe we're actually here?" Carlo asked while looking at the other three. "Thanks, guys, for stayin' here a couple extra days."

"This is great!" Mort replied.

"I'm still in shock that we met most of the group back in that restaurant on the highway and here tonight," Dom offered. "Do you think anyone back home will believe us when we tell 'em about all of this? What a trip!"

"Wanna get a coke and check out some of the girls?" Mort asked.

"Right now I don't care about either," Carlo stated emphatically. "I just want to see Dion and Buddy sing. Maybe we can edge our way a little closer to the front."

The second act did not disappoint. Dion performed "Teenager in Love", "I Wonder Why", and other songs. The Belmonts sang background and did their own modified brand of choreography. They then introduced their partially hidden "new drummer, Buddy Holly."

When Buddy took the microphone, the place exploded. Ritchie quietly took his place at the drum set and played as the man from Lubbock, Texas put on a phenomenal performance.

He opened with "Gotta Travel On", a big hit for Billy Grammer and a song Buddy liked a great deal. He also did his just released "It Doesn't Matter Any More" along with his familiar assortment of "Peggy Sue", "That'll Be the Day", "It's So Easy", "Every Day", "Early in the Morning", "Heartbeat", and "Rave On". For this night only, he added "Salty Dog Blues" (with Waylon singing harmony) and "Bo Diddley".

Toward the end of the show, Buddy called Ritchie and the Bopper back to the front of the stage. Together, they performed "Brown Eyed Handsome Man". With the entire cast, including Dion and the Belmonts singing along, Ritchie concluded the concert with a second version of "La Bamba".

As the entourage left the stage amid huge applause and loud cheers, Carlo noticed it was nearly 11:30. Throngs of girls and guys rushed forward to get autographs and pictures.

As the crowd eventually began to disperse, Carlo and his friends approached the front part of the dance floor.

"Great job," Carlo said to Ritchie. "I knew you played a mean guitar but you were terrific on the drums. It's a good thing you didn't have to ask Mort to fill in."

"I resent that," Mort offered. "But I hafta agree," he quickly added.

"It was fun doing the drums," Ritchie replied. "Thanks for coming all the way from Michigan to see us. Hope you had a better ride down here than we did."

"You and Buddy sounded really neat singing together," Cal noted. "Ever think about the two of you recording a song?"

"Buddy and I have talked about it on the bus," Ritchie answered. "We're planning on doing it after this tour is over."

"Hey, nice bracelet," Carlo observed as he glanced at Ritchie's arm.

Ritchie happily let the guys look closely at it. When he turned it over, everyone could see that it was engraved "Donna".

"So there really is a Donna?" Carlo asked.

"Oh yes. There is," was all Ritchie said.

Just then Buddy leaned over and shook the hands of all four. "When you get back home," Buddy stated seriously, "could you look in on our drummer, Carl Bunch, at your local hospital? Hopefully, he's been released but, if he hasn't, tell him we're all thinking of him."

"We will," Carlo assured, feeling quite honored that *the* Buddy Holly had asked *him* for a favor.

The three friends and Cal then backed away as others sought autographs. Carlo stepped forward one last time to take a mental picture of Buddy and Ritchie mingling in the crowd. The four fans then began to stroll around the ballroom.

At least twenty minutes passed. Mort and Dom met up with a small group from Des Moines and talked with them about their favorite songs.

"The show was fabulous," one of the Iowa girls said. "But I wish Buddy would have sung 'True Love Ways'. It's soooo beautiful."

"That it is," Dom agreed. "But it probably wouldn't have sounded the same without the violins, violas, cellos, and sax. They really make the song."

"Hmmm," she replied, looking rather surprised at the remark. "Are you guys in a band or something?"

Mort now had the opening he was looking for.

Carlo and Cal walked back toward the stage and saw Ritchie signing autographs for three girls. When he finished, he turned and entered the doorway that led to the dressing rooms. Although Ritchie did not notice Carlo and Cal, the two cousins kept walking toward the doorway hoping to get a final look at the stars and their instruments.

When both entered, they saw Ritchie with his back to them saying something to Tommy Allsup. With a clearly reluctant look on his face, Tommy reached into his pocket, pulled out a half dollar, and said "Call it". As he tossed it into the air, Ritchie yelled "heads". The two singers huddled over the coin. Ritchie looked at Tommy and proclaimed with excitement: "That's the first thing I've ever won in my life." Tommy then started walking toward the back door of the venue while Ritchie ducked into one of the smaller rooms.

Carlo and Cal returned to the dance floor to hook up with the others.

"What do you think that was all about?" Cal asked.

"Probably who was going to have to pay for the next meal or who would get the better seat on the bus," Carlo answered while shrugging his shoulders.

Suddenly, an idea flashed into Cal's head.

"What if the winner got a seat on the plane and the other guy had to ride the bus?" he speculated.

Carlo shrugged a second time. "Beats me," he confessed.

When the four guys got back to the car, Carlo had a bold thought and leaned toward his cousin seated next to him.

"How far away is the airport?" Carlo asked.

"About five miles. It's just over in Mason City," Cal replied. "Why?"

"Don't you guys think it'd be cool to watch the plane take off," Carlo responded feeling almost devious in what he was planning.

"I know right where the Dwyer hangars are," Cal offered. "I've flown off those runways myself a few times and, of course, Dad has been doing it for years. Yeah, it might be sorta neat."

"Besides, I'm kinda curious to see who actually is going with Buddy," Carlo added. "Maybe that coin toss we spied on......" He stopped short of finishing his sentence but then, looking into the back seat, he asked: "Whaduya think?"

Mort and Dom looked at each other before Dom spoke.

"Why not?" he replied. "It's been a pretty good day so far. As long as we can stay in the car and not hafta stand outside."

When they arrived at the entrance to the airport, they noticed a station wagon pulling in just ahead of them.

"That's Mr. Anderson's car," Cal observed. "Like my sister said, he's probably the one who made the arrangements with Mr. Dwyer."

Carlo stopped his car well behind where Carroll Anderson had parked. All the guys wanted to remain out of sight so no one would think of them as either stalkers or stargazers. They all admitted to each other, however, that they had become bigger stargazers than any of the high school girls back at home could possibly have been.

When the doors to the station wagon opened, four people got out: Mr. Anderson plus Buddy Holly, Ritchie Valens, and J. P. Richardson. The three singers each shook their driver's hand, then waved to Mrs. Anderson and her son before boarding the small red and white Beechcraft Bonanza aircraft.

Mr. Anderson said something to them but Carlo and his friends, with the car windows closed, were too far away to hear. Ritchie and the Big Bopper got into the back seat of the plane while Buddy sat next to the pilot.

The door closed. After a few moments, the plane began to taxi toward the runway.

"Looks like they're taking Runway 17," Cal noticed. "It's nicely paved. Should be a smooth takeoff."

"Who do you suppose is doin' the flyin'?" Mort asked.

"Probably Roger Peterson," Cal responded. "He does a lot of work for Jerry Dwyer. Pretty nice guy and not much older than I am."

"Really? Hope he knows what he's doin'," Carlo stated as he began to think how his experienced uncle would be able to navigate the plane blindfolded.

As the guys prepared to leave, they noticed the plane was still sitting in the same place.

"That's unusual," Cal observed. "They must be talking, or maybe even arguing, about something."

Just then, the light snow began to fall harder and a brisk wind kicked up. It was still well short of blizzard conditions but the added snowfall was clearly noticeable.

A number of thoughts began to run through Cal's curious mind. If visibility is bad, he reasoned, the pilot would have to rely on instruments. Cal was not certain about this but he now remembered that Peterson was not especially good at instrument flying. He vaguely recalled the young pilot had some problems passing that portion of his flying exam. It now occurred to Cal that Roger might be having second thoughts about taking off. What if he was tired? What if he doubted that flying now was the best thing to do? What if the passengers were trying to talk him into it? Not wanting to alarm the others, he decided not to say anything to them.

Cal also spotted Jerry Dwyer's parked car and figured he was probably inside the tower watching to see the takeoff.

Finally, it began. The aircraft picked up speed on the long runway and, despite some wind resistance, ascended beautifully into the dark night.

"Hey Cal," Mort asked. "How fast can a small plane like that go?"

"It can get up to 180 miles per hour pretty fast."

The three from Michigan all looked at each other some-what surprised.

Carlo noticed it was just after 1:00 a. m. He drove his car out of the airport and back onto highway 18. When they reached Cal's house, they talked briefly before heading to bed. Although exhausted, they reassured each other it was a day they would always remember.

The foursome was awakened the following morning by the sound of police sirens. It was not yet 10 a. m.

Carlo, Mort, and Dom decided they had better get on the road soon if they were going to reach Ironwood that evening. They all thanked Carlo's aunt for letting them stay. She offered to prepare a hot breakfast but Carlo insisted they would pick up some lunch after driving awhile.

As they reached the car, Cal yelled to the three from the doorway.

"You guys take it easy. Wait 'till I tell my Dad the chance he missed last night to fly some big time stars to their next concert."

Another police siren could be heard in the distance to the north as Carlo, Mort, and Dom left the city limits heading eastward. Although a little tired from the previous late night soiree, they still were filled with new takes on that unlikely evening. With no radio to occupy them, the insightful commentaries just kept on coming.

Nearly ten hours later, the threesome crossed the Montreal River on the bridge from Hurley, Wisconsin into Ironwood. They all cheered when they passed the "Welcome to Michigan" sign.

"Let's stop at my place first," Carlo suggested. "We can call some of the other guys and my Mom will probably have some sandwiches for us."

"Sounds cool," Dom replied.

Carlo and the others burst into the front door, anxious to begin sharing their adventure with whomever might listen. His parents were quietly seated in the living room where neither TV shows nor big band music was playing.

"Hi Mom! Hi Dad!" Carlo blurted out. "Do we have a ton of stuff to tell you and everyone else in Ironwood. What a once in a lifetime trip!"

Suddenly, both adults looked more somber than the already stoic looks they had first flashed.

"What's the matter?" Carlo asked.

"Guess you haven't heard," his mother began. "Cal has been calling all day and the radio has been filled with the news. All of you better sit down."

The next day, the three boys headed to the local hospital where they learned that Carl Bunch had been discharged only hours earlier. The nurse said he was flying to Sioux City, Iowa "to play in some band".

"He had frostbite but he's okay," she mentioned. "No gangrene poisoning or anything like that. A nice man named Tommy Allsup called and said he would pay for the hospital bill and the plane ticket."

In the days that followed, Carlo, Mort, and Dom, stunned well beyond mere sadness, barely functioned. The stories they had hoped to tell were now almost too personally devastating to compose objectively. When a reporter from the *Ironwood Daily Globe* got word of where they had been, he requested an interview. They declined.

Aside from telling a few of their closest friends, the young men rarely spoke to others of their trip. When the three were alone together, they rarely spoke of anything else. Every day for several months, some detail of the amazing time they had shared in Iowa resurfaced in their troubled minds. Those reflective moments repeatedly created thoughts filled with a conflicting mix of awe and disbelief.

The Old Lady at the Ice Skating Rink

When Oliver Gilbreath was fifty-nine, his wife of nearly three decades left him for a wealthy banker from Grand Rapids. Now, six years later, Ollie was leading a generally content, quiet life in his longtime hometown of Hartville. His daughter, who always favored her mother in both looks and temperament, resided in an out of state commune and rarely made contact with her father. Still working but close to retirement, Ollie spent his free time with old friends and took part in most public activities, like parades and cookouts, that small town life had to offer.

Knowing he was unlikely to see, or even have, grandchildren of his own, he enjoyed small children whenever he could. Kirk Allison and Huey Becker, fellow workers at the local pipe factory, each had grandsons that Ollie loved to tease and engage in a game of catch. He would even buy them ice cream when the three older men would take walks with the six-year-old boys. Britt and Carlton called him Uncle Ollie, a name their parents did not mind even though both boys had plenty of real uncles as well as aunts to go with them.

Ollie always declined whenever he was invited to anyone's house for a holiday. He respected the need for families to spend time with their own members and had few, if any, joyful memories of holidays with his ex-wife and daughter. At Christmas, Thanksgiving, Easter, and Father's Day, he would amuse himself by watching a sports event or taking a long ride in the country. No sadness accompanied these occasions. Ollie had come to accept the fact that these were times for others to spend together while he mostly reflected on whatever occupied his mind at the moment.

An on-the-job accident limited his exercise that used to include long walks through the park and summertime workouts at the public swimming pool. Two herniated disks in his lower back relegated him to more time on the park bench than its hiking trail.

A few scattered benches also surrounded an indoor ice skating rink that operated year round. Ollie especially enjoyed watching hockey games played by the local junior high and high school teams. Sometimes, these competitions would remind him of his own youth when he was a better than average goalie. In those days, weather was always a key variable since play occurred on a makeshift rink at a local pond. Today, the game was faster, equipment was better, and the athletes themselves were bigger. Ollie often thought how, even if he were their age, he would not be able to compete with today's more physically talented boys.

On some Saturday afternoons, the rink would set up for races where children of all ages could compete for small trophies provided by various local donors. Ollie liked to watch all groups participate but generally paid more attention to the already polished older crowd than to those, say, in the five and six-year-old category. For whatever reason, Britt Allison and Carlton Becker had little interest in ice skating. Ollie regularly chided their grandfathers about this. They in turn blamed their daughters for fearing the boys would be bullied on the ice and injured.

When the races did occur, Ollie generally sat alone at the rink. He frequently waved to other parents who were less worried about their children becoming either physically hurt or corrupted by the hockey culture.

One day when his back was particularly painful, Ollie sat on a small bench to observe the races. Half way through the event, he noticed an elderly white haired lady struggling to walk in his direction with the assistance of a cane. He paid little attention to her and barely noticed as she took a seat next to him on the bench.

"You do not mind if I sit here, do you?" she asked somewhat formally while glancing his way.

"Of course not," the ever-polite Ollie answered as he observed the cane now placed between them. "I left mine at home today," he quickly added, even though he rarely used the cane in his closet, "despite the fact that my back is killing me."

"That kind of pain is potentially quite severe," the lady added in a voice and with a careful choice of words that made her sound rather well spoken.

For the moment, the conversation ended. The lady never offered an explanation as to why she needed assistance in walking. Ollie was mildly interested in hearing what malady troubled her but thought it might be inappropriate to ask. Both merely gazed out at the ice as if the other person were not even present.

After more than five minutes, the elderly lady struggled to rise from her sitting position and began walking very slowly to the see-through wall that bounded the rink. Without looking back, she announced: "I must have a close up view of my granddaughter in the next race."

Ollie did not respond, thinking the lady might not be able to hear him anyway. He did notice her pronounced limp and concluded she likely would not be able to walk at all without the added balance her supporting stick gave her.

When he returned to the area with a cup of coffee three races later, Ollie noticed the white haired lady was far away near the exit. She still moved very slowly and paused every few minutes to rest before valiantly pushing onward. Her full length, loosely fitting coat suggested she was quite frail. Ollie deduced she was probably visiting from out of town and was unlikely to be there two weeks later when the next set of races was scheduled. Now feeling like his back was moderately better, he talked briefly with a family from down the street before heading home.

Two weeks passed. Almost at full strength, Ollie drove to the rink and chatted with several couples his age as the first set of races began. It was much colder outside so the coffee and hot cider flowed freely as everyone sought additional warmth after escaping the harsh winds. When the younger children took to the ice, Ollie excused himself and looked around to see whom else he recognized on the premises.

Much to his surprise, he caught a glimpse of the senior lady he had met earlier as she deliberately edged closer to the nearest resting spot she could find. When she made it to a chair, she seemingly collapsed into it while clutching her cane for balance. All this happened some thirty feet from where Ollie was standing. Had he been able to locate an old friend with whom he might have shared the next few minutes, he probably would have paid even less attention to the lady than he had done two weeks ago.

As his eyes circumvented the large room, however, he saw no one he needed to see. The lady was positioned in a manner so that Ollie could observe only the back of her head and a very small portion of the side of her face. Without the cane and extra slow movement, Ollie may not have recognized her at all. After standing still for a few additional moments, he decided it might be good manners to say hello to someone who appeared not to know anyone at the gathering of locals.

He walked past the chair where the woman sat, did an about face, and moved toward her, still at an angle nearly perpendicular to the left side of her face.

"Back to see your granddaughter skate again?" he offered.

As the lady turned in his direction in a very poised manner, Ollie felt compelled to re-identify himself.

"I met you briefly here two weeks ago," he commented, "although you may not remember me."

"I remember you very well," the lady stated with a broad smile and with complete self-assurance. "You were the fellow with the bad back. Is it better today?"

"Yes, much," he responded almost mechanically. "Thank you for asking. How are you doing?"

"About the same as before," she replied.

There was a long pause. This was the first time Ollie was able to look directly at the woman. He had only glanced at her during their previous meeting. Today she looked distinctly different. Her white hair was shorter which meant that her face was less hidden. He now noticed she had a very soft, smooth complexion like someone several years younger than he had at first assumed. Since she seemed to possess a fairly sophisticated air about her, Ollie quickly concluded she must have visited a first rate plastic surgeon more than once. He now tried somewhat awkwardly to dismiss his surprised thoughts and to act as though he had something else to say to her. He again was curious about her physical condition but decided to proceed in a more general direction.

"How is your granddaughter's skating coming along?" he inquired, believing this was a fitting place to begin.

"I have not seen her in the last two weeks so I am unaware for sure," she replied. "You might say I am monitoring her progress."

"You mean you came back to town just for the races?" Ollie suggested, hoping he was not being too forward. "I'm sorry," he then felt the need to add. "I didn't mean to pry."

"Not at all," the lady stated without hesitation. "You are certainly not being overly inquisitive. I am happy to tell you."

Ollie pulled up a second chair and was careful not to block the lady's view of the skaters.

"For the past three weeks, I have been staying at the Hart House Hotel on the town square," she began. "I am estranged from my only daughter, who lives here. Actually, she is my only child. I drove in from Milwaukee where I have lived for the past twenty years."

"Do you have family there?" Ollie asked.

"My husband died unexpectedly three years ago. Our daughter chose not to attend his funeral. The only way I am able to see my five-year-old Ilona is here at the skating rink. She does not even know who I am."

"I'm so sorry to hear about your husband," Ollie stated with near reverence. "And even more sorry to hear about your daughter and granddaughter. Which little girl is she?"

Pointing to the near side of the ice just a few feet away, the lady proudly identified a lanky blonde child in pigtails.

"Ilona is the one in the short green jacket and dark blue sweat pants," she stated.

Ollie recognized her immediately.

"I've seen her in the park and in the swimming pool with her parents. That's the little Adcock girl. Melvin and Sam are her dad and mom. I've known them, not all that well I guess, ever since they moved here, even before they had the baby."

"Samantha is my daughter who will not speak to me or even acknowledge I am here in town," the lady said sadly. "And Ilona Adcock is my precious little grandchild."

The lady remained poised although Ollie could sense the hurt in her voice. He sat speechless, momentarily at a loss for words.

With almost a tear in his eye and a distinct lump in his throat, he finally resumed with a clumsily stated inquiry.

"What happened? Do you feel like talking about it?"

"Perhaps another time," the lady suggested. "Ilona's race will commence shortly. I do not want to miss even a second of it."

"Of course," Ollie responded as he scooted his chair back to its original place.

"Thank you for listening to me," the lady concluded. "I do not usually open up my personal life to a total stranger. You just struck me as the 'good listener' type."

Not knowing what else to say, Ollie merely nodded and smiled. In return, he observed the most appreciative, and likely the most beautiful, smile he had ever seen.

As he looked away, he began to wonder about the age of the person with whom he had been conversing. Two weeks ago, he would have guessed close to 80. After that last display of her perfect teeth, he thought maybe even less than 75.

Both of them cheered for Ilona during her race. She finished third out of the ten girls participating.

"What did you think of her technique?" the lady asked while looking at Ollie.

"I thought it was flawless," he replied without giving the matter a moment's thought.

"There, there now," the lady responded. "Surely, you noticed she needs to use her arms for better balance when handling the turns. And she could sprint with a little more force during the straight-away stretches. She sure is adorable, though, is she not?"

"No doubt about that," Ollie assured, somewhat surprised the lady knew so much about skating form. "She'll learn from coaches and the other girls."

"Thank you for your encouragement, my dear man", the lady stated with her usual touch of formality before adding: "I do not believe I even know your name."

"It's Ollie Gilbreath. And yours?"

"Evangeline Wickes. But my old friends have always called me 'Wicksy'".

"Evangeline. What a spectacular name," Ollie noted.

"My mother named me after one of Longfellow's most famous characters."

Ollie had no idea what she was talking about so he merely nodded sheepishly.

"Can I give you a ride somewhere?" he offered, quickly changing the subject.

"My car is outside," Evangeline replied. "But I do appreciate the offer. Will you be here at the rink next Saturday? I have been told there is a special practice so the children can prepare for races the following week when skaters from nearby towns will participate."

"You seem to get all the right information," Ollie responded. "Sure, I'll be here. And I'll be cheering for Ilona when she skates."

"You are most kind," Evangeline concluded as she turned to begin the arduous task of making it to the small parking lot outside.

The following two Saturdays, Ollie made a special point to locate Evangeline among the small crowd at the rink. On both occasions, they continued their pleasant exchange but neither spoke much about their personal lives. The major topic of discussion was Ilona.

Evangeline knew only minute details about the grandchild she was forced to love from afar. She lamented that she had sent presents for every birthday and Christmas but their arrival was never acknowledged. Ollie filled her in on the few times he had spoken with Ilona and her parents. His words included praise for the child he considered both delightful and precocious.

Apparently no one at the hotel knew of Evangeline's connection to anyone in town. The only person with whom she shared this information was Ollie who saw no reason to broadcast anything about her.

Ilona performed well in the competition with skaters from the surrounding area. Evangeline even caught her eye as the child stepped off the ice. The loving grandmother smiled proudly and could not help but wave. The curious little girl waved back while wondering why this lady, whom she had never noticed before, was watching her with such interest.

Ollie observed this poignant moment and was filled with sadness as he witnessed the expression of distant love on Evangeline's face.

As they walked toward the door, she spoke first.

"My dear friend, Oliver," she began, "I will be going back to Wisconsin before spending the remainder of the winter in Phoenix. The doctor believes that will be good for these old bones. I will look in on Ilona sometime next spring. Will you promise to keep a watchful eye on her for me?"

"I certainly will," he answered convincingly. "You don't have to worry about that. I hope I'll see you once it warms up around here."

As she turned to leave, Ollie noticed she was walking a little more briskly. He attributed this ever so slight improvement to warmth she must be feeling from Ilona's smile. In some ways, it reminded him of the beautiful smile Evangeline once briefly flashed at him.

The winter was one of the coldest on record in southern Michigan. At the factory, Ollie and his co-workers kept busy doing their routine tasks.

"Thinking about retiring any time soon?" Kirk asked Ollie one afternoon.

"Some Fridays, I swear to myself I'm not coming back on Monday," Ollie replied. "But I can't afford it yet. The work here is dull, as you know, but it's steady and it pays pretty well. I'm not sure I can give that up. As long as my back holds up or they fire me, I'll be sticking around."

Spring arrived later than usual but by early May little league baseball had begun. Ollie went with Kirk and Huey to see their grandsons play one cool Sunday afternoon. When the game ended, Ollie noticed the next group setting up for T-ball. Among the players on one of the teams was Ilona.

Ollie decided to skip the victory celebration with Britt and Carlton at the ice cream parlor. When the game began, Ilona was the first batter. She smacked the ball off the tee, over the head of the shortstop, and into left field. Ollie instinctively clapped his hands and let out a loud "Way to go, Ilona." He then thought to himself how proud her grandmother would be if she could have seen what had just happened.

After waving to Ilona's parents whom he had not seen all winter, Ollie focused on the next hitter and what Ilona would do when the ball was hit.

He was momentarily distracted when a shapely woman in slacks and a colorful sweater quickly walked in front of the stands and climbed up to the third row where Ollie was sitting. As he looked away so as not to appear too obvious, he heard a familiar sounding voice say: "Is this seat taken?"

Up close, the woman had the body of a model and the face of...... Ollie could not believe his eyes. It was Evangeline.

"What are you doing here and where is your cane?" was all he could manage to blurt out before adding more than half seriously: "Do you have an older sister named Evangeline?"

"Hello Oliver," came the reply. "The cane is back in Arizona and I am the same Wicksy you met last fall. I knew I would find you looking in on my Ilona. You just have that honest expression on your face. You would not have said you would keep track of her if you had no intention of doing so."

"I'm genuinely at a loss for words," Ollie began.

"Later," Evangeline stated hastily. "Ilona is about to sprint for second."

When the game ended, both adults walked down the aisle leading out of the stands. Evangeline negotiated the stairs with ease. She was the first to speak.

"I left my car back at the hotel," she said. "So if that offer of a ride still holds, I will take you up on it."

This time, Ollie was a little quicker on his feet. Or maybe he just had a few minutes to think about what he might say when the moment arrived.

"Only if I can buy you a catfish dinner on the way."

"You're on!" she stated as she reached for his arm. "But you had better walk faster toward the parking lot. I do not care to be seen with a slow poke."

As they each sat over a mug of beer in the restaurant, Ollie decided the time for him to be overly discreet was over.

"I have been way too shy about this for too long," he stated. "So now I'm going to ask you two things directly. The first is: what was the problem you had that made the cane necessary in the first place? I never wanted to ask in case you had some life threatening debilitating disease."

"And the second question?" Evangeline interrupted before answering the first.

"I know a gentleman is never supposed to ask a lady this," Ollie continued. "But I've just got to know. Might you be willing to tell me how old you are? I've been wondering all winter. And today, I realize I was way off in what I originally thought."

Evangeline slowly took a sip from her mug before placing it down on the table.

"The answer to your first question is that I had to have a substantial part of my left knee and leg reconstructed due to an auto accident. Both were so badly disfigured that I covered myself to hide the horrible bruises and scars. I did not wear a dress or skirt for several months. The surgery was successful and the rehab was slow but eventually effective. I am 90+ percent back to normal."

"And the second question?" Ollie persisted with a distinct smirk on his face.

"I am 58 years of age. How old did you think I was?"

"I refuse to answer that one," he stated with conviction. "Let's just say you really had me fooled."

Both of them laughed before Evangeline added: "Some day, I will expect an honest answer from you about the age issue. For now, I am enjoying my return to youth."

"So how long will you remain in town this time?" Ollie asked.

"That depends on two things," she replied. "First, I must attempt to reconcile with my daughter and be introduced to Ilona as her grandmother."

"And the second thing?" Ollie inquired.

"How many times do you intend to take me to dinner?" she answered while once again displaying her magnificent smile.

Evangeline's first wish was only partially fulfilled after some difficult moments. She boldly knocked on the door of the modest Adcock house one weekend afternoon. Samantha gave her a cold reception and said she preferred to have nothing to do with her. After much persuasion, however, the younger woman did agree to introduce Evangeline to Ilona.

"Sweetheart," she began. "This lady is your grandmother. She is the one who has been sending you the presents."

"I remember you," the observant Ilona stated. "You are the lady who waved to me at the skating rink. You're beautiful."

"You are beautiful, too, my dear," Evangeline said. "I am so happy to finally meet you. I have been watching you skate. You are very good at it."

"Thank you," Ilona responded. "Can I give you a hug?"

"I wish you would," Evangeline answered.

The moment she had patiently anticipated for nearly six years had finally arrived.

"What should I call you?" the little girl asked innocently.

"How about 'Grandma'?" came the instant reply.

"Can you come and live with us, Grandma?" Ilona offered.

"Probably not," the youthful grandmother answered. "But I sure would like to live here in town and see you often."

"That would be wonderful!" Ilona stated with a glow in her eye.

Samantha eventually agreed to let her mother take Ilona for walks, for ice cream, and for trips to the skating rink. There, Ilona soon realized what an accomplished skater her Grandma was.

On a Saturday evening dinner date, Evangeline related this recent experience to Ollie. Feeling the emotion of the moment, he sensed the time was right to ask yet another very personal question.

"Do you mind my asking what caused the rift between you and your daughter?" he stated cautiously.

Evangeline thought for a moment before speaking.

"When she was 18, Samantha dropped out of college and moved in with a 30 year old man, a bass player in some band. Her father and I were devastated. We threatened to cut her off financially and had to follow through when she refused to accept our advice. When her affair ended two years later, she wanted nothing to do with us. She dated one loser after another until she finally met Melvin. He may well be a decent man, although I have yet to meet him. He seems to take care of Samantha and Ilona plus he does have a steady job. When I unexpectedly lost my husband, I felt that Ilona was all I had left. And I did not even speak to her until yesterday."

"Wow! What a sad tale," Ollie said with empathy. "Somehow, my wife and daughter leaving me pales in comparison. But I don't mean to talk about myself."

"No need to do so at this point," Evangeline replied with her familiar warm smile. "Lita Montoya, one of the workers at the hotel, told me your life story last week. I wanted to be certain you were single before I accepted a ride from you. Proper upbringing, you know. But I would certainly love to learn more about your life so far, whenever you are ready."

Over the next few months, that is exactly what happened. The two soon shared many of their life experiences.

"I knew we had much in common after Lita told me about your wife and daughter," Evangeline openly confessed one evening.

"Besides the family thing, probably not that much," Ollie cautioned. "I had to drop out of a junior college after just one year when my father became ill. After he died, I never went back. You probably went to one of the finest universities on the east coast."

"I do have a degree in British Literature from Wellesley. And my father and husband both graduated from Yale. But most of my adult life, I helped to run the family owned hotel in downtown Milwaukee. It kept me in touch with people from all walks of life. Besides, I also dropped out. After only one semester of work on a master's degree at the University of Kent in Canterbury, England."

Ilona now routinely spent weekend afternoons with her Grandma and her Uncle Oliver. Picnics, baseball games, and, of course, ice skating were all familiar activities. After Samantha and Melvin divorced, he left town while his ex-wife reluctantly began to spend time with her mother.

Evangeline bought the Hart House Hotel and lived on the premises. Ollie retired from the pipe factory and helped her run the business. After the first year, he sold his house and moved into the suite directly across the hall from her.

Miss Lyons

On a cool October morning, Ted Atherton watched the old Ford sedan approach the front of his house. As the car came to a halt and the two girls inside smiled, Ted opened the back door and tossed his books onto the seat before jumping in and quickly closing the door behind him.

The driver, Lydia Kowalski, put her car in first gear and began speaking without looking back at her new passenger.

"Looks like winter is on the way," she stated while reentering the road. "Did you freeze out there waiting for us?"

"Freeze? No," Ted replied. "But I did notice the difference from yesterday. It must be thirty degrees colder."

"It's my fault we're late," the girl riding in front offered. "I had trouble finding a sweater that matched my skirt. My heavy clothes were all stashed in the back of the closet."

"Don't worry, Nola, it's okay," Ted responded. "We won't be late for school. That's all that matters."

Nola Rowan lived just down the country road from the Athertons. Their families had known each other for years. Lydia, the only one of the three with a driver's license, resided with her parents about three miles further to the east.

The three were on their way to the Catholic high school in Indiana City where Lydia was a junior, Nola a sophomore, and Ted a freshman. Since the Kowalskis provided the car, the other parents helped pay for gas so their teenage children could get to and from school.

All three farm families believed their children were receiving an education far superior to that available at the local public school. The small town nearby had limited resources for its school whose student body included many from families of similarly limited means. More than fifteen miles away, Indiana City was larger and had a suburb on the beach where people of considerable wealth lived. Many were active in their Catholic parish.

"Pretty soon, basketball season will be starting," Ted announced. "Do you guys ever go to games?"

"Yeah," Nola answered. "It's kinda fun to see everybody outside of class. I hear the team is supposed to be pretty good. They sure were lousy last year but, thankfully, most of the bad players graduated."

"I can probably drive all of us if the roads aren't snowed in," Lydia offered. "My Dad is pretty strict about bad weather conditions. He's already been giving me the third degree about just driving to school once winter gets here full force."

"Thanks," Ted mentioned dutifully. "I brought it up not to expect a ride but because I wondered if most of the kids went."

"Think you'll ever go to dances?" Nola asked.

"I doubt it", the shy Ted responded. "I don't even know how to dance. What if some girl asked me to go out onto the floor in front of the whole school? I'm definitely not ready for that."

"Most of the kids in your class aren't any better than you are as far as smooth moves go," Nola stated with a laugh. "No pressure. When the time feels right, you'll come around."

A silence settled among the group as Lydia drove onward. Soon, they were within the city limits and only a few blocks from St. Dolores High.

Lydia parked the car in the school lot and everyone disembarked.

"See you guys at 3:30", she stated. "Hope your classes go well and both of you meet the loves of your life today."

Nola and Ted both appreciated Lydia's sense of humor. She easily weighed 200 pounds and was most unlikely to meet any potential suitor any time soon. And yet, she was cheerful and encouraging to her younger friends. As a tomboy all her life to date, she was probably not going to embrace silk and satin just because she was seventeen. Peer pressure was not a concept in her day-to-day existence. She was still more at home on the farm tending to the animals and helping her aging mother and father.

Ted, on the other hand, was starting to notice shapely young girls although he had absolutely no idea what to say to any of them. Nola had some redeeming attributes that Ted sometimes noticed either when she climbed out of the car or reached back into it to retrieve her books. But she was older than he was and probably had her sights set on guys that, say, maybe had a car or knew how to dance.

At the end of the day, the threesome reconvened in the parking lot amid couples who necked as soon as they were free from nunly supervision. A group of senior studs turned their noses up at Lydia's old Ford. Ted, meanwhile, did not want to admit to his new friends that he needed a ride from someone as uncool as Lydia or as average looking as Nola. It would still take a few months before others in the freshman class would realize their "togetherness" was caused by their distance from town rather than some imagined romantic association or even close friendship.

Ted's friends teased him mercilessly about both girls.

"That Lydia you ride to school with is really a babe", one of them taunted. "Do you park on the way home and take turns making out with the two of them?" a less than sophisticated freshman inquired.

Ted learned to ignore them. Deep down inside, he enjoyed talking to Lydia and Nola although he would never share this with any of his classmates. Since he was an only child, the two girls he rode with were the closest things he had to big sisters. At some point, he realized they were looking out for him, even though both had their own social lives, limited though they might be.

Sometimes they would stop briefly after school at an out of the way malt shop where the less than popular crowd hung out. Ted was very self-conscious about sitting with the two girls and even more so when one or two of their equally unattractive friends showed up to join them. When that happened, Ted would keep his eye on the front door and jump up with his malt when he saw someone from his class walk in. Through it all, the older girls were quite tolerant about letting a little freshman boy sit with them and eavesdrop on their comments about junior and senior boys.

One morning on their way to school, Nola informed the others of a rumor she had heard from a friend on the phone the previous night.

"Word is that a new teacher has been hired to handle some of the freshman study halls," she offered. "You heard anything about it, Ted?"

"No. Another old nun like the one we've been having?"

"She supposedly had to retire because of…well, old age, I guess," Nola replied. "This new one is a young single lady. Don't know much else about her."

In his late afternoon study hall, Ted had all the mystery removed. A thin woman nervously walked into the room after the bell had rung and everyone was seated, although not yet quiet. As she stood in front of the desk, she was greeted with stares and eventual silence.

"Hello everyone," the lady began. "I'm Miss Doris Lyons, your new study hall proctor."

No one in the class said anything. The stares continued, adding to the nervousness of the new arrival. She then turned to walk back to her chair and bumped into the side of the desk. Everyone laughed.

When she regained her composure, Miss Lyons looked out at the group.

"I'll expect complete silence," she said. "Now start doing your homework."

"I don't have any," a disruptive boy yelled out defiantly.

"Then read something," came the reply. "Quietly."

"I didn't bring no books," another boy stated, thinking he was being cute, and having that view confirmed as three or four girls laughed.

"There are plenty of books on the shelf over there," Miss Lyons stated pointing to the side of the room. "Go get one."

"I already read all those," he snapped back to more laughter.

After a few minutes, it became painfully obvious the frustrated teacher did not have control of the class. Although the talking eventually subsided when students ran out of things to say, Miss Lyons had not made the kind of impression needed to run an effective study hall.

Outside of class, many of Ted's fellow freshmen were outright cruel in their assessment of their new supposed authority figure.

"Her hair looks like she never combs it," one girl observed. "And there's dandruff all over her sweater. She needs to wear white tops instead of black ones."

"That skirt is two years out of date," another girl added. "She has absolutely no sense of fashion."

"I wonder what her boyfriend looks like," a basketball jock noted. "Can you imagine what kind of loser would go out with her?"

Ted took it all in. While he did not contribute to the conversation, he pretty much agreed with all that was being said even though he knew next to nothing about fashionable clothing.

When Lydia and Nola asked him about his new teacher, he made fun of her much as his classmates had done. The topic was soon dropped since the older girls were not that interested in his unoriginal biased insults. Because they were more mature about such matters, they merely took Ted's comments with a grain of salt.

As the weeks progressed, Miss Lyons was having an increasingly difficult time maintaining order in her study hall. She soon resorted to prowling about the room since students in the back consistently misbehaved when she sat at the desk. While walking between rows of student desks, she was consistently mocked the moment her back was turned toward someone.

Students began to spread the word that she was mentally disturbed because she was becoming prone to fits of anger. Although she had yet to cry in their presence, she frequently did just that the moment she reached either the faculty lounge or the ladies room. A mob mentality quickly got out of hand as students in the room sensed they were in complete control of the situation.

Seeking approval of his peers, especially the girls, Ted soon joined in on the fun. Miss Lyons repeatedly reprimanded him for talking and for being disrespectful.

"I thought you were a more serious student than some of the others in here," she said to him one afternoon.

The others quickly let out a chorus of: "oooouuuuu" as Ted smiled approvingly.

On some days, Miss Lyons did appear to be outwardly troubled even before anyone acted up. She obviously was not enjoying this job and her lack of fulfillment was beginning to take its toll on her.

No one expressed any sort of empathy toward her even when the group was more quiet than usual.

One day, a piece of Kleenex tissue could be seen clinging to the back of her dark sweater.

As the class tried to suppress its laughter, one young boy stated loudly: "It nicely complements her dandruff." The class held back no longer and roared.

Still unaware of what had prompted the comment, Miss Lyons merely began yelling for silence that eventually came amid cynical smiles and glaring stares.

Class behavior improved only when mid terms neared and students felt pressure to accomplish something with their class time. Even under these circumstances, there was always a class clown or two who felt compelled to initiate some sort of disturbance.

After school on a cold Monday afternoon, Ted walked out to Lydia's car where he would routinely wait for the others if they were not yet there. Today, the girls had arrived first so he reached for the back seat door handle so as not to further delay their departure. As he jumped inside, he was more than startled to find someone else seated next to him.

His face quickly turned whiter than the freshly fallen snow on the ground.

Without looking back, Lydia spoke as she began to pull out into the street.

"You know Miss Lyons," she said. "We're giving her a ride because her car is in the shop."

Ted's complexion now turned from white to bright red.

"Yes, I know Ted," Miss Lyons observed with a smile, perhaps feeling in control more than at any previous time during the semester. "How was school today?" she quickly added.

More out of fear than rudeness, Ted did not say a word. Both passengers in the backseat gazed out the window during a drive that seemed to take forever for both.

The silence was broken only when Lydia asked for directions.

"Just keep going down the highway," Miss Lyons instructed. "When you get to Olson Road, you can let me off at the corner. I live just a block or so on the other side of the railroad tracks. It'll be easier for me to walk than for you to get the car up the icy hill. I have trouble with that all the time in the winter."

Lydia and Nola made polite conversation with their guest as the drive continued. Lydia even asked if Miss Lyons needed a ride to school tomorrow.

As Ted tried to shield his fear that she might accept, Miss Lyons stated that her mother would be able to drive her.

When they reached the Olson Road crossing, Lydia pulled to the side of the highway as she had been asked to do.

"Thank you so much for the ride," Miss Lyons offered. "I hope it wasn't too much trouble."

"No trouble at all," Lydia replied. "Happy to do it any time."

"Good-bye, Miss Lyons," Nola called.

"I'll see you in class tomorrow, Ted," Miss Lyons said without looking at him. "Be sure to be there on time."

Ted remained speechless as they waited for the young woman to walk across the tracks. It was one of those crossings where there was only a sign but no flashing red lights. When Miss Lyons reached the other side, Lydia again pulled out onto the highway.

"How could you do that to me?" Ted asked her.

"She needed a ride," Lydia answered. "What could I say? Besides, I didn't mind. It was right on our way. Actually, she seems very nice."

"Yes, she does," Nola injected. "I don't know why you and your friends think she is strange."

Once again, Ted withdrew into total silence.

Over the next few weeks, he was pleased that there were no extra passengers on their ride home. While students in study hall continued to taunt Miss Lyons whenever possible, Ted somehow felt compelled to remain silent. Deep down inside, he began to appreciate that Miss Lyons was much like any other person who was just trying to do a job. He even saw that her initial intimidated manner was not unlike what he felt his first week at a new school.

At the same time, he also refused to feel too guilty about any of his previous actions in study hall and still laughed when the others provoked the anger of their proctor. What kept him in his place was the fear that he might one day have to sit with her again during the ride home.

Thanksgiving brought a welcome four-day break from classes. The kids were especially unruly in study hall that Wednesday afternoon. Feeling more confident that he would not have to face Miss Lyons outside of class, Ted joked repeatedly that day with the cute girl sitting next to him. This drew three or four reprimands that Ted once again felt quite comfortable receiving.

On the way home, he even snickered to himself when they passed the Olson Road crossing where they had dropped off Miss Lyons a couple of weeks earlier. Feeling increasingly mischievous in anticipation of the holiday, he felt the need to make a sarcastic remark.

"Hey Lydia and Nola," he began. "Wouldn't it have been funny if Miss Lyons would have slipped and fallen on her face when she crossed the tracks that day we dropped her off here?"

Neither girl responded.

Thanksgiving dinner at the Athertons was festive as a number of their relatives from Kalamazoo joined them. The rest of the weekend was quiet but Ted was happy being able to stay at home and not worry about any homework.

After church on Sunday morning, Ted perused the comics while his Dad read the front page. Suddenly, Mr. Atherton noticed a story he immediately wanted to share with his son.

"Isn't this one of your teachers?" he asked as he handed the paper across the coffee table.

Ted read the story to himself.

> Doris Lyons, 32, was killed when her car stalled on a railroad track just blocks from her home. A southbound passenger train broadsided the car at 3:30 p. m. on Friday. She was pronounced dead at the scene. Miss Lyons was employed by St. Dolores High School in Indiana City. A former student at Wabash College, she is survived by her mother and father.

Ted did not attend school either on Monday or on Tuesday when he was present at the funeral. No one else from his study hall came to the service.

After Christmas, Ted transferred to the local public high school.

Jeri Christopher

The thermometer outside the kitchen window registered twenty-two below. Fresh snow had not fallen in over a week but snowdrifts and piles from the last round of shoveling were still more than three feet deep. The brisk wind off the southern shore of Lake Superior made it feel much colder than the official temp. Only a few rugged souls had ventured out onto the snowmobile trails over the past week. In the evenings, most locals huddled near the home fire while either watching movies on cable or playing their favorite game of cards.

Ira James Edison was used to the cold but his hometown near the Indiana border usually had an occasional break from extreme frigidity, even in January. That had not happened yet during his first winter in the U P. While he enjoyed sports, especially downhill and cross-country skiing, he was not used to being prevented from participating due to weather warnings. Within the past few days, his favorite winter sport was rapidly becoming checkers.

He was also beginning to feel the type of depression often experienced by youth in Scandinavia. The absence of the sun, the dreary darkness, and the seemingly constant harsh wind were beginning to take its toll on his generally cheerful mental state. The paucity of attractive eligible young women did not help either. Unless some modest form of social life surfaced soon, he was beginning to think about returning home long before his planned August departure.

I. J. was not looking to meet the woman of his dreams at this point but the level of fulfillment produced by whiskey and poker with the guys was quickly approaching diminishing returns. The handful of local single ladies all seemed to possess the same attributes: slightly older, divorced sometimes with children, borderline overweight, either in dead end jobs or living back at home with their parents, and lacking in stimulating conversational skills.

Not that I. J. was either Charles Atlas or a Rhodes scholar. He was, however, taking a year off from college to enjoy the great outdoors while deciding what to do next. His job at the grocery store paid his rent plus a little extra, although there was little to spend money on anyway.

I. J.'s uncle lived alone on the outskirts of town, got his nephew the job, and promised the parents he would keep an eye on him. Once the young man declined the offer of free rent and moved out after the first month, Uncle Hugo's supervision was limited to an occasional phone call on super cold nights or a brief exchange when he bought his groceries.

One day after temperatures rose to nearly zero, I. J. made the short drive to Grand Marais where he had only been once before. The small shops made the downtown area more charming than where he now lived but all still seemed ominously quiet. After stopping here and there, he walked over to the local grocery mostly for comparison purposes. This place was bigger and nicer although business was only slightly more bustling than back at his adopted home.

The one distinctly different feature was the cashier who was close to him in age and far less corpulent than the women he had seen during the past two months.

"Can I help you find something?" the young lady called out seemingly as delighted to see a young person as he was.

Not really looking for anything in particular, I. J. was momentarily caught off guard. The first thing that came into his mind was slow to get there.

"Yeah....," he finally mumbled slowly. "I think I'd like a Coke or Sprite."

"They're in the case right next to where you're standing," came the reply with an accompanying friendly smile.

Embarrassed, he turned his eyes rightward to find both brands within arm's reach. He remained with his back to the check out line until he could think of something to say. When he regained his composure, he was not even sure which can he had grabbed.

"Anything exciting happening in this town?" he asked.

"You definitely haven't been here long, have you?" the lady answered.

"Only about twenty minutes," was his honest but now more easily flowing response. "What about you? Is this where you grew up?"

"Oh gosh, no," she stated promptly. "I've barely been here twenty weeks."

"So what brought you to this wilderness?" I. J. questioned.

"I was going to Michigan Tech over in Houghton," she stated matter-of-factly. "But I wasn't enjoying it and wasn't doing that great. I came here to find myself......whatever that's supposed to mean."

"No kidding," came his now openly enthusiastic answer. "That sounds very familiar, only I was going to Indiana State in Terre Haute. I'm I. J. Edison, by the way."

"Jeri Christopher," she announced. "Mind if I ask what I. J. stands for?"

After giving his reply and explaining that he never used the name he despised, a middle-aged man approached with his small basket of canned food. I. J. stepped aside so as not to impede progress.

When their conversation resumed, I. J. wasted little time and asked Jeri if she'd like to get a bite to eat after work.

Over the next few weeks, there were more dates and fewer poker games with the guys.

The two twenty year olds did their share of skiing, hiking, ice skating, and even ice fishing. An occasional drive to a movie theatre constituted a special night out while a movie at one of their apartments was more common. Whether or not the weather was actually warming and the sun was more prevalent, it certainly seemed that way as life became brighter for both.

When I. J. paused to evaluate where this was all headed, however, his thoughts were inconclusive. Jeri was fun, intelligent, and better than average looking. From what he could observe of her body in heavy winter clothing, she was somewhere between perfect and better than perfect.

When intimacy eventually became common, he was not disappointed.

He did, however, wonder whether all this was happening because neither had other prospects, she was promiscuous, or both were simply bored with their surroundings. When they openly discussed these matters, she assured him none of these reasons were accurate and she did have genuine feelings for him.

She then asked him a similar set of questions beginning, somewhat pointedly, with *his* possible promiscuity. Their openness brought them closer especially after he announced his strong affection for her. Both agreed they enjoyed what they had together but they also felt they were a long way from any sort of commitment.

Meanwhile, his planned return to his hometown grew closer as March became April and then May.

Prompted by I. J.'s parents, Uncle Hugo dropped in one day to see if any decision about returning to ISU had been made. I. J. knew such questions were destined to become more frequent and respected his uncle for giving him some space. The two of them could actually talk rather openly about career plans with Hugo's most persuasive argument being: "You don't want to end up like me."

I. J. said very little about his social life although Hugo had some information because of the speed at which news travels even between neighboring small towns. The elder man thought he would be more effective in planting the seeds of a return to school if he did not meddle in his nephew's personal affairs. Having never been married and not much of a charmer, he also felt he had little credible advice to offer.

After the Big Thaw, I. J. and Jeri at first spent even more time together before limiting their contact to maybe three or four times a week. The guys he knew had all but given up on him as a reliable companion although they did play a little softball or basketball every now and then.

Jeri had her own doubts about her post-summer life. She had little or no enthusiasm for a return to MTU although other options were few in number. She enjoyed the time away from her family whom she missed but did not want to face in light of her indecision about future plans. Most of this she conveyed to I. J. during their more serious moments together. It was almost as if neither wanted to grow up and was unsure if doing so meant making that transition together or separately.

For the moment, reflective long walks along the shore of the big lake, sometimes separately, were common.

During one of these, I. J. decided he had to go back home and return either to his old school or another that would have him. Since it was too late to apply elsewhere, ISU seemed the most likely destination by default. Maybe, once he got there, some new inspiration would come, like a new major, some different courses than what he had already taken, and some new friends. Another winter in the U P just was not in the cards.

When he relayed all this to Jeri, she took it well and admitted she was no closer to deciding her fate than she had been when she first arrived in Grand Marais. For the remainder of the summer, the two of them hung out together and continued sleeping together.

In early August, they took their last walk hand in hand on the beach. During their final hug, she cried and he fought back the tears until he let loose when alone back in his car. Despite the momentary hurt, he knew he was doing what had to be done.

The long drive south was uneventful except for much anxious thought about what lay ahead.

After I. J. graduated, he took a job in northern California as a traveling salesman for a company that sold sports equipment to retail stores. Over the next fifteen years, his work took him to several western states as well as British Columbia and Alberta. He stayed physically fit, made many new friends, and enjoyed an active social life but had yet to marry. His parents had retired in Washington state after selling their Michigan home so it had now been some time since I. J.'s last visit to the Midwest.

When he eventually attended a class reunion at Indiana State, he decided to visit his old hometown and look up some old friends there. Finding only a few, he took the bold step of looking in on Uncle Hugo who was now retired. The combined drive from western Indiana to the U P took some time but I. J. had built up several weeks of unused vacation and the early summer weather made for a pleasant excursion.

When the old man opened his front door, he was more than just a little surprised to see his now mature adult nephew.

"Uncle Hugo!" I. J. shouted as he hugged his father's brother who now required a cane to steady his movement as he walked.

"Ira James!" he responded. "Are you a sight for sore eyes! What brings you to these parts?"

"Came just to see you," I. J. quickly stated. "It's been a long time and I wondered if you were still behaving yourself."

"Hard to do otherwise," Hugo noted. "Especially in this laid back setting. An occasional game of poker is my only remaining vice. And what about you, you handsome devil? No woman has gotten her hooks into you yet?"

During the next two days, the two men had much to talk about. Hugo put together a couple of full breakfasts while I. J. insisted on treating his uncle to dinners at the local dive. When Hugo proudly reintroduced the young man to whomever they saw, I. J. noticed either a grin or smirk as each person shook his hand. He gradually dismissed the gesture although some curiosity remained in the back of his mind.

As he prepared to leave town late one morning, Uncle Hugo poured one last cup of coffee while the two men shared some final thoughts.

"I vaguely remember," Hugo began, "that you had a girlfriend during the few months you stayed up here way back when. Joannie or Jenny, was it? Did you ever reconnect with her?"

"I didn't think you even knew about her," I. J. answered. "It was Jeri. Jeri Christopher. Nice gal. No, we lost touch after exchanging a couple of letters after I left. I think I probably wrote her last. I've thought about her from time to time. But I moved on. Why do you ask?"

"No particular reason," Uncle Hugo snapped back. "Someone once mentioned to me that she moved away from Grand Marais less than a year after you went back to college. I think she settled in Mackinaw City. Right on your way back to the L P. Bet she'd get a kick out of seeing you."

"I doubt it," I. J. offered. "Have you become a match maker in your old age? She's probably married with a house full of kids by now."

Hugo now carefully chose his words. "An old friend of mine in Grand Marais tells me she never got hitched. I'm not trying to fix you up. You're old enough to make your own choices. I just thought you might want to see a familiar face on your way back home."

"Unlikely," I. J. said confidently. "My vacation time is about up," he concluded, even though it wasn't.

As he drove away, he waved to Uncle Hugo and wondered if the two would ever cross paths again. The old man was not that close to I. J.'s father and was not much of a traveler so a trip out west probably was not going to happen.

After a couple of hours on the road, I. J. was getting hungry. Noting he would probably be stopping soon, he glanced at the highway sign that announced "Mackinaw City, 30 miles".

When he pulled up to a hamburger joint on the edge of town, he recalled some of his time with Jeri. After a moment or so of reflection, he initially deduced there was no point in looking her up. He then stretched outside his car and walked inside.

His order was slow in arriving. A bit bored, he decided to ask for a copy of the local phone book. Jeri Christopher lived at 1234 5th street.

The modest looking home was easy to find. Since it was now early Saturday afternoon, chances of her being home were fairly good, he thought to himself. Even after noticing an old Chevy in the carport, he still debated whether to approach the front door. He finally stepped outside while stating out loud: "this one's for you, Uncle Hugo."

A handsome teenage boy answered the door. I. J. instantly noticed the young man looked eerily familiar.

"I'm looking for a Ms. Jeri Christopher," I. J. stated somewhat formally.

"Yeah, sure," the young man said. "She's out back. Come on in."

I. J. took a seat in the front room of the house as he heard the back door open.

Within a minute or so, a woman who still looked good in tightly fitting blue jeans and a halter top entered the room.

"Hello Stranger," he said without rising from his lounge chair. "Remember me?"

A warm smile flashed across Jeri's face but it took her nearly a full minute to compose a response. In the meantime, she sat across from her guest on the sofa while the teenage boy stood near her with a distinct look of curiosity.

"This *is* a surprise," she finally uttered in an understated tone. "How did you ever know I lived here? Someone told me years ago you had settled somewhere in California."

"I just came from visiting my uncle in the U P," he answered. "California? Yes. Settled? Who knows?"

Jeri then turned toward the young man standing nearby. "I see you've met I. J.," she stated almost purposely looking at neither of them.

As I. J. looked over, the young man was now walking toward him before extending his hand.

"I. J. Christopher," he said innocently.

Suddenly, the look of familiarity began to make perfect sense, I. J. Edison thought to himself. This young man looked like a younger version of him.

Now in a state of extreme shock, I. J. clumsily raised his hand to participate in the most awkward handshake of his life. The younger I. J. still had no clue what was happening.

"Well," he finally said. "I'll be back in an hour or so, Mom. Nice meeting you, Sir."

For the next ten minutes, both people still in the room remained speechless, their eyes meeting only once or twice.

I. J. thought about running out the front door but then reminded himself he had already done that. Jeri mostly looked away and appeared to be feeling a mixture of embarrassment and relief. She then reassured herself that the next move belonged to the man seated across from her.

I. J. finally broke the ice.

"Why didn't you tell me before I left or in one of your letters?" he said sheepishly.

"I didn't want to keep you from finishing college or hold you back in any way."

"What did you do when you first found out? Did you move here right away? How did you afford to raise a son, our son, all by yourself?"

"You always did like to ask more than one question at once. I knew I had to leave Grand Marais. It didn't take long for the gossip to begin. I would've been ostracized pretty quickly. I never told you this but my parents have a lot of money. They cut me off when I dropped out of Michigan Tech and told me I had to make it on my own. When I told them I was pregnant, they helped me out some. They also agreed not to track you down and file a paternity suit. I didn't want that. They really made me feel like I made a mess of things. I guess I did."

"You had some help from me," I. J. replied. "I feel terrible. I never meant for this to happen. You were terrific in so many ways. I just wasn't ready to think about anything long term. I would've felt differently if you had told me about the baby. Honest."

"Thank you for saying that. But you don't have to. We're doing okay. I work as a secretary. We have enough to get by. He is really a wonderful son. I'm so happy I have him."

"Does I. J. stand for Ira James?"

"Oh no. I didn't want to do that to him. He is Ian Jacob. But I've always called him I. J. from the moment he was born."

The awkward silence returned. And lasted a bit longer this time. Once again, I. J. spoke first.

"What does he know about his father? Are you going to tell him who I am? What can I do now to make things better?"

"There you go again with the multiple questions. He knows that his father left before he was born and lives somewhere on the West Coast. I don't know what you do for a living so there's not much more I could tell him about you. I just said we spent one marvelous cozy winter together before you had to leave. That's all he knows. Heck, that's all I know. I'll make something up about the visitor I had today. Probably an old friend from high school. That'll be easy enough. I don't expect you to do anything. I never did. I never expected I would see you again. This can be another day just like the last time I saw you at the beach on the big lake. This time, I probably won't cry."

"You never got married?" I. J. asked.

"When we dated, you remember you thought of divorced women with children? To a lot of guys, I probably fit that same mold."

"What if I stayed around town for a few days? I'd like to spend some time with you. And with young I. J."

There was a long pause, as if Jeri had not expected to hear an offer like that. Finally, she responded.

"That's not a good idea. It's better if he never knows who you are. There is a nice man in my life now. A lawyer. He has a son who is the same age as I. J. It took me a long time to get over you. Maybe I haven't yet. But seeing you has helped. Thank you for stopping by. There's no way I want to let you back into my life. I could never be hurt that badly again. I think you should leave now. I'll make it easy for you. Again! I'm going back out to my garden. Just close the front door when you go."

As she exited the room, her magnificent figure was very much in evidence. I. J. could not help but notice. Her stride now ensconced in his mind, he was briefly reminded that his long ago initial assessment of "better than perfect" still applied.

I. J. did not move for a good fifteen minutes. He debated with himself the entire time desperately trying to compose words to say if he walked into the back yard. Nothing seemed appropriate.

As he sulked briefly in his car, a man in a brand new minivan drove up. He walked up to Jeri's front door while buttoning his three-piece suit. He then opened the door without knocking and entered, calling first her name and then I. J.'s.

The flight to California was lonely. Since he never returned to Michigan, I. J. never saw Jeri, Uncle Hugo, or his son again.

Barber Shop Trio

When Abel August was four years old, his father took him to
Carmona's Barber Shop on Main Street. Both men remained regu-
lars there until Abel went off to college. During that entire time,
Roberto Carmona manned the first chair while his brothers, Vito
and Gus, handled the other two. Until Abel was ten, the three
barbers affectionately called him "Little Abel". When he began to
complain that he was no longer little, it was Gus who dubbed him
"Double A".

The barbershop was the only place in town, actually the only
place in the world, where the young boy responded to that fancy
title. In fact, he saw it as a sign of respect that no one else bestowed
upon him. Even though Abel eventually crossed paths with half the
males in town while getting his hair cut, they all called him Abel on
the street and paid little or no attention to the Double A designation he enjoyed in the shop.

The place was much more than somewhere you went for a
haircut. No subject was off limits for discussion. The weather, sports,
and the families of customers topped the list. Of course, everyone
inside was a fan of the Tigers and the Lions, so there was much
to commiserate about during both seasons. Other popular topics
included fishing, which virtually every customer did, and boating,
which only a few were able to enjoy. If there was any envy over
income differences, it never manifested itself.

Proprietors of similar establishments elsewhere tended to
avoid politics and religion. Not so at Carmona's. Most people in
town were Republicans so differences of opinion were few. When

Eisenhower, Nixon, and Ford were in office, much praise for their policies flowed regularly. The only complaint was that none were doing enough to defeat communism or to bully the rest of the world. When Kennedy, Johnson, and Carter manned the White House, each was criticized for getting out of bed in the morning.

Almost all locals were either Protestant or Catholic so God-fearing principles always went unchallenged in any of the three chairs. Some, but not all, of the Catholics proudly spoke of their first Catholic president. Such support was tolerated inside Carmona's since religion in those days still trumped politics. Alternatives to Christianity were few.

The local doctor was Jewish but no one seemed to mind since he regularly cured all who came to him. A Jewish couple also owned the department store where almost everyone shopped. Presumably, both families went to temple in the larger community ten miles away. Occasionally, someone, usually an old timer, was held suspect for not attending any of the local churches. But these concerns were mostly gossip and no one was ever confronted on a face-to-face basis.

As he became more mature and began to think about such matters, Abel suspected he might be attracted to the Democratic Party but he never voiced such views in the barbershop. There was so much else to absorb while waiting for a haircut that Abel never felt disappointed at the wit and wisdom generated there.

Some customers preferred one barber over the others but to Abel it never mattered. When his turn came, he merely sat for whomever was available.

One day while a senior in high school, Abel positioned himself in the front chair as Roberto placed the large white cloth over the young man's clothes.

"Hey Double A," the barber began. "Anything different today?"

"Naw," Abel replied. "I'll just have the usual."

Actually, Abel had no idea what that meant. He just assumed Roberto would make his already fairly short brown hair a little shorter.

"The style of your cut we call a Princeton," Roberto informed him.

"Well," Abel answered shyly, "then a Princeton it is."

All the high school student knew was that he parted his hair on the left hand side and combed it straight across without pushing it back at all. Since the sides were short, there was nothing there to even worry about.

"You decided where you're going off to college yet?" Roberto asked.

"Not for sure," came the response. "It'll probably be either Wayne State, Western, or maybe Albion. I'm even thinking about Valparaiso if I can get in. But it's a pretty tough school."

"When you get to college, you're not gonna become one of those freaky long hairs, are you?" Roberto asked. His tone suggested he was more concerned about the possible adverse effect on his profession than any change in values such an appearance represented.

"I haven't thought much about that," Abel answered. "Right now, I'm just hoping to get into a good school."

"You've got more sense than to do anything that crazy, Double A", the barber offered, obviously paying more attention to the first part of Abel's response than the second. "Just hold onto what you learned in our fine town and you'll be okay."

Abel nodded but was already starting to wonder how much faith he should put into advice from someone who had never gone to college.

"So what's happening with the new construction down the street?" Abel asked, purposely stirring the conversation in another direction.

Each time he left Carmona's, Abel felt he had placed his hand on the pulse of the community more firmly and accurately than when he went anywhere else in town. Gossip was rampant in the coffee shop and in gas stations where he sometimes hung out. The weekly paper put its own unique touch on things but was far more cosmetic than the more natural feel of the barbershop. Now that Abel rarely was present at the same time as his father, the locals seemed to speak more freely of personal events about town. He knew he would miss this camaraderie when he did go off to school.

Abel was accepted at Valparaiso and did well at the school that sat on a plateau overlooking the city. Since he came home only on long breaks, more of his haircuts took place in his college town than in his hometown.

With his degree in hand, Abel entered a corporate training program in Detroit and began the slow but hopefully steady ascent up the proverbial company ladder. The people surrounding him were such that personal attire sometimes mattered more than brainpower. Included in such appearance requirements were routine visits to a hair stylist who charged four times more than he was accustomed to paying for results that were little different than hometown barbers provided.

Since he was fairly well paid, the added cost did not matter that much to Abel. More importantly, he found the hair stylists who catered to the corporate crowd a bit stuffy, much like most of their customers. He eventually began to miss the down to earth conversation at Carmona's.

That Thanksgiving, he waited to have his haircut until he made the trek home to visit his family. Roberto, Vito, and Gus were all glad to see him.

"How's the big time corporate executive these days?" Roberto asked.

"I'm anything but big time," Abel responded. "But I'm doing just fine. How are you guys?"

"We're all behaving ourselves," Gus pitched in. "Vito's boy got himself married last weekend. We even closed the shop. First time we missed a Saturday of work in nearly thirty years."

"Who's the lucky lady?" Abel asked with genuine interest.

"A gal he met over in Benton Harbor," the proud father answered. "She's a real doll. The wife and I are very happy."

"The boy's grandpa is less so," Roberto offered. "Sweet girl? Yes. But she's not Italian," he added in a near whisper.

"You okay with that, Vito?" Abel asked.

"Oh yeah," Vito nodded. "Our Papa's from the old country. He's even suspicious if someone's Sicilian. My son's new wife is a beautiful French girl. We don't care about her nationality. The main thing is that the young couple's happy."

"We asked her about her ancestors," Roberto continued. "Turns out they were from a town in southern France less than a hundred miles from where our family lived in northern Italy. That's closer than the distance from here to Benton Harbor. Papa will come around."

"Isn't it about time you got yourself hitched, Double A?" Gus questioned, mainly to change the subject. "What's the matter with all those big city girls anyway?"

"No one's called me that in ages," Abel noted. "Detroit girls are okay, I guess. I'm in no hurry."

"Good for you," a middle aged man seated in Vito's chair observed. "When the right one comes along, you'll know it."

The man who had just spoken was Ike Cooper. Abel knew him only casually as one of his father's co-workers at the feed store. But he appreciated the homey warmth in his voice.

"People here still cared about each other," Abel thought to himself. At the hair stylist place back in Detroit, all customers would have been seriously bored by everything that had been said so far in Carmona's. No one would have cared much about somebody's son getting married. Or at the very least they would not have let on that they did.

Abel walked out onto Main Street where he stopped to chat three or four times before reaching the small family run department store. He went inside hoping to find a couple of ties since he had already gone through his small collection more than once.

Micah Latman, the long time owner, flashed a big smile when he saw him.

"Abel August!" he belted out in a loud voice. "You look great. I've actually been thinking about you lately."

"Hello, Mr. Latman," Abel replied. "It's nice to be back in town. How's business?"

"Pretty good but it can always be better," came the almost instantaneous response. "That's actually why you've been on my mind."

"How so?" the now curious Abel asked. "I plan on picking up a few ties today. And maybe even some dress socks. Will that help business?"

"That will be fine but that's not what I was thinking about," the proprietor answered. "Our customer base has expanded so much in the last year that I'm having trouble keeping up. I've been 'doing it all' for many years now. The accounting, advertising, hiring help that comes and goes, dealing with the occasional but inevitable customer complaint, purchasing inventory. You name it. I need a full time manager who understands business and who can learn this one fast. Someone who is smart and hard working. Someone I can trust. Someone…well…. like you."

Abel was caught off guard. He had almost bought his ties back in Detroit in which case he would not have gone into this store today at all. He also had several career objectives. Working here was not one of them.

"I'm really flattered, Mr. Latman. I actually only planned to be here until tomorrow morning. I'm pretty swamped with work back in my office."

"I understand all that. If I could get you, I'd be very flexible about when you would start. Even after Christmas would work, although the holiday rush should be something else if it's anything like last year."

"Mr. Latman, I like what I'm doing now and there are plenty of opportunities for advancement. I'm also paid very, very well. More than I ever expected to make at my age. It would be great being back here in town but I just…."

"Let me show you what I can pay you. And you can think about it over Thanksgiving dinner. Talk to your folks. I'll bet they'd love it if you were back in town and closer to them."

Mr. Latman handed Abel a xeroxed job description with the salary listed at the bottom of the page. It was just over half of what he was making now. Abel knew the lower cost of living would make up some of the difference but he also quickly wondered what he would do on weekends. It was not an attractive option.

"I'll tell you what," Abel finally stated, hoping to hasten his exit from the store and the situation. "Let me pick up a few ties and I'll give this some serious thought. I really appreciate that you think so highly of me. You would be a great person to work for."

When Abel brought the seven ties he had selected to the check out counter, he was told to put his wallet away and just take them.

"Just consider it something like the signing bonus that baseball players get," Mr. Latman quipped.

The two men shook hands. Abel began the short walk to his parents' house. When the evening conversation came to a lull, Abel announced his latest job offer. Neither parent was impressed.

"Ol' Micah has been moaning about how hard he has to work for a number of months now," his father observed. "He's made similar job offers to three or four people. They all turned him down."

Abel's mother added her own set of comments.

"Micah's a good man and his family has built up a fine business," she said. "But you have so much going for you, my Son. Some day, you'll be raking in genuinely big money in a city where fortunes can be made. Latman will never be able to pay you what you can make in Detroit. And what you're really worth."

"I know," Abel answered respectfully. "I've just never had anyone surprise me with any kind of a job offer. I interviewed for weeks and got turned down many times before I got the position I have now. The money's great. But the people I work with would stab me in the back the second I stopped looking over my shoulder. I could be let go for nothing I ever did wrong. And then I'd be back doing interviews again."

"We want what's best for you, Abel," his father stated while placing his hand on top of his son's. "We're proud of you whatever you do. You can always come back to this dead end town and do something. You're still young. Don't throw away what you've worked so hard to achieve."

Before his mother could add a second comment, Abel assured his family he was not about to do anything rash.

"I'm not going to throw anything away," he said. "I'll tell Mr. Latman before I leave town that I'm not interested. I've always liked him, though. The man I work for now is a genuine jackass. But I guess I'll put up with him until something better comes along."

On Friday morning, Abel stopped in at the department store on his way out of town. He was sincere and polite when he told Micah Latman he would not be accepting his offer. He also offered to pay for the ties he had been given the day before.

"Just think of me whenever you wear one," Mr. Latman said with his businesslike grin. "Mull it over in your mind some more. Stop in and say hello when you're back in town for Christmas."

As Abel turned to leave, the older man handed him a small bag.

"Don't open this until you're on the road," he said.

Five miles out of town, Abel reached for the bag and found four pair of fine dress socks.

The next three weeks were especially busy. Abel was given extra project on top of extra project. He worked well into the evening every day. When he barely made deadlines, he was chastised for holding up the others. Morale among his co-workers was slipping fast. On December 21, the announcement came that there would be no Christmas bonuses. Two of Abel's more experienced colleagues were unceremoniously given the ax. Abel was asked to take on some of their work. He was overwhelmed.

Employees were given the 24th and 25th off. But all were told they must report at 8 a.m. on the 26th. Most were too exhausted to leave town.

Abel arrived at his parent's house around noon on Christmas eve. After visiting briefly with his mother, he left to do some last minute shopping.

When he walked into the department store, the place was abuzz with activity. Mr. Latman and three of his clerks could barely handle all of the customers.

Abel picked out some shirts for his father and two dressy sweaters for his mom. No one was available to help him. In fact, two older men, thinking Abel was a store employee, asked for his help. His familiarity with the merchandise nearby made it fairly easy for him to assist.

Mr. Latman took notice of the friendly, unsolicited, and unpaid work he was receiving. Two hours later, Abel was still making recommendations to customers about matching shirts and pants as well as which sport coat looked best on them.

One of the customers was Roberto Carmona.

"I didn't know you worked here, Double A," he said. "I could sure use a good idea for a coat for the Mrs."

Abel laughed.

"I don't actually work here," he noted. "I just came in to land some presents for my parents. Somehow, I got mistaken for a clothes expert. Here are the ladies' coats. What's Mrs. Carmona's favorite color and what kind of coat do you think she'd like?"

When things finally slowed down, Abel got in line to pay for the items he had selected.

"You handle yourself well in the store," Mr. Latman offered. "I don't know what we would have done if you had not come along."

He then whispered so no one else could hear him.

"Before you accept my offer of last month," he said to Abel, "add $3000 in annual salary to the figure on the sheet you have."

Abel was understandably surprised but was too embarrassed to say anything. Mr. Latman rang up the sweaters but not the shirts. He then placed them all in a bag.

"You can start as early as January 2," he said. "Tell your Lutheran parents 'Merry Christmas' from their Jewish friends, Micah and Ella."

Even though Christmas day with his family was a pleasant experience, Abel was troubled much of the time. His mind was filled with thoughts of all the mostly uninteresting work waiting for him when he left later that day. He began to wonder how many, if any, of his co-workers he could consider genuine friends. He dreaded facing his overly demanding boss and all the freeway traffic to and from work. He had yet to even mention to his parents anything about the wave of recent robberies in his neighborhood. And the social life was actually nothing like he had expected and certainly a far cry from what he had known at Valparaiso.

When the department store opened on the morning of December 26, Abel entered the front door and walked back to the office.

"Mr. Latman," he said, "I'm headed back to Detroit to give notice. If the offer still holds, I'll be happy to be your store manager as soon after the 1ˢᵗ as I can get here."

The storeowner's face lit up as if he had just sold $1000 worth of jewelry.

"Great! I can't wait to begin working with you," he said. "Oh, and one more thing. From now on, please call me Micah."

Abel's parents were disappointed when he called them from work that afternoon to tell them what he had done. Over the next five years, they changed their tune when the auto industry collapsed, half of Detroit collapsed, and corporations like Abel's former employer laid off all of their young executives in training.

Micah and Abel both prospered as people continued to flock to the department store on Main Street.

More than ever, Abel enjoyed the stories that flowed each time he stopped into Carmona's Barber Shop. As time went on, he added more than a few of his own.

The Magazine

As she hung up the phone, Ariel Salisbury reached for the next file on her desk. For the past three years, she had been the Editor of *Great Lakes Business Review*, a magazine that had been in existence for more than half a century. Its offices were housed in the Institute of Business Research located adjacent to the Southern Michigan University campus. The Institute received most of its funding from the state plus whatever could be generated from the sale of its books and periodicals. *GLBR* published timely articles on current business developments to readers throughout the Midwest.

Ariel drew upon her many connections among faculty at various universities for material. She also relied on two in-house researchers who often wrote polished pieces that quickly passed through the formal editing process. With a background in marketing, Rafael Luzon monitored such issues as sales trends throughout the country along with the ever-changing world of advertising. Angela Eden was a professionally trained economist whose research centered on leading economic indicators and economic forecasting.

While the reputation of the magazine was growing, the Institute itself was something of an enigma. Whether or not it would survive more than just a few years was open to serious debate. The Dean of the Business School at Southern Michigan was a self-made multimillionaire who wanted to use the Institute as his own private research and propaganda arm.

Leland Pitts was used to controlling things. One of his first acts as Dean was to summon the Director of the Institute and inform him that his staff would be subject to the whim of the Dean on short notice. Having held his position for nearly thirty years, the Director essentially told Pitts that was not going to happen. Many members of the Michigan Legislature knew the likeable Director personally. This assured that approval of a relatively new Dean was unnecessary.

Pitts was a clever and, if need be, a patient man. He knew the Director was close to retirement. In a couple of years, the Dean reasoned, he would be able to fill the vacancy with someone more to his own liking and more willing to respond when the puppet strings were pulled.

Inevitably, that retirement happened. Pitts selected an old colleague of his, Dudley Helms, to be the new Director. Dud, now sixty years of age, had been a consultant to the high tech firm Pitts had founded. Actually, Helms had inherited leadership of a well established consulting firm whose staff of specialists was quite competent. All Helms did was send the right group to Pitts whenever his firm needed assistance. When the results proved to be anywhere between adequate and spectacular, Pitts gave primary credit to Helms. The Dean now hoped the Helms magic would be replicated in a university setting.

Both men held doctorates but neither performed any actual research on their own. Instead, they delegated authority to subordinates. This process worked reasonably well as long as the head men commanded the respect of those who worked under them. Since Pitts was tyrannical and demanding, many members of his corporate staff and now his faculty performed out of fear. Helms, however, was unable to inspire such respect now that he was at the Institute.

Everyone who worked there quickly found him to be lacking in just about everything. He spoke in an unconvincing manner. He was unable to provide direction. He seemed unaware of what he was supposed to be doing. He hesitated when asked the simplest of questions before stumbling through a weakly composed answer. Many deduced he may have been prematurely senile or on the verge of becoming so. Others felt he was totally disinterested in his new position and intended to coast for the next few years until he himself retired.

Fortunately for the short term viability of the Institute, its staff possessed a high degree of self motivation. All were extremely capable in what they did. Little direction was needed. Everyone pretty much did what they had been used to doing in spite, rather than because, of their new Director.

Ariel and Brad Smith, her very astute Managing Editor who was better known as "Jonesy", ran the magazine and worked to make it better with each issue. They were an effective team. She solicited manuscripts from researchers while he turned their not always coherent ramblings into readable prose. She also wrote some of the articles herself. Their part time editorial assistant was a delightful elderly lady named Mildred Anderson.

Ariel had faculty experience at other universities before returning to her doctoral alma mater. Her specialty in the regional economy of the Midwest made her a natural for her current post. Jonesy was completing his dissertation in English literature from SMU. His extensive work on raw submissions probably should have been rewarded with co-authorship of several articles but that never happened.

Although she had only completed high school, Mildred was a whiz with numbers. This made her particularly adept at assembling large data sets so essential for researchers to tap. With the aid of a simple calculator, she was able to create tables around which others could base their narratives. She also was responsible for proofing final editions of everything before press time. Mildred had a grown son but no grandchildren and, therefore, loved to spend time with Ariel's small children.

The team also included a superb Publications Editor named Helene Irby. A Ph. D. in English, she made decisions on which books the Institute published and worked tirelessly with their authors to prepare each manuscript for publication. Some of the more trade-oriented books, like a directory of manufacturers in the state, brought in substantial revenue that nicely complemented the state allocation of funds. Her expertise coupled with the ineptness of Dud Helms made Helene in effect the Associate Director of the Institute, although no such title existed.

All staff members were able to do their jobs in large part because Helene shielded them as best she could from the mindless instructions of their supposed leader. Whenever anyone had a problem or a mere question of correct procedure, he or she went to Helene and avoided the person all began referring to as the "Head Cheese."

The magazine was published six times a year, taking its timeliness cue from the more respected *Harvard Business Review*. With ten to twelve articles per issue, Ariel was quite busy securing, well in advance, adequate material that still had to be timely. The mutual respect she shared with Jonesy and Mildred made the oft times intense effort a mostly pleasurable endeavor.

Compliments on a specific issue of the magazine came mostly from other Institute employees, some members of the business community, and occasionally from people at other universities. Relatively few members of the business faculty at SMU cared about the magazine. Dean Leland Pitts never commented either on a single issue or the overall quality of the publication. At times, he publicly spoke of starting a new business school journal as if *GLBR* did not exist.

Dud Helms tried to feign interest but his comments were so off base as to be laughable. The January/February 1982 issue opened with four separate articles dealing with how state tax and expenditure matters affected business in Michigan. After glancing at the copy that had been placed as usual on his desk, Dud dashed into Ariel's office.

"I just had an idea," he opened. "Since the Michigan Legislature is beginning its session in Lansing this week, maybe *GLBR* should run an article or two on what issues they'll be facing."

"Just what issues did you have in mind, Dud?" Ariel inquired in a mild state of amazement.

The response was notably indirect but typical.

"Well..........hmmm....I'm not sure...... I guess......I sort of ....ahhhh......ehhhh......" he began before finally composing himself. "I've only lived, you know, in this state for a few months. The specific issues, I think, would not be that important. I mean, just something that, you know, would get your readers tuned into the fact, you know, that the Legislature is, um, in session."

"Have you seen the first four articles in this issue?" Ariel challenged.

"Oh," came the reply. "I meant something more specific than this. You know....I suppose......well......gee...

Then he stopped.

After scratching the top of his mostly bald head, he continued.

"How soon can you get out another issue?" he asked, now reaching for something positive to contribute.

"From start to finish," Ariel reported confidently, "it takes nearly two months to produce an issue. "We started on this one back in November knowing the Legislature would be arriving this week. We're currently half way through preparing the March/April issue. Most of the articles for that one have been accepted. By then, the Legislature will be well into its agenda. I doubt that one of our articles would get them to shift gears abruptly."

"Do you think the governor might call a special session if we alert the state to something they have not already thought about?" Dud persisted.

Ariel was astounded at the naivete she was hearing.

"I don't think the governor has called a special session based on anything this Institute has ever suggested in the past 50 years," Ariel replied with a chuckle. "You got any ideas?"

"Well, maybe you need to be a little more forward looking with an eye to having a bigger impact on important people around the state," Dud answered as if he were contributing something of value.

"I'll try to remember that," she stated, now biting her tongue to keep from either laughing out loud or calling him an ignorant buffoon.

After Dud left, Ariel returned to her work but only read a few paragraphs before she could no longer resist telling Helene about the pitiful exchange she had just experienced. The women enjoyed some laughs before sharing a glance that revealed how serious the situation was. The emperor had no clothes. When it came to fulfilling their responsibilities, it was quite evident they were entirely on their own.

Both clearly recognized that was not necessarily a bad thing. Each knew what had to be done and only hoped Dud would find something else to amuse himself so he would not sabotage their efforts. The previous Director had given them free reign while making an occasionally valuable suggestion or two. Both women were well equipped with talent and confidence. A bumbling interruption here and there would provide only minimal delay.

In staff meetings, Dud revealed his incompetence again and again. He rarely had an agenda and when he did, it had nothing to do with the mission of the Institute. He always arrived late, had trouble remembering everyone's name, and often lost his train of thought. Nothing was ever decided. His favorite concluding comment was: "Well, let's all think about that until next time." By the following meeting, he had forgotten what had been discussed previously and an entirely new set of unimportant issues was addressed.

One day, Ariel asked Helene if the prestige of the magazine might be enhanced if a well known editorial board were established.

"Do you have some people in mind?" Helene inquired.

"Here's a tentative list," the always prepared Ariel stated as she handed the piece of paper to her friend. "Most are previous authors. The others are well respected in their fields. I know all of them and think I can get them to write for us with a little prodding. They all have numerous contacts as well. I would require all board members to write at least one article for us per year and referee a paper or two. If anyone on the board does not keep up their end of the bargain, I'd boot them and take their name off the title page."

"Looks great to me," Helene replied. "As usual, you have forward looking ideas. You'll have no opposition from me on this. Go for it!"

"Just one more thing," Ariel added cautiously. "I'm a little concerned that Head Cheese will want to add some names of his own.

Probably cronies who would provide window dressing but do us no good whatsoever. How do we avoid that?"

"Easy," came the near instantaneous response. "Just don't tell him about it."

"But what if he gets upset when he sees the first issue with the Board listed?" Ariel added.

"Do you honestly think he'll even notice?" Helene offered. "When was the last time he had anything to say about an article in *GLBR*?"

The women then shared an approving devious smile.

The twenty member Editorial Board helped recruit new authors and did a fair job of writing articles themselves. Six issues (a full year) later, Dud noticed the names of the board members on the inside cover of the magazine. He calmly walked into Ariel's office.

"How long have we had an editorial board?" he asked innocently.

"For quite some time now," was all Ariel said.

Dud nodded and stared at the wall for a few minutes as if to gather his thoughts. He finally spoke.

"If you ever want me to get some of my contacts at more prestigious universities than the ones your people represent to serve on it, just let me know."

"I'll be sure to do that, Dud," she responded while trying to keep a straight face.

Eventually, the Institute did experience some financial difficulty. It was the Reagan era and an "anti-government supported research" attitude was sweeping the nation. Michigan was not exempt.

The state legislature had long wanted state universities to fund their research bureaus out of the general allocation of funds to each school. For some time, all major research organizations at the large universities were listed as separate line items in the state budget. Until now, this never posed a funding problem even though the issue was sometimes debated on the House or Senate floor.

The new Republican governor who rode the coattails of the 1980 Reagan landslide saw an opportunity to engage in budget cutting consistent with the national mood of the day. Using his line item veto power, he simply deleted funding for several research bureaus that had been supported by the legislature. The Institute of Business Research was one of many casualties.

The matter now fell to the Director to convince his Dean and/or those higher up that emergency money was necessary to keep the place afloat. The two most obvious problems were Dud's ineptness and Dean Pitts' indifference. Fortunately, Helene Irby went over both of their heads to lobby the Vice President for Research with whom she had had some interaction on two previous occasions.

When emergency funding was announced in a letter from the VP to Dud Helms, the Director proudly announced the news at a hastily called staff meeting. Totally unaware of Helene's heroic efforts, Dud took full credit for the maneuver. Everyone on the staff thanked Helene for her work on their behalf.

The Dean became slightly miffed that an underling had bypassed his office in communicating the matter to the vice president. He was also smart enough to realize Dud Helms was incapable of such a devious tactic. Instead of being upset with Helene, Dean Pitts saw the episode as conclusive evidence that Helms was not in control of his shop and did not have the respect of those nominally under him. Pitts had suspected this for some time but now knew he needed to begin a search for a more suitable institute director.

In his eyes, such a person had to have more on the ball but also had to be subservient to *his* agenda. It did not take long for Pitts to court a member of the governor's staff who was on temporary leave from his faculty position at the University.

Kendall Hunt was a non-academically oriented professor of management. He was also one of the new breed of wealthy anti-government crusaders who infiltrated state agencies with the goal of shutting as many down as he could.

Dean Pitts knew this but staff members at the Institute did not. The Dean had always regarded the Institute as an uncooperative headache. His aim was now to use its revenue generating activities to help fund a new research organization for which he would secure additional cash from private business sources. Institute staff members knew it was inevitable that Pitts would discover how little Dud Helms was worth to anybody. While they knew little about this fellow Hunt, they reasoned he could not possibly be worse than their current Head Cheese.

Through it all, *GLBR* came out on schedule. The timeliness of its coverage along with improvement in its quality continued but were largely unnoticed by anyone who mattered in a budget crisis. Ariel, Jonesy, and Mildred worked as if there would be no changes in institute policy. There was no reason to think differently. If a new director came along, everyone felt that person would appreciate the magazine for its merits that were clearly evident to anyone with half a brain.

Rumors persisted until Leland Pitts made the official announcement. Dud Helms was out and would fill the vacant position on the management faculty. Kendall Hunt was in and would not be returning to that position any time soon.

Kendall made an effective first impression. Compared to his predecessor, he spoke with confidence and optimism. He promised that the Institute would flourish, that he would secure substantial outside funding for endowed research chairs, and that good work would be rewarded with merit pay increases. While his pitch seemed well rehearsed and almost too smooth, most staff members welcomed a positive approach to no approach at all.

The next day, Ariel asked Kendall if he would be interested in submitting an article for the magazine.

"Sure thing!" he answered in his strong speaking voice. "When do you need it?"

"Sooner is always better than later but I'll work it in whenever you have time to devote to the effort," she encouraged.

Within just three weeks, Ariel found a manuscript on her desk. Somewhat to her surprise, Kendall Hunt was listed as the first author while an unknown graduate student was the co-author. As Ariel read through its contents, it was quickly evident the entire paper was the work of a poorly informed and barely literate business grad student. After seeking the advice of Helene and Jonesy, the threesome decided they would polish the mess to make it readable.

Their disappointment was evident. Kendall Hunt obviously had nothing but disrespect for the magazine and the effort required to put it together. Rather than confront their Director on his outsourcing of the project, they decided to wait and see if his talents lay elsewhere in areas that ultimately would prove beneficial.

Ariel was just finishing a book on the Michigan tourism industry. She had been working diligently on it for the past three years. When Kendall noticed proofs sitting on Mildred's desk, he approached Ariel about her work.

"Look's like a major effort on your part," he began while referring to the proofs. "How about if I write an Introduction to it? Would you like that?"

Ariel did not know how to respond. She knew he had no idea what the pages contained and was not even interested in the subject. He, of course, had nothing to do with its preparation. All of the work had been completed before he had even set foot inside the walls of the Institute. She did not believe he deserved to have his name associated with the project at all.

As all of these thoughts ran through her very perceptive mind, Kendall smiled and walked out of her office. He then turned back and stated bluntly: "I'll have the Intro in Mildred's hands in a couple of days."

Kendall's "Introduction" was two paragraphs he plagiarized from Ariel's first chapter. Visibly livid, she complained to Helene who questioned Kendall about his "input" but was told he would always be writing an opening statement on all books the Institute would publish from this point onward.

His academic dishonesty did not end there. Kendall was invited to give an address to business students at a nearby small university. The Dean there knew Ariel quite well. Before the talk, he had asked Kendall to send him a copy of his resume so that the guest speaker could be introduced properly to the audience.

The small school Dean initially was impressed with the credentials he saw. Up to a point. Something disturbed him as he read through the list of publications. The number of published books was huge. One stood out in a most unimpressive way.

The phone rang in Ariel's office and she answered it.

"Ariel," the voice stated. "This is Luis Carreon. How are things going with the magazine?"

"Very well," came her reply. "How are you, Luis?"

"Fine," he answered before getting to the point.

"Has your book on Michigan tourism come out yet? You did promise to send me a copy," he quickly added.

"You are at the top of my list as soon as it is off the press," she offered proudly. "It should be out early next month."

"Do you have a co-author?"

"No, you knew I was doing it all by myself. Why do you ask?"

"I understood your working title was: 'A History of the Tourism Industry in Michigan.' Is that still what you're calling it?"

"Of course. You were so kind to make recommendations on my second draft. I took your advice and gave you credit in my Preface. I really appreciate your close reading. You were very helpful in filling in some loose ends. I'll always be grateful."

There was a long pause. Ariel could tell something was amiss. Her friend was never short of words. Finally, Luis spoke.

"How is your new director working out?"

"OK, I suppose. The verdict is still out. He's new and we're all giving him some slack until he does or doesn't deliver on his promises. Why the sudden change of direction in your questions?"

Luis was now ready to deliver the final blow.

"Kendall Hunt is scheduled to be a guest speaker here the day after tomorrow. He sent us his resume. On it is a book for which he claims full credit as author. It has the same title as yours and your Institute is listed as the publisher."

"What?!" Ariel shouted in a near scream. "Why that son of a bitch!"

After Luis tried to offer some calming words, he continued.

"There are other books on his list that he claims to have written but I doubt that he has. They sound way too much like the work of other people. In fact, I'm looking at one book right now. It's called 'Recent Trends in the Michigan Brewing Industry' by Kermit Fields, Michigan State University Press, 1978. That's exactly how it appears on Kendall Hunt's resume only he claims to be the author and there is no mention of a Professor Fields. I'm having someone check the titles and authors on a dozen other books. They look pretty suspicious as well."

"The man is a crook!" was all Ariel could manage to say. "I know that book and I know Kermit. He is a very diligent researcher and a skillful writer. I doubt that he has ever had any sort of connection to Kendall Hunt."

"What would you like me to do?" Luis offered. "It's too late to renege on the invitation to have him speak. I could contact your Dean about this, if you like."

"No, that wouldn't help," Ariel replied. "He has no respect for our Institute whatsoever. Only our Vice President for Research might have the guts to face up to this one. I'd better think about this and get back to you."

"Of course," Luis replied. "I'm so sorry to have to tell you this. Do keep up the marvelous work you do. Some day when I have the time, I'd love to write another article for you. And I give you my word, it will be *my* original work."

As time went on, reality set in quickly. Kendall Hunt began hiring expensive outside consultants. Their primary task was soon recognized as carefully interviewing all employees about the work they did. To pay bills submitted by these consultants, the least needed staff members, mostly part time graduate student assistants, were let go. When vital staff left for greener pastures, their positions were not filled.

One day, Kendall posted a letter of praise for the work of the Institute. The business executive who signed the letter attached a donation for the modest sum of $100. When such a pittance was treated as big news, staff members began to question if the million dollar endowments would ever materialize.

One of the consultants was a shifty-eyed middle-aged man who began occupying much of Ariel's limited time. He cared not at all about the content of the magazine, the alumni based readership it served, its importance to scholars elsewhere and to members of the business community, or its PR value to the research image of the University. His only interest was in the revenue that subscriptions brought in vs. the cost of producing each issue.

"Whether or not *GLBR* entirely pays for itself depends on the percent of each employee's time that is included in its cost," Ariel responded to one of the man's more direct questions. "I can give you figures on what the printer charges plus the salary of our managing editor. I spend about half my time on the magazine and the other half on research."

"What about the research you do for articles that appear in the magazine?" the consultant asked. "And the time Rafael and Angela spend doing their articles for you? And the work of this lady named Mildred?"

"The research that all of us do is supported by the research budget," Ariel answered. "Most of that work is published in well established academic sources elsewhere. The Business School sees its national ranking improve because of publications in internationally prestigious journals. We contribute to that ranking. What we all write for *GLBR* are laymen's versions of larger research projects. The time we spend writing those versions is minimal because we have already done the larger more technical reports. Most of our *GLBR* articles are written by people at other universities and we pay them nothing for their efforts. They do it to enhance their own promotion prospects. Some serve on our editorial board for the same reason. But the cost to us for all this outside effort is zero."

"And Mildred?" the consultant reminded.

"Nearly all of her time is spent number crunching for the researchers here," Ariel answered. "When she has a few free minutes, she helps proof articles for the magazine and the books we publish. The proofing does not take more than ten percent of her time."

The consultant nodded several times and took notes but said little. His questions became more detailed with each successive visit. Other staff members were hit with similar inquiries.

Ariel, Helene, Jonesy, and Mildred went to lunch one Friday.

"So what do all of you make of all the questions we are being asked?" the always inquisitive and never bashful Mildred asked.

"I have the same concern," Ariel affirmed. "Something's going on."

"I don't like the looks of any of this," Helene observed. "Our budget is being decimated by consultant's fees. I can understand a new director wanting to learn more about what everyone does but I think he has something more sinister up his sleeve."

"Like what?" Jonesy pitched in.

"There are several possibilities," Helene began thoughtfully. Then she hesitated.

"Well," she finally injected, "the worst case is not pretty. Kendall Hunt obviously has no morals or ethics about him. Worse yet, he is close to the Dean. And maybe the governor, for that matter. The political mood these days calls for a hired hand to infiltrate government funded agencies, see what is potentially profitable, privatize it, and eliminate everything else. The only thing consistently profitable here is our trade publications. The academic books barely pay for themselves. No matter how good it is and how much it contributes to the image of the University, *GLBR* barely pays for itself. That conniving old Dean Pitts has wanted to destroy this place and get his own privately funded research unit going for years. This time, he might be able to do just that."

"And the less than worst case?" Jonesy asked sheepishly.

"Major budget cutbacks," Helene replied. "Keep most of our efforts going but just starve them for funds until they are no longer feasible. The legislature is looking to make cuts wherever it can. If one of us decides to leave, I can pretty much guarantee that person will not be replaced."

"How could I possibly put out the magazine without Jonesy?" Ariel asked, her frustration clearly visible. "And Mildred?" she added out of respect for her friend.

"What a perfect excuse to eliminate the magazine," Helene stated soberly.

Two weeks later, Ariel was called into Kendall Hunt's office. He did not mince words.

"Ariel," he began. "The consultant's report has come back to me and I have now had time to review it closely. The figures on your magazine do not look good."

"What do you mean?" she asked.

"It consistently loses money and many of your subscriptions will expire in the next couple of months," he stated matter-of-factly.

"The circulation data always show subscriptions that are about to expire," Ariel noted. "Readers pay one year at a time. Most of them renew when the reminder is sent. Our subscription base has been pretty steady over the last five years even when we raised rates. There's no problem here."

"That's not the way I see it," Kendall retorted. "I don't think most of the readers will be re-subscribing this time."

"What do you base that on?" Ariel snapped.

"My intuition is usually pretty accurate about these kinds of things," Kendall stated confidently even though he had nothing to support his opinion-based deduction. "My take is that there are real financial difficulties ahead, especially with costs so prohibitively high and rising. Paper is getting more expensive, you know."

"So is everything else, except for salaries," Ariel noted. "None of us has had a raise in five years. We made up the slight increase in printing expenses by raising subscription rates."

"You may not think salaries are that great but all of you combined add a lot to the bill," he alleged.

"What do you mean all of us?" Ariel added indignantly. "There's only half of my salary, all of Brad Smith's, and barely ten percent of Mildred's. That's the information I gave to your consultant."

"I've adjusted those numbers slightly," Kendall responded arrogantly. "Here, see for yourself," he added as he handed a page of the report to her.

After a few moments of close inspection, Ariel was ready to respond.

"This is not right," she observed. "You have all of my salary included as a cost for the magazine, all of Brad's, all of Mildred's, all of one of the secretary's, half of both researcher's---Rafael and Angela---and a big chunk of computer time. You've loaded up costs of a lot of other things we do here onto the magazine. That does not reflect reality at all."

"I think this is more realistic than any other way of doing it," Kendall asserted. "The magazine is costing way too much money. I'm afraid we're going to have to discontinue it."

"That's a pretty rash conclusion based on faulty inflated cost numbers," Ariel pointed out. "*GLBR* has been providing a valuable service for the University for more than half a century. If you ask me, this is a very ill-advised move."

"Actually, I'm not asking you, I'm telling you," Kendall said boldly. "I've made up my mind. There's no room for discussion. The matter is closed."

"So how long do we have before Jonesy and I have to clear out of our offices?" Ariel asked. "The next issue is at the printer. And we have articles accepted for the issue after that. There's a potential legal matter here. Authors may claim a right to sue the University, or at least give us some bad press, if we say we're going to publish their work and then we renege."

"There's no reason for us to get the legal folks involved," Kendall replied. "Go ahead and publish the next issue and the one after that. Then we'll quietly cease publication."

"And our jobs?" Ariel reminded.

"You're not being terminated," Kendall assured. "After the magazine is defunct, you can continue working here as long as you hustle outside grants to pay your way. Maybe you can write your managing editor into a grant proposal and keep him here for awhile."

"Jonesy is not a business researcher," Ariel noted. "He's an editor with literary skills. And he does a marvelous job with the magazine."

"Well," Kendall observed wryly, "we may not be needing him then."

Ariel did not cry because she did not want to give him the satisfaction of knowing how upset she was. She was also too mature to stand up and throw a punch at the cocky bastard although that was clearly what she wanted to do. Instead, she stared at him as she began to leave.

"I'll call a meeting of everyone concerned to announce what I have just told you," Kendall added as Ariel now had her back to him.

The "meeting" began just an hour later. Ariel, Jonesy, Mildred, Helene, Rafael, and Angela were all present.

"Ariel and I have been discussing the *Great Lakes Business Review*," Kendall began. "Because it is no longer financially viable, a decision has been made to discontinue the publication."

The jaws of everyone in the room, except Helene, dropped. She feared this day might be coming but was not surprised.

Ariel could not contain herself.

"Just a minute, Kendall," she stated forcefully. "You make it sound like I had some input into this decision. It was yours alone and, as I told you earlier, it is based on faulty information. This is a gigantic mistake and the responsibility rests entirely on your shoulders."

"Now, Ariel," he responded in a near condescending tone. "I know you have worked hard on the magazine and are disappointed it did not succeed. That's normal. But now we must move on to other ventures."

"It has succeeded for more than half a century in providing valuable information to businesses and to researchers here and elsewhere," she noted.

Once again, Ariel felt the urge to rearrange the man's face despite his larger physical size. Once again, she restrained herself because she knew any response on her part would be futile.

Kendall went on to state everyone's job was momentarily secure until all present could support themselves by obtaining outside grants.

Now it was Helene's turn to speak up.

"I thought you were going to bring in money for endowed research chairs," she stated calmly. "The figures you showed us were in the several million dollar range. That could pay for a lot of research. What we spend on the magazine is trivial compared to that."

"Fundraising has proven to be more difficult than I had originally anticipated," he said displaying borderline humility. "I'm going to need help from all of you in getting outside money."

"We're nearly broke now because of all the bills you have run up," Helene pointed out. "Much of the money has gone to pay consultants. You have also been doing a great deal of travelling with huge bills resulting from those trips. Don't you think you owe everyone present, whose jobs are now in jeopardy, an accounting of what this money was spent on? And how this is supposed to benefit the Institute?"

Kendall dismissed the matter abruptly.

"A director is normally not responsible to his staff to justify his work expenses," was all he said.

"None of us has experience in writing grant proposals," Angela pointed out. "That's not in any of our job descriptions."

"It is now," the Director replied hastily.

An exchange continued for awhile before everyone left the room in disgust. Ariel was too angry to say anything further. When everyone met later without Kendall being present, she apologized to the group before adding that he should have done so. She also said she was committed to seeing the last two issues of *GLBR* completed. She then encouraged everyone to seek employment elsewhere adding that she would probably do the same. She confessed that she had no experience in writing grant proposals and never thought that would be required when she accepted her current position.

Over the next three months, Jonesy completed his dissertation and accepted a job teaching literature at a junior college in Kentucky. Rafael and Angela hustled grants for awhile before moving to a better funded research bureau in Columbus, Ohio. Helene Irby resigned and married a wealthy owner of a construction company. She began writing novels, some based on her research institute experience. Mildred retired and said she would be more than happy to look after Ariel's children whenever her help was needed.

The governor did not veto the next budget for the Institute although the economy minded legislature allotted less than half the money that had been available in recent years. The University made up some of the difference by providing support out of its general fund. Dean Leland Pitts took cash from both sources to establish his new Institute for Creative Capitalism. Kendall Hunt became its first Director. The Institute for Business Research was absorbed into this new entity in name only so that it could still draw state funds that the Dean used entirely at his discretion. None of the employees of the Institute for Business Research were hired to work at the new Institute for Creative Capitalism.

Inside the modern offices of the new propaganda organization was a small room where some books and old equipment from the former library were stored. No one worked inside this room. The sign on its door included small letters that humbly read "Institute for Business Research."

Luis Carreon offered Ariel a full time teaching position in his Department of Economics. She happily accepted. Ariel and her husband remained close friends with Mildred who became the best nanny the couple's children would ever have.

Four Hours in a Hotel Lobby

"May I help you, Sir?"

"Do you have a vacancy for this evening? Just for me. One night only."

"I'm very sorry. We are completely booked for tonight and tomorrow."

Only slightly disappointed, Bailey turned and walked toward one of the lobby lounge chairs to contemplate his next move. He knew several other places would be available but thought he would take a chance on the distinctive 1920s era hotel. Exhausted from the three-day business trip to Toronto, he decided to break up the long drive home by taking a day for sightseeing on the Canadian side of Sault Ste. Marie.

As he sat, he noticed it was one p. m.

Bailey gazed about the room and admired the architecture, noting that newer places where he had stayed lacked this detail and charm. He then casually glanced at the lady seated in a similar chair next to him. Their eyes briefly met before each of them smiled politely and looked away.

Over the next few moments, Bailey could not help but think the woman looked very familiar. What he did not realize at first was that she was having similar thoughts about him. Suddenly, it hit him with the force of a runaway train.

"Kora Gamel?" he asked, now looking directly at her.

"Bailey Loomis?" she replied.

"How long has it been?" he inquired awkwardly.

After pausing to reflect for just a moment, her answer was fairly precise.

"Easily more than thirty years," she stated calmly. "I guess we've both changed quite a bit but that confident yet friendly look of yours is still the same."

"With you, it's your eyes," he replied, "and that unmistakable dimple."

"You remembered that?" Kora noted. "I'm amazed. But you did have some close looks at it."

"That I did," Bailey admitted. "A long time ago. Well…fill me in….how have you been and what are you doing now?"

"I'm a fashion designer," she responded. "I work for a large company based in Chicago but I travel a lot so I live in Niles. I've always preferred the small town to the big city."

"That's the same Kora I remember," Bailey recalled. "You and I had that in common ever since our days in Ann Arbor. So…any kids? Any husbands?"

"Never had either," she answered. "And not even any close calls on the marriage thing. I decided if I couldn't have you, no one else would do."

The grin accompanying that last comment assured she was merely putting him on. Although they had dated for awhile, nothing even remotely that serious was ever part of their long ago conversations. They had had many good times going to football games and parties, but after graduation, each went their separate ways with nary a tear being shed.

"The last I remember," Bailey continued, "you were off to Stanford for an MBA."

"Did that," she replied. "And worked for a few years on the West Coast. But I missed the Midwest, especially Michigan."

"Many years ago, Janelle Rapp told me you came back this way," Bailey offered. "Saw her at a party in Cadillac. But I never knew about Niles."

"Well, what about you?" Kora asked. "Wives? Children? Male lovers?"

"None of the above," came the response. "Almost got married twice. The first gal dumped me just weeks before the ceremony. I chickened out on the second try at a similarly late date. After that, I moved across the state to Ludington where I've lived ever since. My, my. How did two of the best looking UM grads avoid that confining sacred institution all our lives?"

"You do mean marriage and not UM!" Kora suggested with yet another snicker. "Maybe because we both feared it would be confining?"

"Oh no," he replied. "I just said that. I was never much of a man about town, as you well know. After the second near miss, I pretty much gave up on women. And not because I became interested in men either. What's your story? No close calls even?"

"Well, not much of a story, I suppose," Kora began carefully, "but since you ask and since you don't have a wife I might offend, remember how we'd crash at your place after an evening out with your friends. How many times did I spend the night with you? More than a dozen, for sure. We fooled around a fair amount. But you never made the big move. On a few occasions over the years, I've wondered why."

"Wow," Bailey answered with a most surprised look on his face, "I never saw that coming. Nowadays, you get right to the point. I never remember you doing that before. And….I'm a little confused. Are you implying there is some even remote connection between my being timid and your not getting married?"

"Only indirectly. But you're dodging my question."

"Hey, you always seemed like a fairly uptight Church of Christ girl. I didn't think you did that sort of thing. I always figured you'd just say 'no' if I tried. We had a lot of fun together. I guess I never wanted to risk spoiling that."

"When I knew you, I never had done 'that sort of thing'. But I thought maybe with you I might be ready."

"What? I missed out on a chance with someone as gorgeous as you?"

"Yeah, I'm the one who got away, huh? But it was more than that. Later on, when I finally did give in, the couple of different guys were nothing special. I honestly never enjoyed it very much. Not sure why. For awhile, I even began to think I might like women. But I never went there."

"What was the matter with those California men?"

"For starters, they were more experienced than I was. And that wasn't an easy thing for me to hide. None seemed that interested in me. Their good time just routinely included some action. That's all."

"But there must've been somebody special who shared a lot of what you liked."

"Not really. The Stanford crowd was already well connected in the business world. Most of the guys were bright but self-centered and shallow. I wanted to learn as much as I could about business so I could make a good living. And my career has been good to me. But none of the guys I crossed paths with cared about art, music, literature. You did. We always had so much to talk about. Maybe that's why we never had sex!"

The two smiled in unison, with Bailey still thinking about what he had missed, before he mustered a response.

"Stanford guys shallow? I never would've believed that. That's a far better grad school than I ever could've gotten into. I was fortunate to be accepted at Purdue. It was okay but West Lafayette was anything but a hotspot for women. Only after I started working did I do any real dating. And the ultimate results were.......well, you already know."

Bailey stopped before he rambled on any further. Sensing his embarrassment, Kora jumped back into the conversation.

"No doubt there were some terrific men at Stanford. They just never came my way. Once I seriously got into fashion design, men took a permanent place on my back burner. There are plenty of interesting people in that profession. I was never lonesome or anything. At least, I never thought so."

Kora stopped for a second before continuing in an effort to clarify herself.

"Don't get me wrong. It's not like I've been carrying a torch all these years. But you've occasionally popped in and out of my mind. I sometimes wondered if things might've been different if my first bout of real passion had been with someone who actually gave a flip about me."

Not wanting to put him on the spot any more than she already had, Kora quickly resumed speaking before Bailey had a chance to respond. Her line of thought, however, changed direction ever so slightly.

"One thing I often remembered is that we never fought about anything. Maybe it was just because, since we were never serious, there was nothing to fight about. But it was kind of cool. The guys I dated later on? Before too long we were having some detailed argument about the most unimportant thing. You certainly set a standard on that issue."

"We did get on pretty well. I was just myself and you were just yourself. It all seemed pretty natural and easy, I guess."

The two of them looked at each other and nodded before Bailey moved on.

"How are your two younger sisters doing?" he asked.

"See. It's amazing you still remember them. Most of the guys I dated never took any interest in anyone in my family. Gail and Liz are both fine. Each has two children, grown now, but when they were little, they fulfilled my own need for kids. I still see them every once in awhile. They think of me as their widely travelled Aunt Kora, mostly because I always brought them something from the neat places I would go. How did you handle not having kids?"

"It wasn't always easy. I love children. I'm actually the vice president of a firm that sells playground equipment to schools, city parks, and even some churches. I've taken a lot of pride in helping to design safe items. It's very satisfying watching small children having fun."

"Any kids more directly in your life?" Kora persisted.

"My brother has two boys that I watched grow up. In some ways, I was closer to them than to my brother. When the college years came, my contact with all of them became much more limited. A familiar story, huh?"

"Do you remember the different concerts you took me to?"

"Sure. The Kinks. The Association. And.........the Animals."

"I listen to all that music faithfully, even now. Tommy James still lives in Niles, you know. Thirty years ago, I would have fought through a crowd to get his autograph. Today, we say hello at the grocery store."

"Remember when we went to hear the lecture by Eugene McCarthy?" Bailey now recalled.

"Oh yea. Very serious message but not much of a speaker. We were both so disappointed. Still the hopeless dreamy eyed left winger you once were?"

"Pretty much. You?"

"Sure thing. People in fashion are fairly eclectic. Some have no interest in politics or even the news. Others are quite serious about various social causes. A couple of my co-workers and I volunteer at a soup kitchen. We were active in the Clinton campaign. And later we worked for Gore."

"So did I, in both cases. Some of the people I work with got on my case when I supported increases in the minimum wage. Until we got more dedicated and healthier workers. Turnover became less frequent, we wasted less time retraining people, and more of our employees could afford the equipment we were selling. It was a win-win. I don't know why more business owners don't see that."

"I've always been a fan of stylish affordable clothing. Sometimes that's a hard sell when owners want to set trends by appealing first to the wealthy. But I've really enjoyed it when my company has had success with moderately priced items."

"Do you still like high action and mystery movies?" Bailey asked.

"Haven't missed one since you took me to see 'The Adventurers'. Although I've come to prefer a little less bloody scenes."

"So have I. Indiana Jones has been about the right level of action for me. 'Romancing the Stone' was great. I liked the first in the

'Terminator' series but, after that, Ahhnold's limited acting ability really came through."

"I can't believe he's thinking about running for Governor of California. Just when I thought it was impossible for that state to produce someone more simple-minded than Ronald Reagan. Why can't actors just stick to acting?"

"Amen. So I guess we're back to the religion issue. Still active in the Church of Christ?"

"Gave that up after my first month at Stanford. I'm an Episcopalian of sorts, when I do go to church. Dogmatic fundamentalist thinking messed me up in more ways than one. As much as I loved my parents, I can't believe they were still clinging to all those absolute beliefs even as they stared death in the face. Small towns do have some shortcomings. Are you still a Catholic?"

"Gave that up after my first month at Purdue. I attend Episcopalian services during holidays. There are some very sincere people in that church. Most are so accepting of those who are different. And they don't have an idiot pope whose behavior they either have to defend or ignore while inwardly feeling very embarrassed."

"Have you noticed how much we seem to have in common?" Kora noted. "We were more different when we dated than we are now."

"Seems a shame we didn't touch base sooner," Bailey reflected.

There was a long pause. Neither wanted to pick up on that last line but it momentarily haunted both of them.

Eventually, talk resumed, superficial at first but soon they got back on track. Books, museums, and vacation spots all were touched upon. Both were amazed to find their favorite vacations were in Yosemite, the mountains of North Carolina, and rural Wyoming. On those trips, they had actually lodged and dined at a number of the same places, only in different years.

When Bailey finally glanced at his watch, he noticed it was five p. m. Both he and Kora began to invent reasons why they needed to leave even though neither actually had to be anywhere in particular. Their departure was far less dramatic than their initial meeting. It also was a bit strained and formal considering the intimate topics they had just addressed.

She encouraged him to look her up if he ever passed through Niles. Both waved without so much as even shaking hands.

Kora went back to her room upstairs.

As Bailey climbed into his car, he realized he had not even gotten her phone number or email address.

During the next five years, he would occasionally recall some of the details of his chance meeting with Kora Gamel in the Soo.

Daisy's Restaurant

The summer he turned sixteen, Ray Nolan got his first job. A friend of his father had recently bought a restaurant that had closed its doors the previous winter. Cy Stapleton, a local high school graduate now in his late thirties, had tried his hand at several business ventures. Even though the previous owner had not done well, Cy had high hopes for his new breakfast and lunch eatery.

After personally remodeling the lone dining area, he hired three waitresses plus Ray who would double as a waiter and the person who did whatever else was needed. Eager to please and filled with youthful energy, Ray learned quickly and impressed his first-ever boss. Not wanting to disappoint or embarrass his father, Ray initially felt added pressure to do well. With that fear now behind him, he soon found his work satisfying and enjoyable.

Whether he was asked to compute total register sales at the end of the day or merely take out the garbage, each task was performed cheerfully. Ray also did not mind working with young ladies his age or slightly older and therefore more mature in a number of outwardly visible ways.

Cy originally had considered renaming the business but eventually decided that neither Cy's nor Stapleton's nor any catchy phrase was better than Daisy's. He ultimately hoped some name recognition still existed and would attract previous customers. Deep down inside, he believed that those who had lived in Somerville for some time and who could recall pleasant experiences under previous management would return.

Cy also hoped to capitalize on other advantages. Even though the restaurant was three miles from town, it sat on the main highway connecting Michigan to Indiana and eventually to Chicago. Many tourists from Illinois passed the site on their way to vacation spots in the lower peninsula and in Canada. There was also a Michigan Tourist Information Center next door where busloads of hungry travelers often stopped around lunchtime.

After the first month, Ray clearly was happier here than he ever was doing odd jobs for his parents around the house. He felt like an adult when interacting with customers and hoped all his future employers would be as personable as Cy.

One of the waitresses was a high school junior-to-be named Savannah. She and Ray worked well together and had much to chat about when business was slow and both could take a break. Cy did the cooking and, as long as employees were ready to jump into action when the next customer entered, he did not object if they paused to rest and socialize.

"I hear you go to the Catholic high school in Indiana," Savannah asked one day. "What's it like?"

"Okay, I suppose," Ray responded. "Probably not that different from Somerville High. You lived here long?"

"My parents moved here four years ago from Detroit," she offered. "The small town took some getting used to. But I like it now. This is a rare chance to meet somebody new. I thought I already knew everyone who lived here."

Ray took this as encouragement to get to know her better and see wherever that might lead. His inexperience with girls, however, caused him to be both cautious and anything but aggressive. That the two of them had been thrown together by circumstance other than being in the same class was something new to him.

Before long, two separate groups entered the front door so the conversation was cut short. The following morning, Ray worked with Justine who was prettier than Savannah but less outgoing. Ray learned at the end of the day that Justine had a boyfriend who picked her up after work.

The third waitress who was there only on weekends was a total knockout. Ray concluded fairly quickly that, in spite of or maybe because of her looks, Roxanne was clearly out of his league. If he was to get anywhere with any of his co-workers, Savannah was the most likely candidate.

Not that she was merely a third rate consolation prize. Ray liked her for all she was: attractive, friendly, and prone to story telling. Each time they talked, Ray learned something new about her. She was willing to share a number of details about her family and her life back in the big city. She also asked Ray all about himself and his family. Whenever he showed up for work, he hoped Savannah would be there.

As time passed, Ray was also learning more about the operation of a restaurant. Cy even began showing him how to fry bacon and eggs on the grill as well as how to use and clean the waffle iron. One day he took Ray into the walk-in cooler and demonstrated the art of mixing root beer syrup with water before a machine created the bubbles. The young teenager took it all in and soon was allowed to assist in the kitchen when business became brisk.

Ray was especially curious when various suppliers dropped in to take orders or deliver their products. Some items like eggs and tomatoes were bought fresh from a local farmer. On Tuesdays, a frozen foods wholesaler would emerge right on schedule to check if French fries, onion rings, and frog legs were running low. Ray was forward enough that he soon knew all suppliers by name.

During a break one afternoon, Savannah walked up to Ray with a beaming smile on her face. He was not sure what was coming but his heart did begin beating faster than usual. Now almost giddy, she stopped just a few inches from his face.

"Did you happen to notice that dreamy guy who was here for lunch?" she asked.

Ray's heart quickly returned to normal speed. This was not what he had hoped to hear.

"*Dreamy* guy?" he offered meekly. "No. I must've missed him. I was back in the kitchen helping Cy. Why?"

"This is the third day this week he's been here," she added quickly. "Wow! Wavy hair, stylishly dressed, tanned hairy arms."

As soon as Ray regained his composure, he realized he had to offer a polite response despite his disinterest in the topic.

"Have you talked to him?" he asked dutifully.

"Only for a few minutes," came the reply. "His name is Derek and he has a summer job at the golf course. I also found out he'll be a sophomore at Notre Dame."

"Notre Dame!" Ray repeated almost reverently. "It's always been my dream to go there. I've just never thought I'd be good enough, especially coming from such a small school."

Before he could say another word, Cy called him into the kitchen.

"How can I compete with a guy who's already in college?" Ray thought to himself as he walked into the adjoining room. "I don't even have a driver's license."

Cy was direct when he began speaking.

"We'll close down about four today," he said. "Could we talk for a few minutes after everyone leaves?"

"Sure thing, Cy," Ray replied. "Especially if you can give me a ride home."

The owner nodded before turning to some paper work.

Thankfully, Savannah was busy waiting on a table when Ray returned to the dining area. He was greatly relieved that he would not have to hear any more about this Derek fellow for awhile.

When Savannah waved good-bye at 4:15, Cy locked the front door. He and Ray then walked toward the lunch counter.

"Want a coke or something?" Cy asked.

"I'll get it," came the reply. "One for you?" he quickly added.

"Yeah, sure."

Cy got right to the point.

"Your Dad might've already told you I'm also a building contractor," he began.

Ray acknowledged by raising his eyebrows and acting interested.

"Well," Cy continued. "I just landed this new job to build an apartment complex about thirty miles from here outside of Edwardsburg. For the next few weeks, I'll need to be there early in the morning until some time in the evening."

He paused and looked at Ray as if he expected to hear a question. On cue, Ray delivered.

"So what are you going to do about Daisy's?" he said.

"Are you up to running it for me until you go back to school?" Cy asked with an assuring smile that also looked serious.

"Are you kidding?" Ray answered with a tone of fear in his voice. "I've only been working here less than two months. I'm barely 16. If the place catches on fire, I can't even drive away."

"You already know most of what needs to be done around here," Cy responded confidently. "You can cook just about everything on the menu. To complete your repertoire, I'll show you how to make poached eggs. The suppliers will help you decide how much to order. You'll just need to sign for their stuff. You'll be supervising the girls. They're all pretty good at what they do. Oh, and I trust you not to set the place on fire. But if that happens, you know to call the fire department before you run outside, don't you?"

"Of course," Ray stated as his heart once again began to speed up and as both of them grinned.

"I'll stop by your house with the pastries from the bakery and a bag full of money for the cash register about 6 a.m…" Cy added. "I've already checked this out with your Dad. He says he's confident you can do it. As you've seen, it starts to get slow by mid to late afternoon. It's totally up to you what time you decide to close up. When you do, shut everything down, put all the money and the register receipt in the bag, and lock up. I'll stop by your house for the money about 8 or so in the evening. Sound OK?"

"Yeah!" Ray intoned, this time with enthusiasm.

"You'll be the youngest manager in the history of the restaurant industry," Cy concluded. "Well, at least in Somerville."

When he fully grasped what was happening, Ray did not even think to ask if being a manager meant a raise. The thought finally crossed his mind two days later. He then realized it would probably not be very diplomatic to ask. He already told Cy he would do it without even mentioning any added coin. Besides, he thought, how do you ask for more money after only working just a few weeks for someone?

The following week went well. After loading the bakery goods into the car the first morning, Ray and his Dad each had a donut on the way to work. Mr. Nolan waited outside until Ray turned on the lights inside Daisy's at about 6:30. By seven, coffee was brewed and all cooking devices were ready to go. Either Savannah, Justine, Roxanne, or more than one would arrive just before seven when the doors officially opened.

As the days passed, all three ladies were moderately surprised, and impressed, at how well their new "boss" handled things. Daisy's was doing a decent business even though the oldest employee inside was only 17. Somehow, Ray never felt nervous about being in charge even when the place was nearly full. Whatever was demanded, he was up to it.

Eggs and pancakes at breakfast plus sandwiches and soup orders at lunch soon became routine. Hot plates like meatloaf with two sides varied from day to day.

Ray had a list of people to call---an electrician, a plumber, an appliance repairman---in case of emergency. Only once did the refrigerator fail. Ray responded by loading food into styrofoam ice chests until the compressor was fixed later in the day.

His most challenging order came the morning a man in a coat and tie ordered poached eggs. Ray knew he had to crack the eggs and drop them into a small pot of water. What he could not remember was whether or not the water had to boil first. With other orders frying on the grill, Ray dropped the eggs into the water shortly after he lit the fire under the pot. Minutes later, the two eggs looked exactly like they were supposed to be served.

After ten minutes or so, Ray noticed the man in the coat and tie walking out the door. When she cleared the table, Roxanne brought the note that had been left and showed it to Ray. It read:

"Please tell your chef I was unable to cut into the eggs, even with a sharp knife. Next time, you might want to give me an electric drill or an ax."

"Did he pay the bill?" Ray the manager asked Roxanne.

"In full," she replied. "But no tip."

"Sorry, my fault," Ray offered.

At lunch that day, Derek sat at the counter and remained after all the other customers had left. Savannah introduced him to Ray and the three visited for nearly half an hour.

Three days later, Derek returned at just past 2 p. m. The threesome resumed their chat where they had previously left off.

When he had the chance, Ray asked all about Notre Dame. What was it like? How hard was it to get in? Who besides teachers should write letters of recommendation? There were many questions.

Through it all, Savannah remained amused and was just happy Ray was keeping Derek around longer than usual. By this time of the day, the place was practically empty.

As he rose to leave, Derek turned back, faced the two restaurant employees, and acted as though he was about to ask a question. This time it was Savannah whose heart began beating faster.

"Hey Ray," Derek called out. "Do you play golf?"

"I have a few times," came the reply. "But I'm not very good."

"Care to play tomorrow after you close down here?" Derek offered. "I can swing by to pick you up. Maybe it'll give us a chance to talk more about ND."

"Sure thing," Ray stated matter-of-factly.

After the door closed, Savannah turned to Ray and said half seriously: "I hate you. I thought he was going to ask me out, not you."

"Relax," Ray replied. "Maybe I'll put in a good word for you."

"Don't you dare," she responded bluntly. "I don't want you to set me up. I can do this on my own."

"Suit yourself," he said. "You're not exactly doing that great so far."

Derek was an ace on the course. He sank putts from twenty feet with apparent ease prompting Ray to ask: "How do you do that?"

"I play this course at least once every day," he answered. "It's a lot more challenging when I have to play somewhere else. Plus, I help maintain these greens. That makes it easy to see where the ball is likely to break."

The two of them talked about Notre Dame during and after their round of 18 holes. Derek sensed his new friend had what it took to succeed in a first rate university program. He answered all of Ray's questions as best as he could. He repeatedly stressed that coming from a small town, attending a small school, and having parents of limited means were not liabilities.

When he dropped Ray off at his house, he offered one final piece of advice.

"You remember you asked me about recommendation letters?" he began. "Well, I thought about it yesterday. Besides teachers, a letter from an employer like Cy wouldn't hurt. The admissions people would probably be impressed that you can cook and manage a restaurant. But it would really be good if you could get an ND alumnus to write one."

Ray thought for a few seconds before responding with a frown.

"I don't know a single person who went to Notre Dame," he said.

Now it was Derek's turn to reflect for a moment. He then looked at Ray and offered: "How about if I get my uncle who owns the golf course to write you a letter?"

Ray finished out the summer working at Daisy's. Some time after he returned to school, Cy sold the restaurant and became a full time builder. Needing money for school, Ray spent the following summer after he graduated working in a factory that paid well. He heard that Savannah was attending a local community college but otherwise lost contact with her.

Ray was never sure if he was accepted into Notre Dame because of his near straight B+ average and huge list of high school extra-curriculars or the letter from Derek's uncle.

During his second week on campus, he ran into Derek and thanked him for his help.

"No problem," Derek offered with a smile. "Let's play some golf after you get settled. By the way," he added as he started to turn away. "Do you ever see Savannah, the nice girl you used to work with?"

"Not in the last year," Ray replied. "Why do you ask?"

"Just wondering," Derek stated casually. "Once or twice, I thought about asking her out. Maybe I still will.......some day."

"After all this time?" Ray went on. "What took you so long to decide?"

"I guess I'm a little slow with women," Derek admitted. "Besides, I always figured she had a thing for you. You're mostly what she talked about whenever I came into Daisy's."

Happy Hour

Kirby Renfro tossed aside the book he was reading and glanced at the clock on the wall. It was 3:45. Four months earlier, he had met a young lady who worked in an office two buildings from where Kirby had one of his classes. He paused for a moment to reflect on where they were headed together and where his own life might be going. No answer to either briefly felt concern immediately came to mind.

Kirby and Shelly Boswell had organized a late Friday afternoon gathering for friends, friends of friends, distant acquaintances, and anyone else who wanted to celebrate the end of the workweek. Two months ago, the group included eight people. As Kirby would discover within the next half hour, the count this week would reach nearly thirty.

The meeting place was Vitek's, a popular watering hole a block from campus. When Kirby arrived, Shelly was already there sipping on her first beer. They hugged before she introduced him to some of the new arrivals.

"This is Elaine, Vicki, and Tina", she began. "They live down the street from me. We just met last week and they are really neat. We hit it off right away. Guys, this is my boyfriend, Kirby."

Smiles and polite hellos were exchanged. Kirby then waved to the others seated at the long table. There were Dennis and Reggie whom he had known for some time along with Leo and Bonnie whom he had met only a week ago. He remembered the last two for their outgoing personalities and sense of humor. After a few drinks, everyone behaved as if they were old friends. That was the beauty of these gatherings.

Dennis had dropped in and out of school for the past three years. He had some basic smarts and hoped to one day maybe teach high school. For now, he lacked motivation. The college scene was comfortable and some financial support from home was still coming. A part time job here and there provided some beer money and funded occasional dabbling in drugs. Nothing serious, just a little weed every other night.

Reggie was more of a full time student but was also more heavily into hard drugs. An older brother with the same habit but with a steady job was his primary supplier and occasional financial helper.

Kirby met both Dennis and Reggie at a party where they all expressed similar political views. Concern for the environment and poverty plus a disdain for conservative politicians were all part of the glue that drew the three of them together. With Richard Nixon in the White House, there was ample fodder for critical remarks. Despite their vocal support for a range of social issues, none of the young men were especially active in any of these causes.

Kirby had a higher IQ and better SAT scores than his two friends but, as long as the three remained companions, all were going nowhere fast. Only occasionally did Kirby indulge in pot despite the constant urging he felt from those around him.

"So how was school today?" Shelly asked.

"About the same," Kirby replied. "Still uninspiring. Sometimes I wonder why I'm doing this. How was work?"

"It's just a job. The boss was easy on me today. Guess he knew my mind was already on this weekend. So what're we doing tonight?"

"Haven't thought about it much. What do you feel like?"

Shelly just shrugged her shoulders. They had had this same conversation last week and the week before. Kirby ordered a beer and joined into what the others were already discussing. Topics changed quickly. A few jokes were told. In an hour or so, no one would recall much of what had been said. It was not that all soon became inebriated but rather that, aside from a new funny story, few lines were worth repeating. Or remembering.

Kirby talked a little with the threesome he had just met. He found out that Elaine waited tables part time, Vicki did odd jobs, and Tina was unemployed. They were all friendly but a little shallow. Tina stood out as far better looking than the other two.

People came and went as their anything but rigid schedules dictated. When someone left, it was seldom because he or she had to be some*where* else but due more to the fact that it was simply time, for whatever reason, to move on to some*thing* else.

By 7 o'clock, Kirby and Shelly were getting hungry so they finished their last beer before heading out to get a pizza. Kirby knew they'd be jumping into bed together later that evening but it was too early to think about that. Maybe a party or something would fill in a couple of hours although the end of the evening was really all he could think about.

Their conversation was warm. Very little about each of their days seemed worth recalling. The two of them got along well even when little was being said. She was probably thinking about later in the evening, too.

After awhile, Shelly addressed a topic that had been on her mind for the past few days.

"Next weekend, I'm going home to see my father in Muskegon. Want to come meet him?"

"Sure," Kirby replied without hesitating. Driving to another town would at least be something different, he thought to himself, even if it did mean staying in the same house with Shelly and not sleeping together.

"What's the occasion?" he finally added.

"My Dad has a new girlfriend," Shelly responded as she rolled her eyes. "He's invited my brother and me to come meet her. All I know is she's not the one he was seeing when he was still married to my Mom. He gets around, you know."

"Where did you say your mother lives now?" Kirby asked despite being only borderline interested.

"Not long after they got divorced, she moved to Kentucky. She met some car mechanic in town who had family down there. As far as I know, they've been living together ever since. I felt sorry for her back then but I don't hear much from her any more."

"Your dad still owns the truck stop?"

"Yeah. That's where he started fooling around with the waitresses he hired. When he'd dump one for another, they started quitting on him. I think this new one's a maid. He's really scraping the bottom of the barrel. What a jerk!"

"Sounds like it'll be a fun weekend," Kirby offered trying to make light of a serious moment.

As the following Friday approached, he had no idea what to expect. He always wanted to sound optimistic and never focus for too long on anything that involved the more somber side of life. In his present state of mind, there was plenty of time for that stuff later on.

The drive to Muskegon provided plenty of time to talk about several matters. Not every one was destined to be benign.

"You seem to be deep in thought today," Shelly suggested. "Surely, you're not worried about meeting my father and brother."

"Oh no," came the reply. "Of course not. No big deal. Well, I don't mean they're no big deal. I'm looking forward to it and no, I'm not worried."

"Then what is it? Are you disappointed we're missing the happy hour?"

"They'll probably get on okay without us, even though we were the organizers. I wonder how long that tradition will survive?"

"No telling," Shelly answered while still looking at Kirby as if she knew something else was on his mind. "So what *are* you think-ing about?" she added.

"I'm trying to decide whether or not to drop out of school," he stated bluntly.

"Wow! That's a big one. What brought this on all of a sudden?"

"You know it's not all of a sudden. What will I do with a degree in sociology? Sometimes it's really depressing. I feel like a fish out of water. So the world is a messed up place. That's mostly what I'm learning. And I already had a pretty good idea that was the case."

"That's the most serious thing I've ever heard you say. I never knew you had that side. You always seem to be full of fun and not bothered by anything. That's one of the things that attracted me to you."

"Sorry to disappoint," Kirby voiced with a frown.

The conversation reached a pause for a few minutes before Kirby resumed an outward expression of his thoughts.

"This is my fifth year here at Western and I have no idea how close I am to graduating. It's probably still a way's off. So much of what I've taken doesn't apply to my latest major. I should probably talk to an advisor but the last one I had seemed totally disinterested in me. Nobody here seems to care very much about anything except having a good time. I guess that attitude is contagious."

"Hey," Shelly injected, "nobody's pressuring you to do anything. I'm certainly not."

"Maybe that's the problem," Kirby noted intuitively. "I probably need someone to kick my ass."

Shelly did not take the bait. Two years older than her current boyfriend, she had been in the same secretarial position for the past three years after moving to Kalamazoo from her hometown. Over that time, she had registered for a total of four courses and had only finished one. Her relationship with Kirby was the longest running she had experienced in some time although he knew little about her past. Whenever he asked, she would talk in vague generalities before refocusing on the present. Her apparent live for the moment mindset was refreshing to Kirby who found her to be pleasant company when his momentary depression needed lifting.

Her father's house was modern and its yard was well kept. He looked about 50 and his broad smile was welcoming. He hugged Shelly and gave Kirby a warm handshake. Her introduction was unimpressive.

"This is Kirby," was all she said before quickly walking into the house.

"Good to meet you, Mr. Boswell," the young man asserted politely.

After sharing a beer and some light exchange of words, the three of them noticed a young man walking up to the front door. Shelly's older brother had driven down from Cadillac where he worked in a factory.

"Hey Boy!" their father said as he rose to greet his son.

"What do you say, Pop?" Rocky responded.

Kirby noticed the setting was a little awkward. No one in the room seemed especially close. The father asked how both of his kids were getting on and even asked Kirby a thing or two about his hometown but not his family. The younger group's refusal of an offer for a second beer did not deter Mr. Boswell from popping another for himself. He clearly seemed nervous about introducing his kids to his latest love interest. Kirby just took it all in and occasionally smiled at Shelly who was seated next to him.

After a silence of a few minutes, the elder man spoke.

"So Rocky," he said, "are you going to look up Tanya Greene on this trip to town? She's been asking about you. You probably know she's married these days but her husband's out of town a lot and, of course, that never stopped you before."

"It certainly never stopped you, Warren," Shelly stated pointedly and disrespectfully.

"Now take it easy, little girl," her surprised father replied. "What happened between me and your mother is long over and done with. We've both moved on."

"From what I hear, you've been moving on pretty regularly," Shelly snapped. "Still having trouble hiring women to work for you? Have all the waitresses in town heard about you and decided to keep away?"

"I don't want to go there," he replied as he looked at both young men and threw his hands up into the air as if he were seeking support.

No one said anything.

After another long pause, Rocky finally spoke.

"I don't think I'll be calling on Tanya, Pop. There's plenty of other available women where I live now. I'm anything but lonesome."

Warren smiled approvingly. Noticing his facial expression, Shelly flashed a look of contempt.

"So when are we gonna meet the latest whore in your life?" she asked.

"Please don't talk like that," he replied with a sad and pitiful look on his face. "This is a really sweet gal. You're all gonna like her."

"I think I'll take that beer now," Shelly requested.

Warren began to rise from his chair as he spoke.

"Sure, Honey, I'll......"

"I'll get it myself," she quipped.

When she returned, she slapped an unopened can into Kirby's hand and tossed a second in the direction of her brother. No one in the room made eye contact for the next five minutes.

This time the silence was broken when a lady entered the front door without knocking.

"Hello there, my dear sweet Warren," the lady said. "And who are all these good looking people?"

Warren introduced everyone starting with his son. When he finished, he simply looked at the group and stated matter of factly: "This is my future wife, Mona Babb."

The lady probably expected some type of warm greeting or maybe even a word of congratulations.

She got neither.

Shelly and Rocky looked away in disbelief. Finally, Kirby extended his hand much as he had done earlier and mouthed a simple: "Pleased to meet you."

"Let's all sit and get to know each other," Warren suggested in an optimistic tone that could hardly be justified.

There were a dozen or more questions Shelly wanted to ask, all of which would have been insulting, but she decided instead to maintain silence and let the others talk. She already told her father how she felt and his lady was certainly able to pick up on the negative vibes.

Warren looked happy as a teenager on his way to the prom, Mona was eager to please, Rocky was visibly disinterested, and Shelly was having difficulty hiding her disgust.

Kirby spoke not a word and was understandably curious where all this was going to lead.

For the most part, talk was civil. Mona was shy but charming. She eventually expressed to all her love for Warren and desire to make him happy. Her intended used every cliché in the book to describe her looks and personality.

Since Warren's children remained speechless, Kirby eventually felt obligated to say something.

"So how did you two meet?" he stated innocently.

"Our beginning was pretty humble," Mona offered. "Warren had a little too much to drink at a party in the hotel where I work and was unable to drive home. So some of his friends got him a room and carried him up to bed. The next day, I accidentally woke him up around noon when I came to clean the room."

"We hit it off right away," Warren added. "She took care of me and got me going so I could get to work. I called her the next day. And that was that."

The three guests looked at each other but still did not speak.

Warren later took everyone out to dinner at his favorite local restaurant where he toasted Mona, his children, and even Kirby. Afterwards, he asked a friend at the next table to take a picture of the group in front of the fireplace. Although he was invited to join, Kirby eventually convinced everyone it would be better if he were not included.

The generally pleasant evening ended with everyone crashing at the Boswell house. Since Warren and Mona slept in the master bedroom, Kirby joined Shelly in the room she had had as a child. The couple talked for a long time about the hurtful dislike Shelly felt for her father. They eventually drifted off to sleep.

On Saturday morning, Mona prepared breakfast and Kirby helped set the table. Warren announced to all the plans he had for a day of fun. All but Mona quickly found excuses not to participate.

"Kirby and I are going to head back to Kalamazoo today," Shelly announced. "There's stuff we have to do."

This was the first Kirby had heard of any change in plans. Before he could say a word, Rocky expressed a similar desire to leave. Later, when all headed for their cars, he flashed a devious smile and whispered to Kirby that he had decided to look up Tanya Greene that night after all.

Warren was disappointed but thankful his children had spent at least one evening with him and his fiancé with no serious arguments occurring. He said they would receive an invitation to the wedding next month but knew it was unlikely either would attend.

The ride back to Kalamazoo was more subdued than the trip the previous day. More than once, Shelly apologized for dragging Kirby to such an unhappy event. Through it all, he was the good sport she expected he would be.

After Shelly fell asleep, Kirby reflected on what had just happened. He at first realized she had probably needed him to be there for moral support. Although he was anything but vain, he also eventually admitted to himself that he was there to show her family she was capable, despite what must have been a valueless home life, of attracting someone half way normal.

For the next few days, Kirby thought more seriously than ever what the overnight trip had taught him. He continued to see Shelly but they clearly were becoming more distant and she could easily understand why. More than anything, he did not want to hurt her feelings but it was soon clear to both that their days together were numbered.

One evening, some harsh words were exchanged. Shelly expressed anger that Kirby undoubtedly felt she was not good enough for him. Although he denied such feelings, they both knew this assessment was accurate. Almost to seal the verdict, Shelly announced that she had briefly been married shortly after high school but that it had lasted less than a year. Polite to a flaw, Kirby maintained that fact did not matter although he did express disappointment she was unwilling to share that information with him until now.

That was the last evening they would spend in each other's company. It ended before 8 p. m.

Because of their split, it was uncertain which of them would inherit the Friday afternoon happy hour crowd. At first, Kirby wondered if both might attend separately and simply mingle with different people in the now 30+ member group. Dennis and Reggie stopped by Kirby's place on Wednesday evening to offer condolences and assurance that they would keep Shelly company at happy hour so Kirby could sit elsewhere.

Kirby thanked them for their consideration and said he had not decided what he would now do about the welcome to the weekend gathering.

When Friday came, he did not attend. Instead, he got caught up on some reading for his Contemporary Social Problems class.

The following day, he took a long walk by himself. He thought not only about Shelly and their mutual friends but also about his long on the back burner career plans. He knew he would miss Shelly but her unusual family and her own either limited or nonexistent goals assured him they were not a good fit.

He then gave much thought to the crowd at Vitek's Bar. Who, he now asked himself, in that group did he consider his closest friends, ones worth keeping? He pondered this precise thought for over an hour until he reached a seemingly startling conclusion. Among the more than thirty people with whom he had spent almost every Friday for the past few months, there was no one he would consider a close friend.

Dennis and Reggie were nice guys but were so passive about almost everything. They spent most of their free time just listening to music, watching TV, and doing dope. Kirby doubted either would ever make anything of himself or accomplish something of value. All the others were fun drinking buddies who told some funny stories. None of the single girls in the group seemed worth pursuing. Most importantly, there was no one in the Vitek's gang that Kirby ever felt he could look to if he ever needed advice or anything else.

Two days later, Kirby met with his advisor and finalized a degree plan that would allow him to graduate in two semesters if he took 16 hours in each. He also gathered information about taking the Law School Admission Test with a view to studying some aspect of international law, something that had always interested him. He then wrote for the law school catalogues from the University of Michigan, Indiana University, and the University of Illinois. He knew his seemingly sudden bold plan would involve a great deal of work but he finally decided he was up to it.

After his Friday morning class that week, Kirby talked to the young lady who had been sitting next to him all semester. Kelly McDermott was a junior from Battle Creek who was also interested in law school. That Saturday night, they went out on their first date.

Family Freak

When George W. Bush became president in 2001, Evan Zerba took leave from the faculty of Southern Michigan University to become a foreign affairs advisor in the State Department. While Evan thoroughly enjoyed teaching and the research he had been doing, he could not pass up the opportunity to work for former General Colin Powell. The two had met at a conference sponsored by Georgetown University in Washington where Evan presented results of his recent work on governments of the Middle East.

After that conference, he and Powell discussed that troubled part of the world for more than an hour at dinner. Long considered a potential presidential candidate himself, General Powell asked Evan to send him a copy of his latest book. Impressed with the reasoning he found in it, the new Secretary of State requested that its author join his staff to assist in the formulation of U. S. foreign policy.

Evan took a ribbing from his brothers and his in-laws when he accepted the post. Deep down inside, most family members had to be somewhat excited but they still doubted one of their own was fit for such a venture. In addition, many had an inherent distaste for anything in Washington and its federal bureaucracy.

The Zerba family hailed from south central Michigan where Evan's father had set up a small family business. Evan had three older brothers. Virgil was a railway yard worker; Larry was a roofer; Woody was a truck driver. The three had rarely left the Midwest despite the fact that they were now all over sixty. Their parents had passed away several years earlier.

Evan had met his wife, the former Lilalee Priest, when he was in graduate school at the University of Virginia. Originally from a small community in Alabama, she had received a humanities degree from the Charlottesville campus and was working in that town when the couple married.

Lilalee had two older sisters, Cindy Madigan and Denise Wilder, as well as a younger brother, Blake, who was an electrical engineer. Cindy's second husband was a cable TV repairman while Denise was married to a stonemason. Neither woman had pursued a career outside the home. Although all three siblings and their families still resided in the Deep South, it was common for the entire clan to make the trek north for the Christmas holidays.

Lilalee and Evan had always been gracious hosts and warmly opened their doors to all who needed a place to stay for as many days as they wished. His brother, Virgil, provided additional lodging, two restored cabooses behind his house, for all the children, now thirteen in number. Besides seeing Lilalee and her kids, the extended family was also drawn to Michigan by the prospect of a white Christmas. In anticipation of this outcome, they were almost never disappointed.

That Evan had gone to college at all was something of an accident. Neither his parents nor his older brothers had ever provided any conscious encouragement for him to do so. While growing up, Evan became well aware of the difficult manual labor all the men in his family endured. Somewhere along the line, he drew upon his own self-motivation to become a high achiever.

The result was an unexpected scholarship to Ohio University, where he excelled, and later a teaching assistantship to pursue graduate work at UVA. While he appreciated his small town background, something inside his head encouraged him to pursue global studies. Much to the dismay of his devout Protestant family, he was fascinated by the Islamic world and its conflicts with Western culture. All of his family and most of his hometown friends consistently reminded him that such knowledge could never be applied to gainful employment in the U.S.

While studying international relations, Evan also learned much about the Far East and Europe. All of these areas became part of his teaching repertoire early in his professional career. When he did have the opportunity to spend a summer touring several Middle Eastern countries with a government sponsored fact-finding team, he jumped at the chance. This experience no doubt influenced both his writing and Secretary Powell.

Besides Evan and Lilalee, the only other college educated extended family member of their generation was Blake Priest who obtained his engineering credential at Alabama Technical Institute. Blake was a whiz with electrical components but his knowledge of politics and culture was limited to what he had learned in a rural Alabama high school and the small town near which it was located. His children and those of the other southern siblings all received degrees from schools like Liberty in Virginia, Oral Roberts in Tulsa, and Samford in their home state of Alabama. All completed their higher education experiences without having any of their provincial values challenged.

Some of Evan's nephews and nieces received northern versions of narrow-mindedness at such stalwart institutions as Wheaton College near Chicago, Grove City College in Pennsylvania, and Hillsdale College in Michigan. The latter had long been praised by the likes of Paul Harvey, William Buckley and other writers for his *National Review*, and several Fox News pundits.

Evan and Lilalee had two daughters, both of whom had graduated from Cornell and were now employed in the health care field. In the entire extended family, these were the only two who sometimes questioned the hardcore Republican Party line. Those reservations were almost never expressed vocally when cousins, aunts, and uncles were present.

This year's Christmas family gathering was the first since Evan and Lilalee had taken up temporary residence in Washington. She had returned to their Michigan home a week before the others arrived for the long holiday. Evan was scheduled to spend three full days with everyone but knew he would be maintaining telephone contact with his D. C. office.

It was a nationally tense and politically charged time. In response to the terrorist attacks of September 11, the president had sent U. S. troops into Afghanistan where, after prolonged battles, they had not been able to capture Osama bin Laden. Attention had now shifted to Iraq where the American military was in pursuit of Saddam Hussein, his sons, and the troops who supported them.

War on this second front was controversial and a vital part of public debate. As expected, the U. S. role in the world dominated discussion at the family gathering. Opinions, whether informed or not, flowed freely.

Interestingly enough, the opinion least in demand was that of Evan. Everyone else wanted him to hear their views so he would implement them when back at work. Few understood his actual input into foreign policy was minimal, even though he did participate in some fairly high level meetings. He primarily did background research when specific requests for information came from those at the top of the State Department hierarchy.

By far, the two most opinionated family members were Lilalee's sister, Cindy, and their brother, Blake. Cindy had dropped out of high school when she became pregnant but later completed her GED. She admired her brother more for his practicality than his degree. Neither read much but both got most of their information from Fox News. Cindy also kept her ears open during her weekly visits to the beauty shop.

On this occasion, when the subject of Iraq surfaced, it was Blake who got the ball rolling.

"We should've gotten Saddam during the first Gulf War," he opined. "Once we liberated Kuwait from his thugs, our troops should've gone all the way to Baghdad."

"Amen to that," Cindy offered in full support. "That man is a menace to the world and a threat to our security. He no doubt was responsible for 9/11. He and his buddy Osama planned that attack for years. And they caught us unprepared. I'm very nervous about the weapons of mass destruction he has."

Although Evan had reservations about some of what had just been said, he chose not to respond. Blake, however, was not going to let him off that easily. His next comment was aimed directly at his brother-in-law.

"Saw something on the news the other day that your boss has been reluctant to support our going into Iraq," he stated bluntly. "What the hell is the matter with him?"

Evan took a deep breath and began his reply.

"Among those directly involved in setting policy, General Powell is the only career military man. More than anyone else, he understands the horrors of war and that it should be undertaken only as a last resort. He and others at State, myself included, also question the accuracy of some of the intelligence the president is operating on. There is no evidence whatsoever that anyone in Iraq was involved in 9/11. It's unlikely there's ever been any cooperation between Saddam, who in practice is fairly secular, and bin Laden, who claims to be a religious zealot. There's also no proof that Saddam has weapons of mass destruction. A direct threat to us? That's pretty doubtful."

"What do you mean 'no WMDs'?" Blake snapped. "It was reported definitively on the news. Hussein used them on his own people. The news also said one of his top men met somewhere in Europe with an al Qaida rep. Sounds pretty clear to me."

"The supposed meeting in the Czech Republic is pretty iffy," Evan noted. "And Saddam doesn't consider the Kurds who live in the north 'his own people'. He is a Sunni who is trying to suppress the Shiites and the Kurds. The poisonous gas he used has been around since World War I. Plenty of third world dictators can probably get their hands on some of it. Technically, it is classified as a WMD but there is little chance he could ever deploy it inside the U. S. We are in Iraq under false pretenses and that is a dangerous way to begin a military action."

"So you and your boss think we should go easy on that madman?" Blake retorted. "A recent poll said over 90 percent of Americans believe he should be removed from power."

"He is definitely a tyrant who is especially dangerous to the unfortunate people under his rule," Evan suggested. "The Fox poll was misleading because the question was very poorly worded. Who in their right mind would not like to see Saddam removed from power? But at what cost? A more accurately worded poll statement would have read something like 'How many American soldiers are you willing to sacrifice to remove Saddam Hussein?' Or even 'How many of you are willing to see your son or daughter killed in Iraq so that Saddam is removed?' Then there's the even larger question of the number of innocent Iraqi women and children who already have been and still will be killed in the crossfire. Aside from humane implications, killing Muslim civilians severely damages our reputation not only in the Middle East, but all over the world."

"Where do you boneheaded academics come up with all this nonsense?" Cindy pitched in. "War is war. People get killed. Some are innocent. But a greater good is achieved."

"I don't mean to be offensive to you, Cindy, or personal for that matter," Evan replied. "But how many of *your* children are you willing to see killed for the greater good?"

"I can't believe you would say something like that about your own nephews," she yelled. "My boys are not in the service. Those kids who are know what they're getting into."

Blake was equally offended.

"So why do you think we went into Iraq if the premise is false, as you claim?" he voiced with a nasty stare.

Evan thought carefully before beginning his response.

"You understand I can only speak off the record. All of you are my family and I want to be straightforward with you. I don't want to hide information but there are national security issues involved here. Please be discreet in not identifying me as the source of anything I'm about to say. Do I have your word on this?"

As Evan looked about the room, everyone was nodding their heads although this was hardly the kind of response that would stand up in court. More or less trusting everyone present, Evan reluctantly continued.

"Many people at State believe this president and his closest advisors are fighting the last war. Mr. Bush even said 'it's personal since Saddam tried to kill his father'. I don't blame him for being angry about that. But it sounds like a modern version of the Hatfield vs. McCoy family feud. Only this time, it's the Bush vs. Hussein families. Sending American soldiers to their death to defend one family's honor is a bit extreme and probably an abuse of power."

"But there's even more at stake here," Evan went on. "Besides finishing what was not done in the first Gulf War, its veteran participants like Rumsfeld and Cheney have their eyes on a bigger prize. Especially Cheney. His Halliburton energy company would be first in line to get their hands on Iraq's oil. Should Americans die for that?"

"That's the dumbest thing I ever heard," Blake quickly replied. "We need that oil and we're entitled to it. Halliburton isn't the only one who stands to benefit. Other oil producers will as well. And when they gain, so does all of America."

"How many of *your* children, Blake?" Evan stated calmly.

Pretending to ignore that last remark, Blake set off in a new direction.

"We should just take over Saudi Arabia and claim that it is our 51st state," he iterated confidently and bluntly. "That would solve a lot of our problems with those AAArabs."

"I hope you're kidding about that," Evan replied. "If you're not, that's a very good argument for engineers not making foreign policy."

"Not kidding at all," Blake retorted. "We need what they have. Our oil companies are already there. Their workers need protection. It's a simple solution."

"You do mean 'simplistic', don't you?" Evan suggested. "Islamic extremism is quite prevalent in Saudi Arabia. Its roots there go back to the 19th century when a radical cleric established Wahhabism. In the 1920s, the House of Saud was allowed to assume power in the government as long as the Wahhabis controlled the educational system. Over the years, these extremists have established so-called religious schools, or madrassas, where young boys are taught to memorize the Qu'ran and to hate all Westerners and Jews. Do you think a group with that kind of influence and those values would allow us to stroll into their country and take it over?"

Blake was not finished.

"That's all ancient history. People in Saudi Arabia and in other Middle Eastern countries are being held captive by their rulers. If we promise them democracy and freedom, they would happily support us. Once we establish a democratic system either in Iraq or Saudi Arabia, it will easily spread to the entire Middle East. What we should've done after the terrorists attacked us is started leveling cities with atom bombs. That would've sent a message not to mess with us."

"Democracy with bombs, huh? Do you honestly expect me to respond rationally to anything you've just said?" Evan asserted as diplomatically as he could. "Democracy spreading throughout the Middle East? That's a pipedream. And there's no logical scenario suggesting that will happen just because we depose Saddam. If free elections were held in Saudi Arabia today, many supporters of bin Laden would win. Let me also say this. Do you think, if we annihilate cities, that, some day in the future when terrorists do get their hands on nuclear weapons, they would hesitate to use them on this continent?"

"That's why we have to be sure they never get them," Cindy added with complete self-assurance.

"Hopefully they won't any time soon," Evan answered. "But once something is invented, it's hard to 'uninvent' it or keep it out of dangerous hands."

Blake was eager to reenter the fray.

"I heard that Nancy Pelosi accepted over $155,000 from a lob-byist who is trying to influence her vote on an environmental regu-lation of the oil industry. Can you imagine the hypocrisy?"

Evan quickly replied.

"There's only one difference between that and Cheney getting us into war to benefit big oil. It's the amount of money. $155,000 is a drop in the bucket. Iraq is costing us over $10 billion every month. Factor that into the cost of gasoline and a gallon is much more expensive than what we pay at the pump."

There was a temporary lull in the conversation as people refilled their glasses with cider or coffee. Judging from the expressions on their faces, it would have been hard to tell if anyone in the room was giving any thought to what Evan had been saying. When every-one again convened near the recently stoked fire, the topic changed to football.

For some time, a friendly family rivalry had existed about whether college teams were better in the North or South. It was now time for that rivalry to be renewed.

Leroy, Cindy's husband, began.

"With the bowl games coming up, Evan, are you ready for your Big Ten teams to choke again?" he said with a friendly but pointed grin. "The SEC will no doubt prove once more it is the best con-ference in the country."

"When you have the lowest academic standards of any confer-ence in the country," Evan replied, "it's a lot easier to win football games. LSU has the lowest SAT scores for football players of any school in the nation. Their graduation rate is also the lowest. Are they a university or a semi-pro sports team? All other SEC schools, except for maybe Vanderbilt, are not far behind."

"So you're saying all the smart kids go to the Big Ten?" Leroy replied feebly. "What's so great about the colleges up here?"

"Northwestern, Michigan, Wisconsin, Purdue, Ohio State---these are some of the most academically respected institutions in the world," Evan answered proudly. "Not 'all the smart kids' go there but athletes who attend these universities actually have to go to class. Tell me about the academic standing of Mississippi? Mississippi State? And even Alabama?"

"I don't know about good colleges," Leroy answered. "But I do know about good football. And we've got it."

"Hooray for you," Lilalee offered sarcastically.

When her sister Denise announced that her youngest son had received a football scholarship to Baylor in order to be its kicker, Lilalee whispered to her husband: "I thought everyone who went to Baylor was a kicker!"

"So, what's your state's unemployment rate these days?" Cindy asked while looking at Evan.

"We've been living in Washington, as you know," Evan answered. "So we haven't kept up with the numbers. But I know they're high. GM has been in big trouble for some time. And that reverberates throughout the rest of the state. Tourism is at an all time low during the summers. It's pretty easy to find a motel vacancy if you're traveling either here or in the U P."

"That's because we have right to work laws and y'all don't," Blake quickly observed.

"You have a political explanation for everything, don't you?" Evan replied in a slightly unnerved manner. "If what you say is true, every business would be clamoring to locate in Mississippi, Louisiana, and Alabama. Yet these are three of the most economically backward states in the country. How do you explain that? And 'right to work laws' is simply a euphemism. What they really are is 'anti-union laws'".

For one of the rare occasions in his life, Blake had no immediate answer. He smiled for a moment before adding: "We do have more jobs there than you do here."

"Not jobs that pay well," Evan observed. "That's why the poverty rate is still higher in southern states."

"I don't know why I even try to argue with a Yankee," Blake said. "Worse yet, you're starting to sound more and more like a damned Democrat. Is that what being in Washington does to people? The next thing you'll tell me is that Enron is guilty of some crime. Did you see the editorial in the *Wall Street Journal*? It said Enron is completely innocent of the trumped up charges against it."

"That paper *used to be* a valuable source for business news," Evan answered. "Until it was bought by Rupert Murdock. Now it is simply an apology for whatever anyone in corporate America does. It prints all the news Murdock sees fit to print. The criminals at Enron have provided a kick in the teeth to all the honest, hard working business owners and executives out there. If managers broke the law, which more and more appears likely, their top people deserve to go to jail. How can you and Murdock defend cooking the books, defrauding investors, and stealing from employees? That's not what American business is about. Applauding such behavior is more damaging to legitimate business than helpful."

"I was wrong about you sounding like a Democrat," Blake replied. "Now you sound like a raving lunatic."

"When Americans used to hear ridiculous things claimed by *Pravda* in the former Soviet Union," Evan responded thoughtfully, "we learned that whoever controlled the presses, controlled public opinion. As we all know, *Pravda* printed countless lies. How is that different from Murdoch printing lies?"

"Murdoch is pro-business and pro-American," Cindy injected. "That's a big difference."

"Embezzling funds from investors with phony accounting schemes, as Enron has done, *is anti-American*," Evan argued forcefully. "And I 've never thought lying was part of any value system any of us had ever been taught."

Not wanting to admit defeat, Cindy sought a new subject.

"What really gets my goat these days is all the talk about global warming," she stated. "Liberals want to blame oil companies, automobile users, and steel mills. Human activity does not cause global warming. It's simply part of a long term warming and cooling cycle. Besides, if things get warmer, some places where it used to be cold will benefit. Farms may spring up in the arctic circle."

Blake nodded in approval and looked over at Evan to see what he had to say. As always, Evan spoke in carefully composed words.

"Ninety-eight percent of scientists surveyed have said the current global warming is caused by human activity. The view that contradicts this is, therefore, based on what only two percent of scientists believe. That's not exactly a strongly supported case."

"I've never heard that," Blake retorted. "Some left wing group must've made that up."

"That's what I think," Cindy stated, once again in support. "Liberals are behind all the environmental laws that are crippling business. At least Bush got to appoint John Roberts to the Supreme Court. He'll make sure no more unnecessary liberal laws get passed."

For the moment, Evan had had enough. He again stoked the fire before deciding to bring in more wood from outside. When he arrived outdoors, he chose to remain there for awhile.

Even though Evan's brothers agreed with Blake more than Evan on most matters, the Michigan trio rarely backed their brother into a corner in political debates. Instead, they mostly ignored him. They respected the work Evan put into his education and, even though they thought little of his current employer, they knew he was no dummy. For Virgil, Larry, and Woody, merely voting a straight Republican ticket every time was easier than seriously thinking about major issues. As long as their jobs were safe and their taxes did not go up significantly, the intricacies of politics did not concern them.

In addition, they saw Evan more frequently than they encountered Lilalee's family. As a result, the Zerbas had little interest in embarrassing Evan in public. He was their brother, a little odd at times, but still worthy of the family name.

When Colin Powell stepped down in 2005, Evan returned to his teaching position. His faculty colleagues commended his efforts at public service particularly when he and Powell were proven to be accurate in their assessment of false premises in the Iraq War and blatant lies in the Bush/Cheney/Rumsfeld inner circle.

Since Rupert Murdock-owned Fox News put its usual spin on this topic, the Priest family continued to believe what they had accepted all along. When Powell endorsed Barrack Obama for president, Blake and Cindy mercilessly bombarded Evan with emails questioning Powell's patriotism and sanity. Both repeatedly stated that Rush Limbaugh more accurately represented their point of view than the former secretary of state. Both were becoming increasingly excited about the new "tea party" movement and forwarded some of this literature to Evan.

On one occasion, Cindy even suggested that Alabama do what the governor of Texas was threatening to do: secede from the country.

Evan eventually asked to be taken off their mailing list. The following Christmas, he and Lilalee took a long vacation to Vancouver Island, Canada. Three months later during the university spring break, Lilalee visited her family in Alabama. Evan remained in Michigan.

He used the opportunity to spend time with his daughters. Although he had been a lifelong Republican, he now began listening more closely to their views and the reasons they held them.

The Secret

Only a few days after his sixty-second birthday, Logan Bond, a somewhat conflicted man for the past decade, paused to reflect upon all that was bothering him. He longed to retire from his job as a state government administrator in Lansing but feared extreme boredom with so much free time on his hands. Both of his daughters' marriages had already ended in divorce so he often worried about them and their children. Even though he had had suspicions about both of their suitors, he still felt he had failed as a father in not doing enough to discourage youthful poor judgment. After his first wife had left him years ago for a flamboyant millionaire, she incessantly rubbed his nose in his limited income and inability to provide more substantially for their daughters. Of course, she also managed to blame her ex for the young girls' unhappiness.

Logan's hobbies were few and uninspiring. The unchallenging nature of his work drove him to become an avid reader but the more his mind was stimulated, the more he regretted not pursuing a more satisfying occupation. Although he had loved playing handball and jogging, his physical activity had become limited due to back, knee, and foot problems that surfaced gradually over the past three years. Slowly but surely, his energy level diminished and the pounds mounted. He still cultivated a longtime circle of friends who aged gracefully with him but he sometimes wished their combined interests extended beyond watching sports, drinking beer, and playing poker.

What satisfied him most was his second marriage, now nearly twenty-two years in duration. He had met Roberta on the job at the department of human resources office where she had worked her way up the secretarial ladder. Seven years his junior, she still needed to continue working before full retirement benefits were available. This also discouraged Logan from giving up on work any time soon.

Roberta had a grown son who respected Logan when they were together, which was not that often. Since he had lived on the east coast for some time, the young man's visits to his mother were infrequent although the two maintained casual yet friendly contact. Logan and Roberta were both concerned about her bachelor son who still enjoyed big city nightlife and had limited, if any, long term career goals.

The Bonds seldom took long trips but enjoyed visiting old friends in nearby towns plus weekend getaways together in places they found relaxing. They would occasionally spend time with his brother and sister-in-law or with her younger sister and that sister's teenage children. Although Roberta and Logan were anything but jetsetters, their lives together were fulfilling and far less tumultuous than their first marriages.

The couple had resided in the same house for the past twenty years. It had been fairly tight quarters when both girls still lived at home but now seemed more than adequate for the two of them and their rare overnight guests. The neighborhood was well kept and lined with mature trees that, aside from the annoyance of seemingly year round maintenance, provided ample shade for the streets and sidewalks.

Next door to the north lived a childless couple who had been there before the Bonds had arrived. Both were closer in age to Roberta than to Logan. They had become cordial acquaintances who shared an occasional light conversation with the Bonds but otherwise kept to their own circle of friends. Willard had tried his luck at a half dozen or so business ventures and had done well enough to keep the house and pay other bills.

Natasha worked at the local shopping mall, mostly in the gardening section of a family run do-it-yourself store. During summers, she maintained a small garden in the back yard where she raised a few vegetables but primarily cared for flowers. It was this activity that presented Logan with yet another source of conflict.

When the Bonds initially moved in, it was hard for Logan not to notice the bikini clad woman next door pulling weeds and watering plants just the other side of the chain link fence. The initial occasional glances eventually became longing stares once he discovered a vantage point from the upstairs guest room where he could remain for several minutes undetected by anyone on either property.

As the years progressed, the clothing became looser and less revealing but the first set of images persisted. While Logan never so much as engaged in even innocent flirtation with his next door neighbor, several of her poses were hard to dismiss from his perceptive mind. Over time, she appeared on more than one occasion in erotic dreams that produced a satisfied smile when he awoke. His response to all this distraction remained the same for two decades. Fantasies and sometimes even self abuse? Sure. Anything beyond that, including confiding any of this to close friends? Not a chance.

After awhile, he vowed to himself that this was a secret he would take to his grave. There was no need to act anything but neighborly when he casually ran into Natasha. As long as Roberta remained unsuspicious, there was no reason to ever mention to her anything about how Natasha looked or what he might be thinking about her. Others in the community almost always saw her dressed in less provocative attire and no male friend of the Bonds ever even joked about her above average looks. Logan concluded he had a fulfilling hobby after all, one that he need not, and could not, share with anyone.

There were some close calls. Like the time his younger daughter wandered unexpectedly into the guest room and wondered why he was smiling while gazing out the window. Or the time that Natasha's husband walked into the backyard to ask her a question and looked up at the window from which Logan hastily removed himself. Most dangerous was the time Logan was trimming some bushes in his yard when Natasha, not noticing him, spread a blanket and removed her top before lying down on her stomach to sun-bathe. Had Roberta come out the back door, he would have had a challenging time explaining why his tongue was dangling from his mouth.

Over the years, Logan wrestled with himself over the extent of guilt he was feeling or thought he should be feeling. At times, he rationalized that, since no one was being hurt, his deviant thoughts were benign, perhaps even normal. On other occasions, he felt he was engaged in deception in his relationship with Roberta as well as in disrespect toward Natasha. It was almost as if he was stealing something from two people who were unaware of his crime and were not yet outwardly affected by it. But how could he possibly make any retribution to either party without creating a most deli-cate situation? How could he do anything without making things worse rather than better?

Each time he closely examined his conscience, he concluded that keeping the entire episode to himself was the only logical course of action. He sometimes hoped that the couple next door would move away or that age would take its toll on Natasha's appearance. Neither happened.

While Logan continued to loathe his job, he performed it duti-fully if sometimes unenthusiastically. Some days were better than others but all concluded with the belief that he was accomplishing little or nothing professionally. He oversaw programs of public assis-tance whose specifics were mandated by law. He managed a group of twenty underlings, many of whom appeared similarly dulled by their responsibilities. There was no room for creativity of any sort. Even when he felt compassion for the impoverished recipients of state aid, there was little he could do besides follow administrative procedures to the letter.

One afternoon when he was especially feeling the burden of merely putting in his time until he could walk away from it all, one of his employees approached him.

"Logan?" he asked. "Our group has finished the report and made the changes you requested. Who was it you said should receive a copy before it goes upstairs to the front office?"

After pausing briefly, Logan remembered he had in fact requested that an advance copy be sent to someone. He just could not remember who that someone was.

In an effort to cover himself, he replied with hesitation: "I'll double check and get back to you."

The employee walked away filled with both confusion and concern. This was the third time in the past month he had stumped Logan with a routine question, the type he had answered effortlessly dozens of times over the past decade.

Logan himself returned to his office and wondered why he could not remember the name of someone whose face he could picture and whom he had known for many years. Try as he may, the name just would not come to him.

Roberta also had been observing similar behavior in her husband. After several recurrences, she finally convinced him to see the doctor.

Multiple tests confirmed he was *already beyond* the early stages of dementia.

The decision of when to retire was now made for him.

Six years passed. Roberta lovingly cared for her husband as his condition slowly deteriorated.

He eventually reached the stage where he would sometimes go in and out of conscious reality every few minutes. After an astute observation or two, he might quickly degenerate into gibberish or might talk about his parents and little brother as if the boys were still small children and their parents were still alive.

Through it all, Roberta was patient each time she had to reexplain to Logan that his parents were dead, that his brother was no longer five years old, and that he had two daughters. Most of the time, he did not even recognize them.

One day with Roberta lying next to him, he lay back in their bed, closed his eyes, and began reciting aloud a passionate litany he had run through his own mind many times.

"Natasha!" he said with a beaming smile on his face. "You are the most beautiful woman I have ever laid eyes on. I have always wanted you ever since the first time I watched you in your bikini in the back yard. This time, let's make love in my guest room. Oh Natasha, you are so hot and an amazing lover. I never seem to get enough of you...."

As these last words were spoken, he drifted into slumber.

After a sleepless night, a shocked Roberta understandably visited her next door neighbor, who was unaware of Logan's deteriorating state, the following day. Not wanting to appear accusatory or confrontational, she approached the matter quite gingerly. She began by offering in some detail how badly her husband's memory had degenerated over the past few months and that much of what he often said made little sense whatsoever. She then repeated nearly verbatim what he had uttered in a near trance the previous day.

Quite distressed over this latest information, Natasha first made it clear she had not spoken to Logan in several months. She then assured her neighbor that in years past she did not even recall so much as shaking hands with him. What few conversations they had had, she continued, never involved more than barely meaningful small talk. She quickly added that neither Logan nor she had ever voiced anything along the lines of this most recent revelation. Had he ever said anything like that to her, she insisted, Roberta would have been informed immediately.

Finally, Natasha apologized if her backyard dress habits were ever inappropriate but she was never aware that anyone had ever watched her working there. Considering the nature of the topic of conversation, both women remained surprisingly calm.

Roberta seemed quite satisfied at what appeared to be a sincere explanation and expressed regret that she even had to bring it up. The two women hugged, something Natasha and Logan had never done, but whatever neighborliness they might have previously felt was now probably damaged irreparably.

From that day forward, Roberta never looked at her husband with the same fondness she always had. She debated whether or not to mention this whole episode to him the next time he appeared especially lucid. She concluded it probably would not be worth it. Minutes later, he would likely forget their conversation.

On the charge of infidelity, Logan was vindicated. But his long time personal secret did not quite make it to the grave.

Night Train

The evening humidity made for an uncomfortable walk from the chemistry lab to the row of apartments four blocks from campus. Early September nights were not usually this oppressive. More than usual, flowers wilted in their beds along the sidewalk lined with small shops that catered to students. All were now closed except for a coffee shop and an ice cream parlor, both popular hangouts.

Over the past three years, Gideon Nichols had taken this route often. On some days, the journey was made as many as three times. Grad students in the sciences sometimes got their best ideas back in their residences. After such inspiration, it was not uncommon to return to the lab where more formal tests could be conducted.

Tonight's thoughts were of a more personal nature. A few days back, the aspiring chemist had endured a breakup with his girlfriend of nearly a year. Given how little they had in common, the split was inevitable and, in retrospect, not all that troubling. She was two years older than he, had been married before, and sometimes even angered him with her outspokenness and propensity to flirt with other men in his presence.

At this juncture, Gid wondered why he had stayed with her as long as he did. Their meeting had occurred at a party where, sure enough he now recalled, she had made eyes at him first while sporting her most recent of several bourbon and gingers. That they ended up in his bed a few hours later was hardly a reason to have even a first date the following weekend. The most that could be said was that she was easy on the eyes and her flippant personality nicely offset his empirical scientific seriousness.

None of this seemed to matter now. Looking forward, Gid reasoned that he needed to exhibit more discriminating tastes and stop wasting so much time with unchallenging conquests. For a sweet treat before returning home, he decided two scoops of ice cream would hit the spot.

The Night Train was unique, at least in this town. All of its creamy homemade favorites were diced with just a touch of liquor. The added flavor came from various brandies, rum, or fruity vodka. The content was never potent enough to cause a high but it occasionally introduced its mostly youthful crowd to after dinner drinks somewhat more sophisticated than cheap whiskey. Tonight Gid ordered one scoop of kahlua-enhanced Mexican vanilla and a second of Dutch chocolate laced with peach brandy.

For ten minutes, he sat alone and stared out onto the street in deep thought. As the last spoonful was savored, he rose from his chair and vowed that his next date would be more "straight arrow" than his most recent company and some of the ones before her.

Two days later, he called the younger sister of one of his fellow grad students. Their quiet evening together was pleasant, stimulating to the cerebellum, and otherwise uneventful as well as unmemorable. The next weekend, he shared dinner with an introverted gal who lived in the apartment complex next to his. She was wholesome, athletic, and only moderately interested in men. Both dates caused Gid to ask himself exactly what it was he expected to find among the less flamboyant crowd.

An attractive lady he would meet at the undergraduate library the following Wednesday night caused him to again reexamine this question.

Erika Ingram had an All American smile that announced an outgoing positive attitude. She only spoke kindly of others and shyly laughed at Gideon's sometimes strained attempts at humor. Ordinarily, her over-niceness would have nauseated him but, given his newfound philosophy of following the narrow path, she seemed to be within his acceptably defined range of potential companions. Their first and second evenings together were laid back although she seemed a little uncomfortable and her conversation seldom touched upon anything of significance.

"So what's your major and where are you from?" Gid asked over coffee after a movie on their first date.

"I'm in elementary ed," Erika replied. "And my hometown is Wayland. Know where that is?"

"Yeah. It's in between Grand Rapids and Kalamazoo Not far from Cutlerville."

She did not seem all that surprised that he was so well acquainted with her part of the state.

"What about you?" she asked after a few moments of silence.

"Home is Michigamme in the U P," he answered on cue. "And I'm working on a doctorate in physical chemistry."

"Oh," she added, seemingly unimpressed or at least only moderately interested. Perhaps her short answer revealed either her academic distaste for science, or an intimidation, or even an age difference she had not yet considered. Gid could not tell. Her response clearly did suggest he needed to nudge the chat in a different direction.

Such awkwardness would emerge repeatedly in dialogue that often died before going anywhere. Gid initially took this as more of a sign that she was merely guarded in her verbal expression rather than unintelligent. He even thought her relatively quiet demeanor might grow on him.

Erika did convey a warm interest in small children but indicated she preferred to one day teach in a suburban environment rather than an inner city school. Gideon did not necessarily think this demonstrated an elitist attitude particularly when she cited the lack of safety that often accompanied working with the disadvantaged. He was not terribly socially conscious himself and regarded his interest in chemistry as a ticket to a faculty position at as prestigious a university as would accept him. For the moment, their common interest in education would become their conversational mainstay.

By their third date, Gideon deduced he was the more fun loving and the more broad-minded of the two. Erika did not care much for dancing, although she moved about out on the floor as much as she could. Her dislike of serious themes and sex in movies was soon evident. Her interest in sports and hiking was limited to only short walks, a fact that may have at least partially explained her pleasantly plump appearance.

At the end of this evening, Gid asked Erika if she would like to stop for a drink at a watering hole not far from her apartment.

"I don't drink," came her terse but still polite reply.

"That's fine," he stated. "We can get a coke or something, if you like. Any particular reason you avoid the sauce?"

"It's against my religion," she announced proudly. "I'm a devout Baptist. Never had even a single drop of alcohol. And never will!"

"Well, I suppose that says it all," he answered while raising his eyebrows in surprise. "You wouldn't even have a nice glass of wine with dinner at a fancy restaurant?"

"Nope!"

"How about champagne at your graduation? Or someday at your wedding?"

"No way. But you go ahead. I don't mind if you have a beer or something tonight," she quickly added.

Gid was amused. He did order a Hamms draft which he nursed as Erika sipped on her Fresca. Although he did not pursue the matter further at this point, he began to wonder where they would go from here, especially once he revealed his own fallen away Catholicism and tendency to tie one on after a major exam or whenever he was frustrated with his course of study. When alone later that night, he began to wonder whether the "straight arrow" world was really to his liking after all.

All the same, something still drew him to this young lady who was undoubtedly very different from anyone he had ever met. She was affectionate although not passionate. She was pretty although not ravishingly beautiful. And she was bright if not scholarly.

He sure was neither wanting nor needing to hook up with a female chemistry grad student. The three he knew were decent lab partners but not anyone he wanted to spend time with away from the test tubes.

And yet, there were times when Erika was not any more fun than his grad school acquaintances. His male friends found her to be......nice, but nothing special. At one of their birthday parties, Gideon overindulged a bit on spiked punch and made a few advances afterward that Erika let him know she did not appreciate.

He apologized.

After some reflection, he admitted to himself that he had stepped out of line. Putting himself in her place, he realized how disgusting it probably was for someone who was stone sober to have a drunk slobber all over her. On the other hand, even though his hand was only there for a split second before it was slapped, her left breast had felt nice and firm.

Classes became ever more challenging as mid term exams approached. Always the conscientious student, Gideon worked diligently and for the moment gave little thought to Erika. Lab experiments were especially demanding and time consuming. Late in the evening, he would sometimes share a beer or two with one or more of his colleagues who were similarly involved in the stress of work. Those who were married seldom saw their wives at this time of year. It seemed only normal that Gid also was taking a break from an active social life.

And yet, something still motivated him not to write off Erika completely just yet. There remained an unexplored portion of their "relationship" that he felt needed to be addressed, as soon as he determined what that was. Both physical intimacy and a night of debauchery were clearly off limits. A deep discussion of world events was not going to happen. While he sometimes thought of pursuing a serious inquiry into her specific religious beliefs, he quickly decided he had little or no interest since he was rapidly becoming an agnostic. She looked great when she got all dressed up but no such occasion was likely at this serious middle of the semester time.

Hoping she had forgiven his recent roamin' hands episode, he reluctantly called her just to chat. Her response was warm and she eventually informed him she also was busy with projects as well as preparation for mid terms. They briefly discussed their fall break plans to visit family back home.

More or less on the spur of the moment, an idea suddenly fell into Gideon's head.

"How about if we go get a quick late night dessert?" he offered.

"Dessert? Just what did you have in mind?" she asked in a tone that Gid took to be suspicious of his innocent intent.

"Maybe cake and coffee," he replied quickly as if to reassure he had not meant a roll in the sack. "Or some fruit juice at a juice bar?"

"Oh, I don't know," she answered in a most hesitant tone. "I still have so much to do. Some of this stuff just can't wait until tomorrow."

"You probably could use a break from it all," he said persistently. "Come on. It'll be fun. You need to catch me up on all you've been doing."

"Oh.......okay," she concluded. "But only for a little while. Time is so precious now."

When he arrived at her place, she was anything but glamorous. Actually, she was a mess in blue jeans and a sweat shirt with her hair barely combed in an effort that must have taken only a second or two after he had rung the doorbell. He looked the way he usually did: casual and borderline unkempt.

"Hi!" he offered. "This won't take long. Ever been to the Night Train for ice cream?"

"No," she replied. "Never heard of it. Is their ice cream any good?"

"The best there is," he stated convincingly with a slightly mischievous look on his tired face.

The crowd seated at the tables was sparse, much like most of East Lansing at this time of year. Erika ordered a single scoop of "cherry vanilla". Gid countered with "cream de mint." Despite his huge appetite, a small amount would suffice tonight, he thought to himself.

The conversation was light. After a few minutes, she launched into a line about how different the two of them were. The words were the sort that usually precede the "don't want to see you anymore" speech. He had heard this before and knew where she was headed.

When she paused to collect her thoughts, he noticed her cup was empty and seized the moment to interrupt.

"Did you like that ice cream?" he asked.

"Uh…sure," she answered. "It was okay. Why did you ask me that now?"

"Remember how you once told me you have never had even the slightest touch of alcohol?" He then quickly added: "And that you never would?"

"Of course," came the puzzled reply.

"Well, I hate to have to break this to you," he said trying desperately to hide his pleasure. "But your virgin lips have become tainted. The cherry flavor in your ice cream was from cherry vodka. Tvarski's, one of the cheapest brands no less. It wasn't so bad now, was it?"

Anger filled her face as it reddened uncontrollably.

"Gideon Nichols!" she shouted. "Why would you do this to me?! You are a terrible person! May God forgive you!"

As Erika stood up, she gave him one final hateful stare. She then ran from the Night Train and walked by herself all the way home. She quickly forgot the name of the place where her fundamentalist Christian principles had been violated and never even returned to that particular street near campus.

Gid never saw her again.

Two years later, a friend of his from Detroit showed him a photo and article from his hometown newspaper. The short blurb announced that Erika Ingram had married a preacher whose brushed back, well-groomed hair made him look like Conway Twitty. She was now living in a suburb of that city where her husband was an assistant pastor at the First Baptist Church. The last sentence stated that the couple would reside in a home on Night Train Lane.

Gid's friend knew the area well. He said the street had recently been renamed in honor of Dick "Night Train" Lane, a former Detroit Lions football player.

"Want to go and get some ice cream?" his friend offered with a devious smile.

"Two scoops," Gid replied.

The Run Home and the Home Run

As he walked up the stairs of his hometown church, Ernie Preston hoped this weekend trip would land him a summer job. Barely nineteen, he was about to finish his freshman year at Western Michigan University where he was majoring in music. Deeply religious, he recently learned the long time parish organist had abruptly announced she was about to retire. Already accomplished on several instruments including keyboards, Ernie dreamed of a career that would combine his love of God with his passion for all forms of composition from classical to contemporary.

So interested in making a good impression on those who mattered, he had not even stopped at the home where he had grown up and where his parents were expecting him. Before seeing anyone, he felt the need to kneel in the empty front pew and pray for worthiness plus direction as he pursued this first professional step in his young life. While attending the parish high school and shortly after graduation, he had played the organ at selected masses and wedding ceremonies when no one else was available. As he now recalled the many positive comments he had gotten from those in attendance on those occasions, he was encouraged and felt positive about the inquiry he was about to make. Of course, he never took action without seeking the divine inspiration that guided his every step.

After genuflecting in the aisle, bowing reverently, and making the sign of the cross, he knelt and immediately launched into silent prayer, many of which he had been taught in early childhood. These included the Our Father, Hail Mary, Glory Be, and Apostle's Creed as well as selected biblical verses he had committed to memory. He then reached for the beads that remained in his pocket wherever he went. After kissing the crucifix and again crossing himself, he recited the entire rosary. Only then did Ernie begin to compose requests in his own words.

He first asked that, if it were God's will, he would be forever grateful for a summer job at the church plus a second part time opportunity somewhere else to help save money for school. He then requested a strengthening of his faith and patience in dealing with his imagined human frailties. Finally, he prayed for continued purity in thought and in his limited dating experience with young women. During the past year, he had strayed from the path twice when his roommate showed him the latest Playboy centerfolds. While he had obtained forgiveness in confession only days after each event, he now paused to recite a formal Act of Contrition for even thinking about what he had seen. Of course, he had never observed an actual naked woman and vowed to maintain that spotless record indefinitely.

After nearly a full hour of prayer and serious reflection, Ernie sat back in the pew and stared at the various artifacts strategically positioned throughout the building. His eyes slowly and smoothly flowed from the golden tabernacle that housed the Blessed Sacrament to the statues of the Virgin Mary, St. Joseph, St. Francis of Assisi, and St. Peter. He then focused upon the Stations of the Cross and felt conflicted about whether or not he should actually walk through each. After deciding he would not be severely punished for merely observing the plaques from the vantage point where he sat, he dwelt upon the suffering Christ endured leading up to his crucifixion. Ernie shed a brief tear as he recalled the drama of that fateful walk.

As he paused to reflect upon his own recent transgressions that included one or two little white lies and an occasional taking the name of the Lord in vain, he reminded himself of the need to go to the regularly scheduled noon confession tomorrow. It had been nearly three weeks since his last trip to the sacred sin admitting box, a longer absence than had occurred since his confirmation into the faith some seven years earlier. He now paused to reprimand himself for this oversight while quickly promising to make amends for his lackadaisical behavior.

When he was finally able to gain a grasp of present reality, he became concerned about how he would approach Father Milton Stelmach with his more immediate need. His relationship with this man of the cloth had been mostly positive over the past five years. The crusty cleric in his mid forties seemed to like his young protégé who showed more signs of accepting official Catholic doctrine than any of his more secularly oriented contemporaries. Ernie hoped to draw upon his past service as an altar boy and member of the choir to persuade the pastor that, despite his youth, he was ready for center stage on Sunday mornings, at least for the upcoming summer.

His feelings toward the priest were mixed. Pastor for the last eight years, Father Milton was anything but buddy-buddy toward high school boys and outright indifferent toward the girls. He often seemed to have his own agenda as his mind wandered from whatever young people were saying to him. The priest's sermons, although less than inspiring, provided minimal value to those willing to absorb lessons that appeared to come from someone barely motivated to deliver them.

Having befriended priests in college who were more intellectual, more athletic, and more sympathetic toward young people, Ernie was beginning to wonder why local parishioners considered Father Milton such a big deal. In addition, through the eyes of someone in his late teens, Ernie saw the local priest as unattractive in the extreme. While not yet wrinkled, his face was drawn, much like that of someone prematurely disinterested in life. His thinning hair revealed a dome that, under direct lighting, nearly blinded onlookers. His waistline displayed a significant bulge while his manner of dress, when he was not clad in official black, resembled that of a homeless beggar more than that of a man about town.

All in all, he represented a challenging hurdle for someone hoping to win approval as a potential employee. Ernie pondered all of this as he sought a combination of courage plus a heavenly escort to the next building. He remembered that Father Milton admired his musical talent and enjoyed joking with him more than he did with other students. His love of Cubs baseball star Ernie Banks caused the priest to refer affectionately to the young musician as "Slugger", even though this Ernie had limited athletic talent. Armed with keyboard ability, deep religious faith, a recent litany of prayer, and a respectful personality, he wondered if maybe he was ready to make his bid.

As he contemplated his next move, Ernie thought of another person he needed to see during this trip home. Demanding and sometimes even authoritarian, his high school music teacher showed little patience for anyone other than the most dedicated students. Ernie clearly fell into that category although he was still intimidated by the nun who was barely thirty years of age.

Sister Rosemary Ruth possessed impressive credentials but had only officially been in the convent for six years. Looking upon students as if she had something to prove to them, she came off as more of a disciplinarian than nuns thirty years her senior. High schoolers were not sure what to make of this, especially those who sought friendship among an aging group of mentors. Freshmen and sophomores were often rebuffed by the teacher whose inner persona they were incapable of penetrating. The boys thought of her as unusually "decent looking" but few ever expressed this viewpoint even to their closest friends. To all recent graduates, including Ernie, this nun, who seemingly lacked any pretense of outwardness or humor, was merely someone from whom to learn in a most businesslike fashion. She was tough and rarely gave a compliment. She was hard on herself and everyone around her. If she had a warm or religious side, few of her students experienced either.

Despite this teacher's seemingly negative attributes, Ernie felt the need to touch base with someone whose knowledge of music and artistic creativity he respected. He hoped that, after he presented his case to the pastor, he would be able to summon a reference from Sister RR at the nearby convent. Seeing both, he reasoned with the mixture of awe and fear he held for each, was far more important than any time he could have spent with either family or friends.

Much as he wanted to take the next step, Ernie could not motivate himself to rise from the church pew. Despite his supposed divine encouragement, he was still hesitant to approach Father Milton whose ability to keep his distance and his occasionally abrasive demeanor now served as roadblocks to the young man. For a moment, he thought it might be best to launch into another round of prayer. As he began doing just that, he quickly realized he was merely delaying the inevitable. After one final sign of the cross and a deep breath, he rose from his seat where his legs had nearly fallen asleep.

To the right of the main altar stood a statue of St. Anthony, patron saint of special causes or some similar theological designation. Just below the statue's bare feet lay six rows of small candles housed in red glass containers. Lighting one of these, saying a special prayer, and making a small monetary offering was a combined ritual often undertaken by those in need. Ernie went through all three steps further delaying his exit from the holy premises.

As he stood from his kneeling position, he noticed several rows of even larger candles begging for his attention. This was, he reasoned, an especially important moment in his life worthy of yet additional prayer and money. When he rose this time, his knees ached, an appropriate discomfort, he thought, as if this self-imposed pain somehow would aid his case. He then looked about the entire massive room to be certain he had not missed a single opportunity to bow before an icon or give away more cash.

Before walking to the rectory next door, Ernie thought he would check the sacristy, the small set of three rooms behind the altar where priests dressed before each religious ceremony and where supplies were kept, in case Father Milton might be working there. The first door was wide open so Ernie entered without saying a word. He immediately noticed the stash of collection baskets, the closet where the altar boy's cassocks were kept, and the table where a gallon of sacramental wine sat half full.

During this last glance, he recalled the time he and a fellow server opened a similar bottle with the intention of sneaking a sip. Even though both chickened out at the last minute, they could not resist inhaling the pleasant fumes after the cap had been removed. Although he had told of this terrible misbehavior in confession the following day, he paused to again seek forgiveness for this now nearly decade old temptation and near fall from grace.

The second room also prompted several recollections. Missals for the pews and a stack of sheet music were scattered among other reading materials. As Ernie walked through the open doorway, he began to peruse what lay on the table and immediately recognized a number of pieces he had played on the church organ. Two or three brand new books also attracted his always-inquisitive mind, especially when the topic was religion.

As he started to page through one of these, he heard rumblings from behind the closed door of the third room. His initial inclination was to respond with a forceful "hello" which he delayed doing as other sounds soon emanated through the walls. Always willing to accept guilt for every awkward situation, Ernie reasoned that he was an intruder of sorts and did not want to disturb any prayers being said. He also wanted to be cautious just in case the commotion was initiated by someone who actually was seeking to rob something of monetary value.

Now standing perfectly still, Ernie began to hear voices that simulated pain and perhaps even shortness of breath. At first, he wondered if Father Milton might be going through an exercise regimen. Some of the expressions even sounded like the beginning of a hymn or chant. For a few moments, they subsided. When they resumed, Father Milton's voice sounded higher, almost feminine. Ernie began to worry of a possible heart attack or other affliction that required the help of another. No longer willing to stand by idly, he opened the door that thankfully was not locked.

Ernie was astounded to find a naked Father Milton lying on his back on top of church vestments that served as a cushion. On top of him with her habit raised to her neck was a nearly nude woman whom Ernie quickly recognized as Sister Rosemary Ruth.

"Hey Slugger!" the priest stated softly. "What's up?"

Ernie froze and remained speechless.

The nun did not dismount or even turn around although she did cease her rhythmic up and down hip motion. Instead, she tried to hide her face but her identity was already evident to the shocked teen.

Not familiar with the nickname "Slugger", she was probably unaware who the interloper was. She did reflect for a moment, however, on the fact that her days in this parish were now probably limited. Her transfer notice would eventually arrive in just over a week.

Only a few seconds passed before an embarrassed Ernie finally covered his eyes and briskly left the scene. He said nothing of the incident either to his parents or to any of his local friends, all of whom he felt would not have believed him. He never again took part in the sacrament of confession. Only after several weeks did he return to a religious service, this time at a Lutheran church. For his summer job, he worked at a factory a few miles from his home. When he began his sophomore year at WMU, he changed his major to psychology and joined a rock 'n roll band in which he played a mean lead guitar.

One day after a couple of beers, he finally told his college friends of his shocking experience the previous spring. Toward the end of his account, he reflected on what he had observed.

"What a pitiful person I am," he stated with a look of disgust. "I wasted all that time being overly scrupulous. And the first time I actually see a naked woman, it has to be a nun."

Everyone chuckled before Ernie added one final comment.

"From the angle I had, though, she didn't look bad at all."

The Claustrophobic Agoraphobe

When he was twenty-five years old, Mick Stillwagon survived a plane crash in Indiana. After being pinned under seats and the side of the fuselage for nearly three hours, he was finally rescued. Although more than thirty passengers died in the incident, Mick escaped with only minor injuries.

Over the next ten years, he thought he had put the trauma of that incident behind him. Although he never flew again, he travelled widely by car and train throughout the Midwest and Canada. He was fairly settled in a career as assistant manager of a small movie theatre in his native Battle Creek. Still single, he had many friends who shared his interests in the outdoors and in the latest film releases. His pipe dream was to one day write a script that would be made into a financially successful film.

Wednesday was Mick's day off. He would often use it as an escape from the routine of work or as a chance to get some personal things done. It was on such a day in January that he made a trip to the grocery store. After filling his basket with more than the usual amount of items, he proceeded to the check out where only one clerk was available.

The line moved slowly. As Mick neared the front, two more clerks arrived and motioned to some of the customers who were behind him. Within seconds, a problem developed with the customer just ahead of him. Sensing the solution might take some time, Mick attempted to back up but found himself trapped by those who remained behind him.

A very strange feeling of anxiety came upon him. Within seconds, he felt as helpless as he had been in the downed airplane. His logic told him the two situations were anything but similar but panic soon displaced whatever rationality he could muster.

He eventually pushed aside the customer ahead of him and ran from the store, leaving a full basket of unattended groceries inside. Despite the freezing temperatures, Mick broke into a deep sweat as he struggled to insert the key into his car door.

While sitting inside the car, his anxiety did not dissipate. After fifteen minutes, he determined he had better get home. Driving cautiously did not help. The more he drove, the more enclosed he felt inside his roomy SUV.

Upon arrival, he slowly maneuvered his way into his living room where he immediately sat on his couch to collect his thoughts. They were troubling and disruptive to his peace of mind.

Two hours passed before Mick began to feel almost normal. He ultimately reasoned that it had been an unusual virus attack. He popped two aspirin even though he doubted this ritual would have any effect. He merely felt it might be wise to try something.

The rest of the day passed without incident. By late afternoon, he missed the groceries he had nearly acquired but was too embarrassed to return to the store. The following morning he shopped elsewhere.

Work was fairly routine for the next two weeks. On a Saturday night, the theatre was filled to near capacity. Mick had to be on his toes since he was fully in charge. When one of the popcorn poppers failed, he calmly made the necessary repairs himself. When an inebriated patron became unruly, Mick escorted him into a back office and called a cab. When one of the workers became ill, Mick pitched in at the refreshment counter until the crowd died down.

Half way through the feature, Mick did what was standard procedure: quietly walk down both aisles, flashlight in hand, and make sure all was on the up and up. When he walked in front of the audience, he turned to face them. Only four or five of the hundred-plus people looked at him as he began to ascend the slight incline.

Suddenly, however, Mick felt as though all eyes in the theatre were upon him. When he stopped walking, more people did notice his presence. His face soon became flush, perspiration ensued in a matter of seconds, and he even shivered as a chill ran through his upper body. When he looked at the walls, they somehow now seemed closer to him. What had been a large room quickly shrank to what seemed like a fraction of its previous size.

Struggling to regain some semblance of poise, Mick slowly stumbled toward the back of the theatre as if he were fighting the effects of alcohol. His employees could not help but notice his distress as he made his way toward his humble office. Perspiration now dripped from his face and upper body. One of the young ladies brought him a cup of ice water. He took a few sips but little change in his condition was forthcoming. As he lay on the couch, he asked that he be left alone until he had time to compose himself.

Thirty minutes later, he was able to sit up but lacked the initiative to resume any work related duties. At the end of the evening, one of the male employees drove him home in Mick's car and made sure he was safely inside.

Incidents such as these soon became increasingly commonplace. Although Mick had kept these episodes from his friends for several months, he eventually decided it was time to confide in those closest to him.

Ken Carson and Clay Witt had known Mick since before his plane crash incident. Ken worked in a bicycle repair shop while Clay was a TV cameraman. Both expressed concern when Mick informed them of his recent bouts with anxiety. At first, neither saw a connection to the now more than decade old air mishap.

"Have you seen a doctor?" Ken inquired.

"No, 'cause no matter when this happens, I'm better after a couple of hours. Sometimes, even sooner. I'm just never sure when it's gonna come on."

"Are you ever concerned it could be your heart?" Clay asked. "Any heart problems in your family?"

"I'm never actually short of breath. I do get a little dizzy for awhile but then that goes away, too. I'm not sure what to think. Maybe I'm just goin' crazy."

Ken and Clay looked at each other before the latter spoke.

"What can it hurt to get checked out? Maybe there's some pills you can take. If it is all in your head, ol' Doc Watson can probably suggest something for that. He sure did a great job of stitching up your leg after that plane crash."

"The plane crash!" Ken injected. "Maybe that's it. You might be having some kind of delayed fear that whole thing brought on. I'm no shrink but I have heard of people being haunted by past memories."

"Don't be ridiculous," Mick stated confidently but defensively. "What does that have to do with feeling weird in a grocery store or when I'm on the job? I've been doing stuff like that for years without anything out of the ordinary happening. Go back to fixing two wheelers."

"We just think you should jump on this before it gets worse," Clay replied. "What if something like this happens when you are about to get laid? Wouldn't popping a pill be better than telling some hot number she needs to go home unsatisfied?"

"You guys are no help," Mick offered. "Why do I even tell you anything?"

"Just know you can always call either one of us in an emergency," Ken assured. "Especially if you need some help with some hot chick!"

"Let's all go get a beer," Clay suggested. "Maybe you need more time in a bar to help you relax."

"That's anything but profound," Mick retaliated. "But for now, I suppose that'll work."

The familiar setting of a local nightspot induced no trauma. Mick even confided to his friends that he appreciated their listening to him. For the moment, all seemed fine.

Two weeks later, another more serious episode occurred.

Mick took a date to a minor league baseball game between the Lansing Lugnuts and the South Bend Silver Hawks. Over 12,000 fans were in attendance at Cooley Law School Stadium in the state capitol. The couple had fairly good seats just three rows behind the first base dugout. In the bottom of the fourth inning, a pop foul headed their way. Mick tried to catch the ball but dropped it. As it rolled away, some of the nearby patrons jeered at him while others were more positive in thanking him for allowing a little boy to come up with the souvenir.

In either case, Mick found himself at the center of attention at an event where he had hoped to be an anonymous spectator in the large crowd. Even while humbly seated as the game continued, he could not dismiss the thought that he had somehow humiliated himself in front of a near capacity crowd and a pretty young lady.

In less than a minute, the usual symptoms appeared: dizziness, heavy perspiration, a flush face, and moderate trembling. His date tried to offer comfort but was unaware of any previous similar events. Fortunately, three kind men came to his assistance and helped him to the nearest exit. Mick nearly collapsed to the ground three different times during the short walk.

A stadium usher offered to call an ambulance but Mick refused.

"I'll be alright in a few minutes," he assured everyone, even though he had no basis for making such a promise.

Each time the crowd overhead cheered, Mick was filled with renewed anxiety as if their cheers were somehow aimed at him. One of the men brought him a coke from the concession stand. When Mick feigned bravery, all but his date returned to their seats. Mick remained on the small bench for more than half an hour before he attempted to rejoin the crowd.

After twenty or so steps, he collapsed onto the concrete ramp but did not lose consciousness. This time, he did have chest pains.

"Nadine", he called out. "Will you help me up? I'm not sure what's going on here."

"Let me get a doctor," she stated instinctively as she assisted him to his feet. "One of the men said there is a team doctor in each dugout. I can have one here in a second."

"No," Mick replied. "I'll be okay in a minute. I just have to sit for awhile."

"Are you sure?" Nadine asked. "I want to help if I can."

"Don't worry, I'm not going to drop dead on our first date," Mick offered, trying to lighten the moment.

There was silence for the next several minutes as both sat on chairs near the concession stand. Nadine kept a close eye on Mick but no one else paid either of them any attention.

"I really know how to show a girl a good time, don't I?" Mick finally said with a slight grin.

"Don't worry about that," Nadine answered. "I'd really feel better if you got checked out by someone. Has this ever happened before?"

"Yeah, once or twice. But I rallied. I'm starting to feel better. I don't think I want to watch the rest of the game, though. Do you mind driving my car back to your house?"

Mick really was not feeling any better. He just wanted to get away from the site of his latest disaster. On the trip back, he tried to behave normally even though he still was experiencing tension, muscle pain, and a headache. Since the chest pains had stopped, he was less worried about being in any immediate danger. Although he was still struggling with his inner thoughts, he managed to make the short drive by himself from his date's house to his.

"How did the Lugnuts do?" Clay asked him the following evening when the two of them met for a pizza.

"Okay, I guess. We left early. Nadine had to get back to do something or other."

"So you struck out, huh?" Clay teased.

"She was actually very nice," Mick responded. "But I probably won't see her again."

"What was the matter with her?" Clay continued.

"We just didn't hit it off that great. No big deal. Forget about it."

"Hey, the last thing I want to do is pry."

Mick never even mentioned what had happened at the game. Since the whole incident was out of town and none of his friends knew Nadine, word never did get back to Battle Creek. For now, that's the way Mick wanted it.

Nadine did call to check on him but he politely told her he was fine and not to worry. He never called her back.

Ken stopped by the theatre one night when Mick was working. They chatted for a few minutes in his office and made plans to go fishing the next day.

That night, Mick was unable to sleep. This was the third or fourth time the problem manifested itself. Before that, he had always slept like a log.

In the morning, he felt nauseous. Then came the sweats along with chest pain, muscle aches, and very troubling thoughts. Mick deduced that more and more he was experiencing an exaggerated sense of stress even when not in stressful situations. This was accompanied by an inability to relax no matter where he was.

Through it all, he forced himself to get dressed and meet Ken down by the river.

When he arrived, his tension level had diminished somewhat. He assumed some casting from the riverbank might bring him the peace of mind he so desperately sought.

Things took a drastic turn for the worse when he saw Ken.

Instead of driving up, Ken approached in a small rowboat he had rented. Sensing where this was leading, Mick quickly felt a surge of anxiety that rivaled the worst he had ever experienced.

"So what do you think?" Ken yelled. "We can get a lot closer to the good fishing holes downstream in this excuse for a yacht than we can from shore. Grab your pole and tackle. Jump in. Rent is paid for the next four hours. We can keep it longer if they're biting."

Mick's first inclination was to run back to his car but he resisted. Before saying anything to Ken, he told himself he had to beat his fears.

"Sure thing," he replied while struggling to mask the hesitation in his voice. "How about meeting me over at the dock? That way, I can get in without getting my feet wet."

Ken rowed the hundred or so feet back upstream as Mick reached for his gear and began walking. His legs felt rubbery. His arms felt like he had lifted hundred pound barbells instead of a light pole and tackle box. He began to tremble uncontrollably.

As he walked onto the pier, Mick gave himself a serious pep talk. It was now or never, he decided. If he was going to beat these irrational fears, getting into a harmless little boat with his friend had to be the first step. He reminded himself he was a better than average swimmer, if the need arose. "What could be more relaxing than sitting in the middle of a river he knew well?" he reminded himself. "And wouldn't it be a thrill to land either a northern pike or a largemouth bass?"

A calm momentarily came over him. He handed his gear to Ken before stepping into the boat himself. He more or less confidently took his seat.

"We can take turns doing the rowing," Ken suggested. "I'll go first since I've already started. You can bail me out if my arms get tired."

"Yeah, sure," Mick stated as he watched the rapidly flowing water.

Ken slowly guided the boat some seventy to eighty feet from shore before letting the current take them around a bend toward a spot he suspected might harbor some fish.

Mick kept telling himself he was going to be fine. For the moment, his positive attitude seemed to be working. The trembling slowed and his muscle pain was less severe.

"What kind of lures did you bring today?" Ken asked.

"I already got one on my line," Mick answered, trying not to think about anything that would require special effort. "You all set?"

"I guess I can find one in here that pike can't resist," he stated as he looked through his tackle box.

Both men spoke softly so as not to scare away anything from beneath the water.

To get his mind off of his worries, Mick began casting. Ken soon followed in the opposite direction.

After ten minutes without a nibble, Ken whispered: "Maybe we should move on."

He then motioned "one more" before taking his thumb off the reel and re-grabbing it as the lure hit the water. This time, just twenty or so feet from the boat, he felt a sudden jolt on his line. He quickly pulled hard in hopes of hooking his prey.

"I got one," he yelled with excitement. "Get the net and help me bring her in."

As Mick reached for the net, he rocked the boat more than he thought he would. He regained his balance but began to focus on the current that seemed to be flowing much more rapidly than it had been just seconds ago.

He froze and sank back into his seat.

"Over here," Ken shouted. "I almost got him."

Mick did not move.

"Okay," Ken now stated with a puzzled look on his face. "So you're gonna make me do this all by myself. If he gets away, it's your ass."

Fortunately for Ken, he was able to yank his catch into the boat without the aid of a net.

"It's a trout," he noted. "Pretty good size. He gave me a decent battle for something that's not more than a couple of pounds. Maybe we should stick with this hole a little longer."

When Mick failed to respond, Ken looked up to find his friend looking and acting quite strange. He had an expression on his face that seemed more than fear. Something on the order of being completely petrified. Despite the still cool temperature, he was perspiring and shaking.

"Are you okay?" Ken asked.

Mick said nothing. He stared at the fish almost as if he were sorry Ken had pulled him from the water. His muscles tightened. His legs tingled. His mind wandered beyond his control.

He looked out at the stream that now appeared to have waves reminiscent of those on Lake Michigan. To him, the boat seemed to be moving uncontrollably. Even Ken was a blurred image.

"Mick?" Ken called out. "What's going on? Say something!"

After a brief pause, Mick looked around. His anxiety accelerated and he concluded it still had not peaked. He wanted to stand up and run but quickly realized that was not possible. He felt totally trapped as if he were enclosed in a closet.

"Mick?" Ken said one more time as he reached for his friend's arm.

"Don't rock the boat any more than it already is moving!" Mick replied. "I've got to get out of here. I need to be back on shore. Now!"

Before Ken could do anything to stop him, Mick dove head first into the water. When he surfaced, he was breathing heavily. He immediately began taking uneven strokes in the direction of the shore.

Ken quickly began rowing after him in case he tired and needed assistance. When Mick sensed the riverbed was now shallow, he tried to walk the remaining distance but stumbled several times before lying on his back in two or three inches of water. He had great difficulty catching his breath.

Ken dropped anchor a few feet away. He rushed to Mick's side and tried to lift him but Mick motioned he wanted to stay where he was.

"Where does it hurt? What can I do to help?" Ken asked, visibly frustrated at his momentary helplessness.

"It hurts everywhere," Mick replied before motioning Ken to move away.

Ten minutes passed during which Ken noticed that Mick was breathing less rapidly. He now insisted that he provide help in getting Mick to his car. As he dropped him into the back seat, Ken pulled the keys from Mick's soaked pocket and started the engine. He headed straight for the emergency room at city hospital.

When they arrived, Mick was trembling severely and was barely conscious. Within minutes, doctors were doing all that was possible. Ken provided all the information he could. When he was asked to leave the emergency room, he feared the worst.

Over an hour passed. Ken phoned Clay who soon made his way into the waiting room. An hour later, the doctor appeared.

"Your friend is fine," he said. "He can leave whenever he feels like getting out of bed."

"But......," Ken interrupted.

"He has a form of GAD or generalized anxiety disorder," the doctor continued. "He has all the classic symptoms that can be brought on by fear of closed in areas coupled with fear of open spaces. His heart checks out and all his vital signs are consistent with those of someone his age. He is meeting with our staff psychologist who will refer him to a colleague of hers for more extensive therapy."

"What will he have to do?" Clay asked.

"I've prescribed an antidepressant," the doctor responded. "There'll be a program of physical exercise. He should avoid caffeine and even cough medicines, both of which can spike this type of anxiety. Most patients can feel better after 3 to 4 months of cognitive behavioral therapy. It may include a technique called desensitization where the patient is gradually placed in a setting that has brought on the anxiety in the past. Through specific breathing or relaxation exercises, he'll eventually learn to cope with the situation and break its past mental connection to fear and panic. This condition is not all that uncommon and it is very treatable. I predict he'll do well."

"What caused him to get this?" Ken inquired.

"He's giving details to the psychologist right now," came the reply. "But I did hear him say something about being in a plane crash. That's a likely source."

"It's good that you got him here when you did," the doctor continued. "When not treated properly, the situation can get progressively worse and can lead to all kinds of irrational behavior. Some patients go so far as to contemplate suicide. Just continue being good friends and keep him in touch with his family. If they're not an important part of his life, they need to be now. He could benefit greatly from an active support group."

"Thanks, Doctor," both young men said in near unison.

The MD smiled and walked away.

Ken and Clay looked at each other before Ken spoke.

"Family? His parents deserted him when he was sixteen, joined some religious cult in the Philippines, and haven't seen him since. His only brother married a Portuguese girl and moved to Lisbon. Who else is left?"

Total Break Up or Total Break Down?

When Cedric arrived home, Jeanette was seated on the couch waiting for him. Before he could utter a word, she stated softly but directly: "I can't go through with this. I'm moving to Oregon." After a brief pause, she added: "And I need to go there alone."

Cedric promptly set his stack of books on a nearby table before dropping into an old lounge chair directly across from her. For a few moments, he only flashed a forlorn facial expression but said nothing.

The couple had met three years earlier when Jeanette was a senior and Cedric was half way through his doctoral studies in political science. After graduation, Jeanette began a master's program in biology that she was now close to completing. Cedric was finishing his degree as well but had yet to pursue serious job opportunities elsewhere.

Over the past year, the two had made detailed plans for their life together including likely residence locations and number of children. Although they officially lived separately, they spent more nights together than apart. Everything from career ambitions to common entertainment interests to more than gratifying intimacy seemed to be a perfect fit.

Now stunned into silence, Cedric hardly knew how to begin his response. He had absolutely no inkling this drastic change of plans was even a remote possibility. Although he was trembling inside and close to that outwardly, he did his best to project a calm in his carefully chosen words.

"What's the matter?" he began. "When did you decide this? I guess you were accepted into med school at the University of Oregon?"

"This is the hardest decision I've ever had to make in my life," she replied. "It wasn't easy. I'm so sorry. I don't mean to hurt you. I just can't handle med school and a husband, too."

"I thought we've been over this more than a few times," Cedric persisted. "Wherever you were accepted, I'd find a teaching or research job nearby. It doesn't matter to me where we live or what I do as long as I'm with you."

"I just can't do that to you," Jeanette stated gracefully and seemingly sincerely. "You are an outstanding teacher and researcher. I don't want you to put your career on hold for five or six years until I'm ready to open a practice or work in a hospital somewhere. By then, you could have tenure at a highly respected university."

"I don't care about tenure. There's plenty of time for that later. I do care about you. More than I ever imagined possible. I've always known you are brilliant and I've always encouraged you to go after whatever career you want. I'm so happy you've been officially accepted. I'm happy for us, not just you."

"You're not getting what I'm saying. There's not going to be an 'us'. I can't do that now. There'll be too much else going on."

"Do you think I'll expect you to come home to cook me dinner and to watch the evening sit coms with me?" Cedric asked rhetorically. "I'll be as busy as you are. You'll need some financial help and I'm more than willing to work for the both of us. That's what couples do. We don't even have to get married right away. The piece of paper doesn't matter. You do."

Jeanette looked away as if she did not know what to say and was having difficulty looking Cedric in the eye. She was clearly troubled but also convinced this was her only and most logical course of action.

During the silence, Cedric sat back in what was under more normal circumstances the most comfortable piece of furniture in the house. At this moment, however, he was so squeamish that comfort could not even be imagined. He tried to retain some sense of poise despite his inner fear that his world was falling apart.

Perhaps his whole life was not flashing before his eyes but the last three years certainly were. He and Jeanette had shared so much together. They had spent long hours side by side in the University of Michigan library and even more time in some quiet room or coffee house on their laptop computers. They enjoyed concerts, movies, and distinguished speakers who came to campus. When alone, they had extraordinary difficulty keeping their hands off of each other.

"How and why could all of this suddenly and inexplicably be ending?" he thought to himself.

This time, Jeanette broke the silence.

"Maybe you're more mature than I am," she offered somewhat feebly.

He was 28; she was only 23. Their five-year age difference had never seemed to matter before. He could not even begin to accept this line of thinking.

"You are unquestionably more mature than I am," he retorted. "I've always believed that. Are you sure your parents are not influencing you on this?"

Cedric always felt a little intimidated around Spencer and Elke. He was a pediatrician while she was a psychiatrist who specialized in treating young children. Together they ran a successful clinic that included a young doctor whom Jeanette had briefly dated. The parents always hoped their daughter would one day join the practice. They also made no bones about the fact that they preferred the young M.D. for her rather than some globally fixated Ph. D. in a non-medical field.

"I've talked to my parents about this," Jeanette replied. "But I've made the choice on my own. And I have no interest, by the way, in going back to Leon. There was never anything between us. Certainly nothing like you and I had."

"Why 'had'? I still don't understand what is prompting this," Cedric asked. He had yet to even raise his voice but his tone clearly suggested he was growing increasingly frustrated.

"Maybe I've just used you for good company while I worked on my master's," she suggested.

"Now you're stretching," he rebutted instantly. "I know you're not like that. Why are you trying to invent fictitious explanations while avoiding the real reason?"

"Maybe, when it comes right down to it, I'm just not the marrying type," Jeanette stated bluntly, her eyes now staring at the floor. "You almost had me convinced otherwise. You are as wonderful a man as there is. If I can't see myself married to you, I can't imagine living like we have with someone else."

"So that's it?" he questioned in his most befuddled manner yet.

"There is one more thing," she injected reluctantly. "I'm absolutely certain I never want children. I know we talked about having two or three but I just don't ever see that happening. My parents are so career oriented. They thoroughly neglected my brother and me. I've really come to resent them for that. Some people shouldn't have kids. They shouldn't have. It's almost like they gave all their attention to their little patients and were 'childrened out' by the time they came home. I see myself with a similar professional drive. And I definitely don't want to be either a pediatrician or any kind of shrink. Surgeon is where I'm at. I'll bet you now think I'm cold and detached enough to cut into human bodies with ease."

"You've already cut into mine," Cedric offered meekly.

Over the next two weeks, he spoke with Jeanette face to face on four separate occasions. Each time, he held out some hope that he could probe more deeply into the matter, eventually convincing her to reconsider and not throw away all they had built together. By the conclusion of their fourth session, he realized it was a losing cause. When he left her apartment, he knew they had spoken for the last time.

Neither attended formal graduation ceremonies. Jeanette returned to her parents' home in Ontonagan in the U P where she would spend a few days before leaving for Portland.

Cedric briefly visited his mother in Union Pier, the beachside community in southwestern Michigan where she now lived. He then returned to Ann Arbor where one of his professors belatedly agreed to include him on his one-year research grant sponsored by the National Endowment for the Humanities. While studying recent U. S. relations with Poland, Cedric pursued the academic job market more aggressively than he had the previous year.

He also became more introverted and reluctant to seek any type of even casual relationship. The demands of his work caused him to spend long hours gathering data and writing reports for his mentor. No longer teaching or otherwise professionally involved with the campus community, he had little or no contact with anyone female. All but a handful of his grad school friends had taken jobs elsewhere.

When he was finally sent to Warsaw to work on the next phase of his project, Cedric seriously contemplated not returning to the states. In some ways, he felt as alone in Poland as he did back in Michigan. While he was meeting several fairly high-level Polish government officials, his diplomatic skills were declining as he grew increasingly uncomfortable in social situations. Once effervescent and outgoing, he saw himself slowly but surely becoming a loner.

He now appeared far more comfortable plowing through stacks of documents than interacting with people anxious to socialize with Americans. The local counterparts on his research team were eager to please and highly respectful of Cedric's insights. He did enjoy discussing U. S.-Polish relations with fellow academics, many of whom were close to him in age. Even though three of them were bright, attractive young women, he made no effort to spend time with any of them other than in a large group.

When his one month stint was over, he reluctantly prepared to return to U of M. Had he not been in such a personal funk, he might have more openly inquired about some source of continued financial support in Poland. He concluded it was not worth the effort, especially since his current passport limited the length of his stay and he was not into renegotiation with the necessary authorities. Besides, aside from seeing more of the countryside, there was little reason for him to remain longer. It was time to formally write up his final research report, something he could do more comfortably in more familiar surroundings.

The Ann Arbor winter soon struck him as far more harsh than others in recent memory. Within weeks, Poland seemed as much in his distant past as Jeanette was. Intellectually, he had let her go but his altered personality was living testament to the fact that he could not forget her. What remained in his heart was a mixture of fondness and disdain, the latter growing more rapidly than the former. Formally trained to think logically even in the uncertain world of international diplomacy, he could find no logical explanation for Jeanette's behavior.

The job market was a difficult one. Although Cedric would one day likely produce two or more publications from his doctoral dissertation and his current research on Poland, at the moment he had nothing either in print or accepted for publication. This put him at a distinct disadvantage compared to other applicants for every position he was seeking. His interviews at such places as the University of New Hampshire and the University of Delaware, both respected institutions, did not go well.

Told by his mentor that there would be no extension on his grant support because funding had ended, Cedric had little choice but to lower his expectations and seek whatever work would pay the bills. Running out of options, he eventually began to court community colleges in the state. His old professors could not comprehend how one of their more promising graduates was unable to find employment commensurate with his abilities.

His lone offer came late in the summer from Lake Michigan College, a two-year school in Benton Harbor. Humiliated, he packed his meager belongings into his ten-year-old Nissan Sentra and rented an apartment in nearby Baroda. All of his research materials went with him but would remain packed or stored on his computer files indefinitely. Both his newly emerging disinterest in these topics and a demanding teaching load of five courses would guarantee the materials would not be looked at any time soon.

Cedric found his new students to be far less motivated than those he had taught at U of M. He had expected something like this to occur but the gap was far greater than he had initially imagined. Getting through the first semester was a grind not unlike a summer job he had undergone in a plastics factory when he was still an undergraduate. Both were equally unstimulating. It was hard to accept that just a few months earlier he was rubbing elbows with government leaders in an eastern European country while he was now trying to invigorate students, most of whom could care less if there even was a Poland.

Over the holiday break, he dreaded having to return to the classroom. He knew he had taught with little enthusiasm during the past semester and had been reminded of that by his department chair who was concerned after reading his lackluster teaching evaluations. With even less mental energy this time around, he dragged himself to his first day of January classes. As he prepared to give the same opening lecture for the fifth time late in the day, he paused to take roll one more time.

The fourteenth or fifteenth student on his list was a young lady whose first name was Jeanette. Cedric looked up from his roster to observe the student whose hand was raised. He stared at her for at least ten seconds. Although she looked nothing like the Jeanette he had known, he could not stop finding similarities in the two countenances.

As other students began to mumble and the young lady became confused as well as embarrassed, Cedric rose from his chair and walked from the classroom leaving all of his notes and other belongings behind. The following morning, he loaded some of his clothes and other personal effects into his car. He then left town and headed north.

Soon afterward, he stopped briefly and walked out onto the bridge that crossed the Kalamazoo River. As he gazed down upon the briskly moving cold waters below, Cedric tried to find some inspiration that would rekindle his scholarly interests. A couple of hours later, he again rose from his car and looked out onto Lake Michigan from a cliff a few miles off the main highway. This time, his thoughts were more intense, and more disturbing.

They included warm memories of his parents, of his college years in Nebraska, of his frequent travels abroad, and of the promise he had displayed in his graduate studies. He also recalled how much of his recent time had been wasted, how the death of his father traumatized him more now than it had ten years earlier, and how he had let down the professors he idolized. More than ever, he did not know what he would do.

He was, however, certain he would never again work at any educational institution.

As Cedric continued driving along the lake, he began to tremble and weep uncontrollably. When he eventually regained his composure, he was entering a small town whose name he had not even noticed. On its main street stood a post office with a "postal carrier wanted" sign on its front door. Still disheveled, he walked inside and began filling out an application.

Before he had finished, he returned to his car and once again began to tremble. With his hands still shaking, he tore the application into several pieces.

Momentarily composed, he started the car engine. After a few minutes, he pulled away from the post office, once again heading north.

The Pedophile Defense Fund

Felix and Carolina Armas lived with their four children in one of the poorest neighborhoods of East Los Angeles. Although they struggled to make ends meet, both worked steadily: he in a tile factory, she as a waitress. Both believed that what held their family together was their faith and their active involvement in the local Catholic Church.

Despite their limited means, the couple routinely donated ten percent of their combined income to the church. They did this not only because the Bible said to do so but also because they knew the money would be used to assist those who were even less fortunate. Both understood that every church in the Los Angeles area sent some of their funds to the headquarters of the archdiocese. For many years, this body listed the California charities along with overseas missions they were helping in selected reports to member churches.

The Armas family took pride in the admittedly small role they were playing and vowed they would always tithe a portion of their earnings. They also believed their family would be rewarded for their efforts because of promises made both in the Bible and by their local pastor.

In the summer of 2006, this view seemed to be confirmed. While rumors of layoffs persisted at the factory where Felix worked, he heard from cousins in Michigan that factories in Flint were hiring. With a promise of steady work at higher wages in the Midwest, Felix quickly moved there. After two weeks in a job that clearly was a step up, he sent for his family to join him.

It did not take long for Carolina to find work. Because a local family run restaurant was well established and did a booming business, both the hourly wage and tips were better than what she was used to in California. The children easily adapted to their new location and made many friends both in school and in the modest neighborhood where they lived.

The family frequently offered prayers of thanks for their newly found good fortune. In addition, they pledged to their pastor back in East LA that they would continue to donate money to his church.

"It's the right thing for us to do," Carolina voiced to her family. "Because we supported the church there, we were blessed with this new life here. And East LA is where all of us were born. We owe something to the congregation there. We can make small contributions to our new parish here. God will understand our loyalty to everyone back in California."

Felix and the children all nodded in approval.

"Maybe we can do some volunteer work here," Felix suggested. "Like bringing communion to members of the parish who are old and sick. Or just visiting them to cheer them up. Once we are all settled, we can talk to our new pastor about what is needed. He sure seems like a friendly and holy man. We are so blessed to be here."

His highly focused work ethic caused Felix to be noticed by his superiors at the factory. After only six months on the job, he was given a raise.

After announcing the good news to his family, he immediately stated that they would be increasing the amount of money sent back to their former church in East LA. No one disagreed.

Felix and Carolina were both high school graduates who did not have the opportunity to receive additional education. Both were highly intelligent and, despite the enormous demands of work and parenthood, made it a point to follow current events as best as they could.

They were understandably deeply troubled when increasing numbers of Catholic priests were accused of being pedophiles. At first, they refused to believe such a travesty could even be possible.

As the evidence mounted, however, they reluctantly accepted the reality of this tragic situation.

Predictably, their first response was prayer, for the victims and for repentance among the perpetrators. Initially, they tried to shield their children from the news, a strategy that proved to be futile as well as counterproductive. Other children soon were discussing specific press accounts with the young members of the Armas family. Felix and Carolina soon found themselves having open discussions with their children about matters they never imagined having to discuss with them.

Through it all, the entire episode still was something abstract and a great distance from their present home. No one in the family knew any victims and, thankfully, that was not going to change.

One day, Carolina took her three youngest children to the grocery store. As they unloaded their basket at the check out counter, inquisitive fourteen-year-old Adriana noticed a disturbing headline in the local newspaper. It announced a major sex scandal in the Catholic archdiocese of Los Angeles.

"Look at this, Mom," the teenage girl stated.

Carolina noticed but pretended not to do so. She quickly told her children to wait for her at the front of the store. When they were not looking, she grabbed a copy of the paper and motioned for the check out clerk to charge her for it as she placed it into one of her already packed bags.

That evening after all the children were asleep, Carolina retrieved the newspaper and began plowing through its top story as Felix tended to some chores in the garage.

More than ever, what she read was beyond belief. Half way through, she could read no more. When Felix entered the room, he found his wife in tears.

"What's the matter?" he asked. "Are you and the kids okay?"

As Felix sat next to her, Carolina handed him the front page.

"You've got to read this," she said. "It will make you sick."

His hands still dirty, Felix began reading. After just a few minutes, he tossed it aside in disgust.

"Dear God in Heaven," he stated sadly. "What is happening?"

The gist of the story was that the archdiocese of Los Angeles had settled *over 500 lawsuits* filed against priests charged with sexually molesting boys between the ages of 3 and 16. The amount of the settlement was *$660 million*. After initially refusing to allow the LA county district attorney to access church documents, Cardinal Roger Mahoney now offered a belated apology to victims. In addition to the boys, one woman had been abused by seven different priests beginning when she was 16 years of age. Her legal battle had lasted 23 years.

For ten minutes, neither Felix nor Carolina spoke. Both contemplated prayer but neither could muster the desire to pray at this time. And precisely what, they wondered, would they be praying for?

Felix finally broke the silence.

"Ten percent of our hard earned money over the past fifteen years has helped to pay legal expenses for pedophiles and settlements for their victims," was all he could manage to voice.

"I feel so betrayed," Carolina added before stopping abruptly.

The couple once again lapsed into silence. Felix began to pace about the room. He experienced various emotions ranging from extreme sadness to anger. The latter lingered.

"Many of the people we trusted and much of what we believed…" Carolina struggled to say. "It's all one big lie."

Felix wanted to say something to comfort her but appropriate words did not come to him. He could only admit silently that she was correct.

Eventually, they began to discuss specifics of the article.

"Cardinal Mahoney would only release correspondence with pedophile priests and records of their seeing psychiatrists when the Supreme Court required him to do so," Carolina began. "How could a man of his standing in the church shield sex offenders he knew were guilty?"

"Across the country, bishops have routinely protected priests -- I think the story said over a thousand of them -- by reassigning them to other parishes," Felix recalled with anger still in his eyes.

"Unsuspecting children in these new parishes soon became victims as well."

"And this was not only happening in Los Angeles," Carolina added. "Also in Santa Rosa. San Diego. Seattle. Boston. Dallas. Santa Fe. And who knows where else."

"Countries in Europe, too," Felix acknowledged. "Ireland. Germany. France. This plague is worldwide. What has happened to our beloved Church? We were taught in elementary school catechism classes that it was the one true religion."

"There is concern that the cover up goes as high as the Vatican itself," Carolina stated in a near whisper as if it were irreverent to even speak of such a thing. "The successor to St. Peter, the representative of God himself on earth, may have known about this? And covered it up?"

"I thought it said somewhere in the story that victims were forced to sign confidentiality agreements before receiving settlements," Felix now remembered. "That means the full extent of the crimes may never be known. Why is our church protecting the guilty and only reluctantly compensating those poor children who had to suffer for years in silence? As if any amount of money could make up for the pain they have endured. This is all a bad dream! We had heard some stories but I never believed them."

"I'm sure there are many secret settlements that never even made it into the papers," Carolina postulated. "And if all that money is going to victims, it is not going to schools, hospitals, charity work. That's what our religion is supposed to be about. Not protecting sexual predators. I think I am going to throw up."

Carolina left the room. Felix sank into his tattered twenty-year-old lounge chair. He thought of all the things he had asked his children to do without so that the money could be used for a more worthwhile cause. He thought of the vacations he had denied his family that ten percent of their income would have paid for. He even wondered about their local priest back in East LA. He was probably innocent of any of these crimes but how could Felix know for sure? Everyone in the clergy was supposedly serving God. But some were only serving their own pathetic sexual appetites.

When Carolina returned, she sat across from her husband.

"What are we going to tell the children in the morning?" she asked. "Are we going to take them to church this Sunday? Will we ever go to church again? I never thought I would even think of such a thing."

"The kids will find out even if we say nothing," Felix assured. "We have to let them know there are some very evil people who claim to be doing God's work. I thought Jimmy Swaggart and Pat Robertson were charlatans. They apparently have plenty of company in our own religion."

"How can we possibly describe to the little ones what these priests did?" Carolina voiced. "They're too young to understand what that is all about."

"We have a lot to contemplate," Felix admitted. "And I don't even know how we'll resolve this in our own minds, let alone in the minds of our still very innocent children. I never thought that as parents we'd ever have to address anything like this."

The next morning, it was off to school and work as usual. The older children heard the latest news from some of their peers. That evening, they had many questions for their parents who did the best they could to answer them.

Sunday morning was more difficult. The Armas family attended 10 o'clock mass as they always did. They all prayed that the latest awful situation would somehow be resolved justly. Carolina and Felix knew their prayers were asking for a lot. In his sermon, the priest did not address the situation in Los Angeles or in any other city.

Over the next few weeks, the family could talk about little else. All agreed they would never again contribute a single penny to an organization that might use their money to defend such repulsive criminal behavior.

Other questions were even more serious and challenged the very fiber of their beliefs.

Should they become Episcopalians? Methodists? Lutherans? All of these religions held views not terribly different from the Catholicism that had been central to the Armas family for generations. All in the family agreed their belief in God should not be shattered because of this horrendous scandal.

The following Sunday, the Armas family said the rosary at home but did not attend any religious service. They continued to pray for guidance in the future direction their faith was to take.

One week later, the inquisitive Adriana began the family prayer session with a request.

"Mom and Dad," she began. "I think we should make a decision this morning or at least very soon. What are we going to do about church? I miss going to mass. I've been reading about different religions. I think we should take a family vote to see where we go to church from now on."

"That is very thoughtful," Carolina began. "What have you learned about different religions that has apparently helped you make a decision?"

"My friend Melba is a Baha'i," she replied. "Her parents are very spiritual people. They pray together, not every day, but whenever the family has a special concern. I think that's neat."

"What do you know about Baha'is?" Felix asked respectfully but pointedly. "Before we all convert to a religion, we have to know more about it besides the fact that one of your friends and her family practice it."

"That sounds fair, Dad," Adriana answered. "I'll be glad to tell what I have found out about it. But I'm also willing to hear what everyone else in our family thinks."

"You are very mature, Adriana," her mother offered. "Has anyone else thought about this?"

Olga, the oldest at 16, said she would be anything but Catholic while Tess, the youngest at only seven meekly stated that she would like to keep on being Catholic because that was the only religion she knew. Ten-year-old Jose said he had not had time to think about it yet because he was busy playing baseball.

The parents knew they had a difficult situation on their hands. Neither had done as much homework as Adriana but both were understandably reluctant to change beliefs they still held. Studying the major tenets of different religions was something they had never expected to do. They knew that attending another religious service and seeing what the people there were like was probably a better approach. Doing so, however, was so contrary to everything they had been taught.

As time dragged on with no definitive solution in sight, Sundays became increasingly chaotic. Adriana began attending Baha'i services with her friend Melba and Melba's family. She felt comfortable there but could not persuade other members of her family to go with her.

Olga was more than willing to continue praying at home with the family but said she was not going to any church for awhile. While her parents tried to persuade her otherwise, they eventually understood the reasons for her behavior and, for the moment at least, accepted it. Tess went to the Catholic Church with one or more of her parents when they did go. Sometimes, Carolina could not make herself attend mass. Jose was the most spiritually uncommitted person in the family and belatedly convinced his parents he was staying home on Sunday mornings with Olga.

After several weeks of this lack of togetherness, only Felix and Tess attended mass together. Soon afterward, Tess stayed home on Sunday mornings.

Carolina began talking at length with women she had met about their religious beliefs. One lady had recently become a Presbyterian and spoke highly of the experience. Another was a devout Baptist while yet a third was a lifelong member of the Church of Christ. Carolina became more uncertain than ever.

She and Felix began to argue over the example they should be giving their children. He took the view that the Catholic Church would eventually purge itself of its evil element and return to its core mission. Carolina doubted this would ever happen. Meanwhile, the scandal continued to widen, thereby confirming Carolina's worst suspicions. Word even came from friends in California that a priest who had been at the parish next to theirs was now being charged with rape of a child.

The Armas family continued to pray at home but Olga and Jose, severely tarnished by the entire ordeal of the scandal, began to lose interest in religious matters. Tess looked to her parents for guidance but saw conflicting signals. Only Adriana appeared happy as a fully practicing Baha'i.

The cement that had long held the family together was now crumbling.

A few more months of indecision passed. Felix went to church alone while Carolina jumped between different congregations with the women she knew. Their marriage suffered. After a time Felix accepted the fact that his wife was no longer a Catholic. He and she found it more difficult to adjust to the fact that three of their children were moving away from religion in general.

Distracted by the family crisis, Felix began to make errors on the job. On an assembly line, this can be quite dangerous to co-workers. After several incidents, he was let go.

Unable to find work, Felix turned to alcohol. Olga dropped out of school and moved in with her 18 year old boyfriend who had dropped out three years earlier. Jose joined a gang and moved out of the house. Tess and her mother became Presbyterians but Carolina never felt entirely comfortable with all of the new beliefs. She sought something more structured but less so than the fundamentalism demanded by the Baptists.

After she and Felix divorced, he moved back to California. Three years later, Carolina was on public assistance, Jose was in prison, Olga walked the streets, and Tess was a neglected child who was sent to a foster home.

Adriana was now a college student who had become increasingly involved in the Baha'i faith. When asked by a friend why she practiced this particular religion, her response was clear and straightforward:

"Because they have no priests."

Corporate Etiquette

A week after her honeymoon in Acapulco, Daphne Sands was comfortably settled in her home in the wealthy Detroit suburb of Grosse Pointe. Still getting used to people calling her Mrs. Tyler Sands, she knew her new role would include a demanding social schedule.

Her father-in-law was a senior vice president at General Motors while her husband, barely two years with the firm, was on the fast track in a planned ascent to senior management. Both men were very well paid and lived a country club life style that was the envy of lesser peers.

Daphne hailed from more modest beginnings. While certainly not poor, her childhood in Harbor Beach on Lake Huron was simple yet happy. Her father was a surveyor, her mother a nurse. She had two older sisters who had married high school sweethearts and remained in Harbor Beach. All three girls were graduates of Michigan State.

It was there that Daphne and Tyler had met. President of his fraternity, he was a dashing man about campus who primarily rubbed elbows with other overprivileged semi-serious students. Impressive family connections made a detailed understanding of Shakespeare both unnecessary and impractical. Spring breaks were spent in places like Bermuda or Hawaii while family Christmases often were celebrated in Vail or Whistler.

While at MSU, Daphne pursued an elementary teaching certificate and took part in various volunteer efforts. She never joined a sorority and always spent school holidays back at home with her family. She loved art, music, and poetry.

Their chance meeting at a pep rally resulted in an instant attraction and subsequent whirlwind romance. To Daphne, frat parties were little different from the loud social gatherings she had already attended. Over time, she reluctantly admitted to herself that the world inhabited by Tyler and his friends, although at first foreign to her, was not without its interesting moments. She enjoyed having fun and he clearly provided her with ample opportunities to do so.

Tyler had a warm and curious side that she fed rather well. She would take him to art galleries and even an occasional poetry reading. Their mutual love of music made rock concerts, and sometimes the symphony, an enjoyable Saturday night experience.

While initially overwhelmed by the Sands family wealth, Daphne found Tyler's parents to be outgoing, knowledgeable, and generous with her. Early on she suspected they mainly thought of her as an asset in their son's career goals. Despite these reservations, she eventually convinced herself that the attention they gave her was sincere and perhaps even loving.

Tyler seemed to relate well to Daphne's family, especially her father, who admired his ambition and pleasant demeanor. The two men would sometimes play golf together and Tyler routinely let his future father-in-law win, a habit not entirely lost on the elder man. Daphne's sisters both worked in businesses owned by their husband's families, a fact that allowed Tyler to express often his support of small business ventures.

No one among Daphne's family or friends ever found a single trait in Tyler that caused them to question his integrity or his intentions. His family wealth was merely considered an added bonus.

Of course, Daphne was required to sign a pre-nuptial agreement that would leave her only a token sum in the event of divorce. Tyler assured her it was a mere formality required by GM lawyers. The legal team, he maintained, was concerned about possible squabbling over stock options and property owned jointly by the corporation and a select few of its executives. Her family encouraged Daphne to go along in order to assure her in-laws-to-be she was not a gold digger.

During the early months of their marriage, there were frequent business trips. On some of these, Daphne and other corporate wives were encouraged to participate. On others, it was "men only". The time Tyler spent away from home was fairly short in duration. During her husband's absence, Daphne would either busy herself in her worthwhile volunteer work or spend time with other left behind wives, whose company was not always that enjoyable.

Less than a year into their marriage, Tyler received a significant promotion. This meant more of three things: responsibility, travel, and income. Daphne benefitted by having seemingly unlimited access to funds for clothing, jewelry, lunch gatherings with corporate wives, and trips home to see her family.

Only the last of these was important to her. She could care less about fashionable attire that she was forced to maintain with the company she was required to keep. On each visit to Harbor Beach, she observed the enormous difference between her own shallow lifestyle and the genuineness of the small town life she had left behind.

Even the charity work she was doing in Detroit was somehow credited to the corporate family of which she was a member. At company parties, she was a major hit because of her attractive appearance, outgoing personality, and knowledge of the arts. At all such gatherings, however, she could sense the jealousy of her peers who appeared to be having less success in shining up to company brass. This made her feel very uncomfortable since mingling for success only was not part of her social repertoire.

At home one evening, Daphne felt the need to clear the air with her husband.

"Ty," she began. "Do you think the other wives resent my talking with the VPs?"

"Huh?" he replied appearing to be only moderately interested, if at all.

"What do you mean?"

"At the last party, I talked a little longer than usual with some of your Dad's fellow execs," she stated. "Not only did I notice an ugly stare or two but, since then, no one has called me to have lunch. When I left a message for Gretchen Willoughby, she never called me back."

"I can have a word with Gretchen's husband, if you like," Ty responded. "I can use my influence to get her back in line."

"I don't want you to do that," she shot back quickly and with a distinct note of dissatisfaction. "Is that what all this hobnobbing is about? You use your pull to get women to be nice to me? So I don't have any real friends, only puppets who are put in their place if they don't play the game properly?"

"Now Daph," came the almost condescending introduction to a canned speech. "You know how things work. These women think you already have an advantage over them because of my Dad. They're just trying to help their husbands get ahead and they probably saw you as preventing them from making their case to the big boys."

"I only talked to the so called 'big boys' because they initiated conversation with me," she snapped. "Most were pleasant at small talk and a couple even asked me about the art museum. It was okay. Come to think of it, that old goat Sumner Foote did seem a little flirty. He couldn't take his eyes off of my low cut dress."

"Don't let him bother you," Ty offered. "He's like that with all the young women. Just play along. Main thing is not to offend him. He's really close with the CEO. We can't botch anything now that we've gotten this far."

Now Daphne was visibly upset.

"So I'm supposed to let some perv look down my blouse so you can get promoted faster"?

"He's harmless. He just looks. I don't think he's actually ever put his hands on anyone."

"So undressing women with your eyes is fair game in this corporation?"

"C'mon Daph. It's not worth getting all upset about. The other wives all understand this is part of what you have to do. They're okay with it. It doesn't really hurt anybody and we've got a lot to gain from a little innocent flirtation."

"So you can't get promoted on your own ability plus your father's connections. I'm also supposed to shake my ass for the right people?"

"Nobody said you have to shake anything. You look fine just the way you are. Don't get so upset over nothing."

"Nothing? I can't believe what I'm hearing. I *look* fine? So I'm just this little ornament that has to show up looking pretty at the right time? Is that what all the other wives do?"

"Hey relax. This Christmas, I'll take you on a Caribbean cruise. The company's paying for about ten of us couples to go. It'll be a lot of fun."

"And that's supposed to make everything better? I don't want to go on a cruise at Christmas. I want to be with my family. And I'd be happy to spend some time with yours. But I don't want to be stuck for a week on a boat with all these other couples that I have nothing in common with. Will I be expected to wear a bikini for old Sumner Foote?"

"Now listen. It'd be an insult to turn this down. For some of us, it's a working trip but you can just enjoy yourself. Play some tennis, go swimming, great food."

"You're not hearing a word I'm saying."

Daphne stormed out of the room, walked down the hallway, and shut the bedroom door behind her. She remained speechless when the couple went to sleep later that evening.

Tyler left for work early the following morning. Still fuming over the previous evening's discussion, Daphne stayed in her pajamas all morning while reevaluating her priorities, and her life.

Of course, her husband returned home that evening with a dozen roses, bought by his secretary, and an apology. The couple agreed to talk more about what was bothering Daphne.

In the conversations that followed over the next few days, Tyler did a better job of listening and appeared at least outwardly to be more sympathetic to what his wife was feeling. Among other things, he assured her that she was more than a cog in the machine geared toward his business success.

For the moment Daphne acquiesced, sought refuge in her own interests, and reluctantly returned to the role of the good corporate wife.

Tyler began travelling more, mostly to rural Ontario where he was in charge of establishing local GM dealerships.

As December approached, plans for the Caribbean cruise were being finalized. Daphne spent Thanksgiving with her family in Harbor Beach while Tyler worked most of the weekend in Detroit.

For the next few weeks, things between them were at best awkward. Their social life consisted of lavish dinners with his business associates. They did not spend a single evening alone together until it was nearly bedtime which was already becoming less adventuresome despite the brief tenure of their marriage.

Daphne was dreading the cruise but had vowed she would go. Three days before Christmas, they flew to Miami and boarded the ship the following day.

Activities followed a steady pattern. After a group breakfast attended by all twenty in the GM crowd, the men held a business meeting that lasted through lunch. They then played tennis before taking a lengthy dip in the pool. After dressing in designer slacks and sport coats, a mid to late afternoon social gathering in the bar preceded the fancy dinner.

The women either strolled or sunbathed after breakfast before playing several rounds of bridge. They lunched together before breaking into two groups: one went swimming while the other caught a movie. The swimmers vacated the pool area long before the men arrived there. Women were invited to join their mates for cocktails but only a few did and these arrived after most of the men were already borderline intoxicated.

The food at dinner was fabulous, the conversation decidedly less so. Dancing followed dinner. A full orchestra did their best Glenn Miller imitation and was reasonably entertaining.

On Christmas eve, executive bonuses were announced and sealed envelopes indicating specific amounts were given to each couple.

Except for the last ritual, the range of activity deviated little from day to day.

Daphne grew increasingly bored with the entire routine and felt quite claustrophobic in her cabin each night while waiting for her slightly incoherent husband to return from his late night game of bridge. She especially dreaded having to dance with the other men, some of whom seemed to take near inappropriate pleasure in holding her.

On the last night before returning to port, Sumner Foote cornered Daphne for one of the last dances. While nearly slobbering in her face, he reached below her waist and began to rub her left cheek.

"No way, Mr. Foote," she said angrily as she pulled away.

"There, there, Mrs. Sands," he quickly answered with a well-rehearsed line. "Some women pull away from me at first until I guarantee them a hefty promotion for their husbands."

"You can shove your threat," Daphne stated with an appropriately harsh glare. "If Tyler gets promoted, it'll be on merit. Not on me being receptive to an old letch."

She turned abruptly and took a first step toward the stairway.

"Don't be so hasty, my dear," he said fairly loudly. "You might be a bit more cooperative after I tell you of your husband's new Canadian girlfriend."

"What are you talking about?" she asked, now more troubled than ever.

"Men get lonely on business trips," he offered. "Some of the small town dealerships are run by women. One in particular is a real dish. Ty took notice. Hey, he's only human."

Daphne hesitated and looked away before composing a response.

"Why are you telling me this?" she said lividly while struggling to keep from letting the tears flow. "How could you possibly think that, if what you say is true, I'd be more receptive to your crude advances?"

"My dear, we're all one big happy family here, more or less," Foote responded confidently. "New arrivals need to learn how the game is played. Your husband has figured it out quite nicely. Now you........."

He stopped as if it was understood where his train of thought was heading. After a brief pause, he resumed speaking.

"Now, shall we resume dancing?" he stated in a businesslike tone without even cracking a smile.

"Go to hell, you old bastard!" she replied as she headed straight for her cabin.

Even before arriving, the tears did flow big time. More than ever, it was clear she had made a major mistake in marrying into this wealthy, deceitful corporate family. She decided not to confront her husband that evening and merely pretended to be asleep when he arrived much later.

Daphne behaved as if all was well during the flight back to Detroit. Only after they arrived at their home did she bring up what was on her mind.

"You told me that old Foote guy never put his hands on a woman," she began. "Well I now know first hand you're dead wrong about that."

"What do you mean?" he asked feigning surprise.

"What he did is not that important," she replied forcefully. "I can take care of myself and I did. What he told me, however, was *very* eye opening."

"Like what?" he answered still appearing to be in the dark over what was coming.

"He basically said the young wives give into his advances if they want their husbands to get ahead," she stated while looking straight at Tyler. "He said we need to learn how the game is played here. Then he said you've learned quite well. Something about a woman who owns a dealership in a small town in Ontario? Who is she?"

"Old Foote may have bribed a woman or two in years past," Tyler admitted. "And their husbands did get promoted. He's very well connected and has more power in the company than my Dad does. I hope you turned him down gently. He plays for keeps. He actually helped my Dad get to where he's at."

"Are you saying your mother.........?" Daphne asked not believing she had the courage to even partially voice such a thing.

Ty just put his head down and looked away.

"And the Canadian woman?" Daphne persisted.

"He's way off base there," Ty responded. "I don't do things like that. You have to believe me. That's not my style."

"Then why would he say it if it wasn't true?" Daphne retaliated.

"He probably thought you'd sleep with him if you believed what he was telling you," Ty offered.

"You've been acting strange and distant lately," she continued. "If that's the kind of values your parents have, how do I know you're any different?"

Ty remained silent. He then walked out into the cold night and drove away.

On the way back to their bedroom, Daphne paused at the entrance to Ty's study. She then walked in and looked around. Sitting at the desk, she went through the drawers, examined the papers in his briefcase, and even checked his email. Buried in the two dozen or so unopened messages was one from a Desiree Morningstar that stood out like seductive silk hosiery.

Daphne read it.

"I sure did enjoy our late night meetings on the ship. There's more where that came from but you'll have to meet me in Ontario next time. Thanks for buying my cruise ticket. Maybe some day just the two of us can take one without all those other people around. I've got the hots for you! Desiree."

Instinctively, Daphne checked if any old messages from the same person could be found. If they existed, her husband had carefully deleted them.

She did print two copies of the email she had just read and left one on their bed.

When Ty came home later that evening, Daphne was not there. She spent the night in a hotel before returning the following day after Ty had left for work. After packing most of her immediate personal belongings including clothing, she began the three-hour drive to Harbor Beach.

The divorce, handled by her parent's attorney, was uncontested. The small amount of money Daphne was awarded helped her to resettle in a rented house down the street from one of her sisters.

Harbor Beach Elementary School had an opening for a fourth grade teacher. Daphne felt right at home working there for the next five years until she married a local dairy owner. The only times she ever visited Detroit were on class trips to the museums. All of her family and friends enjoyed driving their Toyotas wherever they went.

Over the next few years, the federal government bailed out GM more than once when profits vanished due to inept management. These handouts of taxpayer money assured that generous executive bonuses and cruises were uninterrupted.

The Train Show

When he was only five, Barney received his first electric train. It was an American Flyer complete with smoking steam engine, colorful boxcars, and lighted caboose. Over the next few years, he and his parents added bridges, switch tracks, and assorted buildings to his slowly but steadily growing layout. Neighborhood kids and out of town cousins would all marvel as Barney donned his engineer's cap and operated the train for their enjoyment. As is true of many boys, his interest waned when he began high school and girls entered the picture.

Some years later, he married one. Their first child offered the perfect excuse to unpack the stored boxes and reassemble the old Flyer under that year's Christmas tree. A budding adult hobby was beginning to take shape.

At first, it was something to share with both children as Barney took his son and daughter to hobby stores and to train shows. In both places, the threesome met other adult collectors and their children. When the kids outgrew trains and discovered computer games, Barney was on his own, at least among immediate family members. Now well known among local collectors and dealers, he vowed to pursue this avocation as a positive distraction from his work.

With his children now in high school, their own interest in hobbies strayed much as his had a generation earlier.

At a local hobby shop in Flint, Barney bought train magazines and occasionally responded to ads in which collectors from all over the country listed items they were selling. He sometimes visited with the store owner and other train enthusiasts but his naturally shy demeanor kept him from making close friendships among this group. There were collectors who worked together at each other's houses but Barney preferred to go it alone.

When shows were held in various cities around the state, he would spend the better part of a Saturday looking at the large stock of items that dealers were selling. He spent money sparingly but wisely so that his running layout and displays grew.

The four bedroom family house was eventually reduced to three as the fourth room became known simply as the train room. Having amateur carpenter skills, Barney built tables on which several trains could run simultaneously and shelves on which older, more delicate trains could be displayed. His ever tolerant wife sensed she was destined to become a train widow if that had not already occurred. On those rare occasions when she would complain about the amount of time he spent alone in his play room, his response would generally win her over.

"My dear Stella," he would say, "isn't this better than me hanging out in a bar or chasing women? And most of the time when I'm doing this, I'm right here in the next room."

Sometimes Stella would accompany her husband on one of his out of town day trips. After dropping him off at his show, she might do some shopping or check out local sights of interest. Then they might catch a late lunch or early dinner together before heading back home.

Most of the time, Barney would make the trip solo, especially when he wanted to check out local hobby shops after leaving the show. Stella generally preferred not taking an entire day away from home since she had her own interests close by.

For several years, Barney attended as many as eight to ten shows annually. Now in his early forties with his children away at college, the day trips were a perfect getaway that fed his increasingly strong interest in his hobby. He got to know dozens of dealers throughout the state plus several who hailed from Indiana, Ohio, and Illinois. His collection soon outgrew his hobby room so, at some shows, he even sold off some of his excess supply of railroad goods, a practice common among collectors.

One day at the show in Detroit, Barney noticed that he was arguably the youngest person there. None of the older paid guests had grandchildren with them and young adults simply were nowhere to be found. When one of the dealers was not busy, Barney approached the subject with him.

"Ralph?" he asked. "I know we are all aging but doesn't it strike you as a little odd that no young collectors are here today?"

"You haven't noticed that's increasingly the case?" he replied, surprised that his friend had yet to observe this before.

"I've seen that older dealers are more prone to collect pre-World War II tinplate trains," Barney answered, "but I always thought the people walking in the aisles represented all ages and all walks of life."

"When you go to as many shows as I do," Ralph observed, "not only in Michigan but all over the Midwest, fewer and fewer young people are around."

"Why is that?" Barney requested innocently.

"Do you have kids?" Ralph began to respond to a question with one of his own.

"Sure. I have two."

"Are they interested in the hobby?"

"Well, not any more. I took them to shows when they were little but they're in college now."

"What have they been doing for fun the past few years?"

"Well...., besides parties and dates, I guess they've been into computer games."

"Bingo!" Ralph stated emphatically. "Have you noticed how video game stores are replacing traditional hobby shops?"

"Yeah, I suppose they might be," Barney responded. "But I just assumed they coexisted, each filling different preferences."

"Let's get another view on this," Ralph suggested as he leaned over toward the dealer table next to him.

"Hey Harvey," he called out. "Tell young Barney here what happened when you set up a train set for your out of town grandchildren to play with when they visited."

"It was pretty sad," Harvey noted while scratching the top of his head. "After about five minutes, one of the five kids looked at the others and said: 'all it does is go in a circle'. Then they all turned and walked away."

"Most young adults have never been on a real train the way many of us had done when we were kids," Ralph added. "Unless they've gone to Europe. So they have no real experience to draw on."

"Guess I never thought much about that," Barney admitted.

"Some people think this hobby is genuinely dying," Harvey injected. "Who will get your trains when you move on to the next world?"

"My wife and kids, I suppose," Barney reflected, "like whatever else I might have when that time comes."

"And what will they do with them?" Ralph inquired. "Think they'll display them or run them as proudly as you do?"

"Now that you mention it, I suppose not," Barney stated with a frown followed by a strained smile.

"We've got more than twenty years on you," Harvey offered while looking at Barney and pointing to Ralph. "Whichever of us does not go first might buy some of the stuff from the other's wife. For top dollar? Not likely. And there aren't that many other buyers. Why do you think we're selling now?"

"I used to tell my wife trains were a good investment," Ralph added. "And they were, for awhile. The more recent price guides show a lot of this merchandise going down in value. Not a lot but a trend has begun."

"I've got to run," Barney said. "Thanks for your thoughts. They were sobering for sure."

On the trip home, Barney thought about other demands on his time. His stressful job. The illness his wife's sister was experiencing. The possible need to help finance graduate school for both children.

He concluded that maybe he should spend less time on hobbies and more on the serious realities of life.

For the next ten years, that's exactly what happened. His job became more demanding than ever before he finally switched to something less mentally taxing. Stella's sister recovered but her period of convalescence was lengthy and required much outside support. Son and daughter needed financial help while in graduate school before eventually marrying and establishing themselves in careers.

Over that decade, Barney claimed he could count the times he had been in his train room on the fingers of one hand. While a slight exaggeration, time for fun clearly had all but disappeared.

Sensing a new opportunity, he vowed to once again immerse himself into something he had dearly missed.

The reaquaintance was a slow process. Engines required maintenance. Parts of the layout needed to be redesigned. Dust was everywhere.

Maybe most importantly, Barney had lost contact with his fellow collectors and dealers. The local hobby shop, his source of supplies and information on timing of shows, had closed.

An internet search uncovered the date of the large annual show in Detroit, luckily just three weeks away.

Barney looked forward to attending, not so much because he needed to buy, or sell, anything specific but to again engage in "train talk" with other knowledgeable enthusiasts. When Stella sent him off, she was pleased to see a gleam in his eye that had not been there for some time.

Upon entering the civic center where the show was held, Barney initially observed things looked pretty much the same. He felt as if he had returned to a hometown or some other fondly familiar place.

Some of the items for sale looked vaguely familiar as did some of the dealers whom he did not know well. After browsing for a half hour, he addressed an elderly gentleman seated behind his table of goods.

"Hey, how you doing?" he began.

"What can I help you with today?" the old gent asked.

"There are two guys I used to buy from in years past, Ralph and Harvey. Are they still dealing in trains?"

"Ralph died about three years ago," came the reply. "And Harvey's back at the table over in the corner."

"So sorry to hear about Ralph," Barney stated sincerely. "What happened?"

"Heart attack. He was 75. Otherwise seemed to be in good health and spirits. One day he just dropped."

"How's Harvey doing?" Barney asked.

"Go see for yourself. He's had some problems but he's okay."

Barney put his head down and walked away. His first thoughts were of Ralph's combination of good cheer and realism. He then remembered the beautiful Chesapeake & Ohio passenger set Ralph had sold him and how it was still sitting atop one of his floor to ceiling display shelves. Finally, he recalled Ralph's forecast that their hobby was falling on hard times.

Two rows over, Barney ran into a dealer with whom he had often spoken years earlier. For the moment, the name escaped him but Barney noticed his specialty, restored early postwar Lionel steam engines, had not changed. What did change was the man's appearance.

Barney remembered the man as vital, energetic, and outgoing. Now, he was humped over, walked with a cane, and barely made it to his chair. His hair was fully white and his strained speech suggested he had been the victim of a stroke.

"Hi, how are you?" was all Barney could say as he walked by the man's display.

The man smiled but said nothing.

When Barney reached the corner of the large room, he could barely recognize the man seated there. With plastic tubes hanging from his nose and his feeble arm resting upon a dolly that supported two large oxygen tanks, Harvey's glazed eyes looked out as Barney approached.

Barney tried to downplay his old friend's deteriorated condition. "How's business today?" he said with a smile.

After staring for a moment to get his bearings, Harvey struggled to utter the words: "Not bad."

Clearly he did not recognize the younger man in front of him.

"I haven't been to a show in more than ten years," Barney offered hoping to spur additional conversation. "It sure was too bad about Ralph."

"Yeah," Harvey mumbled. "Some of these bridges and cabooses were his. He was a good friend for many years. I miss him."

Barney noticed that getting through those few words seemed to have worn out the man who spoke them. He occasionally rubbed his chest and looked away as if to regain his breath and gather his thoughts. If someone had wanted to steal something from his table, the old man probably would not have noticed.

Although he wanted to extend their brief conversation, Barney realized his efforts were futile. He looked for a few minutes at the items for sale hoping to find something to buy but there was nothing there that he needed.

"You take care, Harvey," was all he could say as he began to leave.

Harvey merely nodded and waved the arm not resting upon his breathing aids.

Among the customers, there were fewer young adults and children than Barney remembered at the last show he attended a decade or so earlier. As he continued to mingle in the crowd, he realized he was by far the youngest person in the room.

As he neared the exit, Barney walked up to the table where fliers announcing future shows were exhibited. None were there. The table contained only a few ads left by individual dealers.

"No announcements for other shows elsewhere in Michigan or northwestern Ohio?" he asked the man still selling admission tickets to this show.

"None have been sent to us," the man replied with a somber look. "This show may not even survive next year," he added.

The drive home this time seemed longer than usual. When he arrived, Stella smiled and walked toward him.

"How was the show?" she asked.

"Very, very sad," he replied.

He then walked into his hobby room and stared at his magnificent collection. An hour later, the doorbell rang. When Barney answered the door, he noticed it was a neighbor accompanied by a small child.

"Hi Barney", the elderly man said. "This is my great grandson, Axel. I told him about your hobby. Is there any chance you can show him your train room?"

"Sure thing", Barney replied without hesitation. "Well hello there, Axel. And how old are you?"

"I'm seven," the boy replied confidently and alertly.

"Do you like trains?" Barney continued.

This time the boy thought for a minute before finally uttering, with a confused look on his face, just three words.

"I don't know."

On Trial

For the past twenty years, Autry Clevenger and his youthful wife Edna had cultivated a small circle of friends. As the group experienced various crises while passing through different stages of life, they had become increasingly close. Whether it was a teenage daughter on drugs or an auto accident that required weeks of rehab, support emerged instantly and lovingly.

Autry was a research botanist at a nearby state park where his responsibilities included developing new methods of caring for some of the oldest trees and assorted plant life in the area. Edna had worked as a telephone operator until that occupation had become technologically obsolete. With their three children now grown, she gladly embarked on a life of semi-retirement while pursuing various avocations like volunteering at the local library.

Kent McKeon and his wife Clarice were both retired military and now managed a small apartment complex. Their virtues included a strong work ethic, an unquestioning patriotism, and consistent success in playing the stock market. Financial security enabled them to travel extensively whenever they could persuade one of their two grown, but less than ambitious, sons to look after the tenants under their charge. Kent and Clarice treated the Clevengers much like younger siblings and were occasionally prone to offer sincere but pointed advice when it was neither expected nor desired.

Milt and Delia Bishop were the local florists whose business had flourished for more than two decades. Despite their religious zealotry, they got along well with other members of the immediate group, and of the community at large, all of whom were less devout.

Like the McKeons, the Bishops were more conservative politically than the Clevengers but these and other differences never impinged on their friendship. Their mutual interest in the outdoors and in things that grow kept the Bishops and Clevengers on the same page more than whatever each thought about the actions of a president or governor.

Michaela Carmichael was the youngest member of the group. Recently divorced from an abusive husband, she reentered the labor force as a retail clerk and provided as well as she could for her ten-year-old daughter. Meticulous to a flaw in all she did, Michaela assured all she knew that she had little interest in pursuing male companionship. Instead, she embraced single parenthood and worked long hours, especially since her ex had moved out of state and was not always prompt in child support payments.

At times, the group appeared particularly occupied with, and committed to caring for, their most unusual member. Colette Cantrelle had most recently worked as a beautician after dabbling in various occupations earlier in life. Her three failed marriages and more numerous affairs had left her with little more than a lengthy collection of memories, some more pleasant than others. Now sixty-two, she chose to take early retirement because of her distaste for the work situation in which she found herself. This included an overly demanding boss and a host of customers whose every whim she no longer felt compelled to satisfy.

Collette carried her age well. Like Michaela, she had grown suspicious of most men. Unlike her younger friend, she had already gone through most eligible males in the county. Others in the group felt compassion and some sorrow for Collette who was probably confronting an element of loneliness for the first time in her previously active life.

It was quite common for this group of eight to gather for an evening of dinner and chatter. All shared much detail about every aspect of their lives. Children, work, past friendships, and recent experiences all were discussed at length. Wine flowed freely at these get-togethers, a fact that sometimes loosened tongues a bit although no one consistently drank to excess.

Occasionally, Collette became more reflective than the others after a second glass of whatever was offered. At times like this, the others could sense her inner hurts. She always seemed genuinely interested in what everyone had to say about their children despite the fact that she had none of her own. Over the past few months, however, she had become increasingly nostalgic and borderline fatalistic over what she perceived as rapidly approaching old age.

"I really need a vacation," Collette lamented one July evening. "I just don't have the money to do it."

"Could you visit your sister up in the Soo?" Clarice offered.

"I've probably worn out my welcome there," Collette responded. "Besides, her kids get on my nerves. I'm getting too old to deal with rowdy teenagers. I'd like to go someplace where there's peace and quiet instead of chaos."

"Would you want to spend a night or two renting a cabin on the lake?" Edna suggested. "Some of the places between Alpena and Tawas City aren't that expensive. They're not luxurious but they're clean. And it is quiet. Autry and I stayed there a few years back. It's a nice getaway."

"I don't know," Colette answered, expressing a recurring doubt that was becoming increasingly evident no matter what the conversation was about. "It's not like I'm under a lot of stress any more. Having all this extra time on my hands is taking some getting used to."

"We always need volunteers over at church," Delia injected. "And we do a lot of worthwhile stuff: helping at the hospital, bringing meals to those too old to get out, going camping with kids. We not only do for others but it's a lot of fun for us."

"Yeah, I know," Colette admitted. "I already run errands for an elderly lady down the street from me. I don't mind helping out. But I'm not anxious to commit to anything else just yet. Maybe later, in the winter."

"Ever think of taking up a new hobby?" Kent asked. "Painting? Writing poetry? Gardening? Sewing?"

"None of that appeals to me," Collette stated with an obvious look of disinterest. "I take long walks, drink a lot of coffee, do some baking. Once in awhile, I'll read a good romance novel. Living vicariously, you know."

"What have you been doing in your free time, Michaela?" Edna asked, trying to steer talk away from the moody Collette.

"Free time? What's that?" Michaela retorted quickly.

Collette was not going to let the group off that easily.

"Maybe I should take a course at the community college," she interrupted. "There might be some older men teaching there. Or, what the heck? Maybe even some younger men."

"People usually take a course so they can learn something," Edna stated with just a slight tone of sarcasm. "Like a second language, cooking, history, art."

Edna stopped abruptly, recognizing she was getting nowhere with her appeal to logic. She had no intention of making Collette feel badly. There were times when Edna and the others just wanted to shake Collette mercilessly until some sense entered her mostly open but not always absorptive mind.

After a few moments of silence, Collette launched into a lengthy tirade about how well off all the others were while life had dealt her a less than benevolent hand. This was not the first time such an outburst had occurred. As usual, the group tried to be sympathetic and supportive listeners. Even their seemingly tireless patience, however, had its limits.

Tears flowed from Collette's weary eyes as she began to leave. Such waterworks were becoming increasingly common especially after a second or third glass of wine.

"Autry," Edna called out. "Maybe you should give Collette a ride home?"

"Of course," he responded.

"Thanks, everybody," Collette voiced in a near whisper. "Sorry I lost it. I'll try to be more fun next time."

Autry waved to everyone as he looked through the beautifully designed and welcoming glass frame at the top of the front door.

Mentally exhausted, the remaining members of the group collapsed into the sofa and chairs.

"What are we going to do about her?" Michaela began. "Should I try to get her on part time at the store where I work? She has the time and obviously needs some money. I'd be a little worried, however, that she might jeopardize my current good standing there. I need the job more than she does."

"Maybe I could go stay with her a couple of nights at one of those cabins on Lake Huron," Edna offered. "But, in all honesty, I'd rather spend a couple of nights away with my husband. It'd be a lot more fun."

"She obviously could use a man," Delia stated. "But our past efforts at setting her up have not been all that successful. The last time I mentioned her to one of the nice single men at church, he politely walked away. He has avoided Milt and me ever since."

"She needs to look out more for herself," the rugged individualist Kent suggested. "Sure, she's our friend but we can't be trying to meet her every need when we have our own lives to lead. She has single handedly turned this otherwise sane group into a soap opera. I miss the conversations we used to have about......everything else besides Collette."

Autry reentered the front door and hung his jacket on the hall tree.

"How did it go?" Michaela asked.

"She didn't say much," he answered, "other than repeating herself a lot and apologizing for ruining our evening. I told her not to worry and get a good night's sleep."

Within a few minutes, the others thanked their hosts and bid farewell.

"Next time, dinner will be at our place," Delia assured. "I've got a new pork roast recipe I'd like to try out on you guys."

"Sounds great," Clarice said with a smile. "We'll be there."

Two weeks later, the same gang of eight assembled at the home of the Bishops. Half way through dinner, Autry received a call on his cell phone. A disappointed look emerged from his face as he hung up.

"What's the matter, Honey?" Edna inquired.

"Some vandals destroyed one of the large flower beds at the entrance to the park," he replied. "The police are there with two of the park rangers. They need me to come right now."

After kissing the top of Edna's head, he apologized to everyone and headed out the door.

"He works so hard," his wife lamented. "People don't realize how much extra work comes up besides just researching the latest methods of caring for bushes and ivy. It's always something."

Dinner conversation soon returned to normal. After desert was served, Collette seized the moment.

"I'm not sure how to say this," she began. "But something is on my mind that I need to share with all of you."

"What is it?" Delia stated dutifully, assuming the role of the dedicated hostess.

"I've really felt uncomfortable around all of you lately," she mumbled softly.

"What's the matter?" Clarice asked. "Have some of Kent's dumb jokes been offensive?"

"It's not Kent," Collette replied. "It's actually been Autry."

"What's my husband done?" Edna questioned with only moderate surprise. "Has he run on at the mouth about oak wilt decline?"

"It's more serious than that," Collette stated somberly. "He's been staring at me when none of you notice. It's almost like he is desiring me. I can see it in his eyes. Women can sense these things, you know. I'm sorry but I know what I see."

As Collette bowed her head, a prolonged silence descended upon the room. Everyone glanced at Edna, sensing that the next spoken words should probably come from her.

"C'mon, Collette," she finally offered. "Do you realize what you're saying? The only thing Autry looks at with desire is roses.

Might you be misinterpreting his natural look of concern that we all have for you?"

"Oh no," Collette responded. "It's been going on for some time. It was especially evident when he drove me home from your house. He couldn't take his eyes off of me. I was worried he was going to hit another car."

The others now joined in.

"Did he make any kind of move on you?" Michaela asked.

"Well….no," came the reply. "But we talked about a lot of personal stuff."

"Like what," Edna inquired curiously.

"You know, how nice I looked. My hair and my smile. That kind of thing."

Edna instantly deduced none of this had happened. Her husband's mind was too scientific to notice such things. More importantly, she knew he did not have a wandering eye. He had proven that over and over again during the past thirty years.

"I don't believe you," Edna finally pronounced bluntly. "You're having another one of your fantasies. Only this time, you are way off base."

"I'm sorry to have to tell you this, Edna," she replied. "I haven't wanted to hurt you. But I'm not mistaken. The man has lust in his eyes. I've had experience in recognizing that look. And he's definitely got it."

Edna looked away as the others focused on her. After a few moments and with tears dripping down her cheeks, Collette rose to leave. This time, no one offered to give her a ride.

After the front door had closed, Edna stood up and began to speak.

"I can't believe it," she voiced emphatically. "That woman has finally lost it. I've put up with a lot of her whining crap for a long time. This time she's gone way too far."

Expecting immediate support from everyone, Edna was more than a little surprised at the silence that followed her comments. At some point, she began to look directly into the faces of her friends as each looked away. She was uncertain how to read their unspoken emotions.

"Is anyone going to say anything?" she finally blurted out.

"I know this was a shock to you," Clarice finally stated. "Collette is obviously very hurt about something. Maybe we should give her a chance to fully speak her peace."

Delia was the next to break her silence.

"Women sometimes do misread a man's look," she observed. "But maybe she sees something none of us do. I don't think we should totally dismiss what she's saying until we hear her out. She was clearly upset tonight and left in a hurry before offering any details. Maybe we should meet with her privately. Maybe even without you being present, Edna."

"I can't believe what I'm hearing," Edna said, now raising her voice. "I feel like all of you are ganging up on Autry. And he's not even here to defend himself. In fact, he's totally unaware of any of this."

"I hope that's the case," Kent suggested unconvincingly. "The girls here just want to give Collette a chance to state her case. Clarice and I have had to deal with plenty of lawyers in our business affairs, especially in handling employees. Every charge needs to be investigated thoroughly before any definitive conclusions can be drawn."

"Lawyers? Definitive conclusions? Employees?" Edna yelled. "Autry is *not* one of your employees. I thought he was your friend. What is the matter with you people? Collette is prone to some pretty irrational behavior. Her life has been one high-drama near-disaster after another. How can you take anything she says with an ounce of credibility?"

"Why would she make anything like this up?" Milt injected. "She may be mistaken but she deserves to be heard. God will see to it that justice is achieved. I think the ladies should talk to her and I would be more than willing to join them. Edna, we need to have compassion and consider Collette's feelings. She's been going through a lot."

"What about Autry's feelings?" Edna snapped. "He's working while all of you are sitting here honoring Collette's accusations with no proof whatsoever. He has never done anything to cause me to doubt him. Michaela? Where do you stand on all of this?"

Michaela began cautiously.

"I have no reason to accuse Autry of anything. But men can be bastards. I never doubted my husband at first. Then I learned he was playing around and making a fool out of me. I'll be glad to meet with Collette and the others."

"Well, you do just that," Edna snapped a second time. "I have nothing to say to her. If all of you think you are qualified private investigators, be my guest. Frankly, I'm totally disappointed and just a little disgusted with all of you."

One by one, people began to leave. Edna was the first to head for the door. When Clarice offered her a ride, she said she would rather walk.

A half hour after she arrived home, an exhausted Autry entered and found his wife sitting in a dark living room. He could instantly tell something was amiss.

"What's the matter, Babe?" he inquired.

"Collette thinks you have the hots for her," she replied.

"What?" he answered indignantly. "How did she arrive at that conclusion?"

"She says you look at her with lust in your eyes or something like that."

"When did I supposedly do that?"

"She claims you've been doing it for a long time. And that's not all. She said you told her she looked pretty when you drove her home and that her hair was nice."

"Not much was said by me during that short drive. But I know I didn't say that. She did all the talking and it was more of the same self-pity."

"I know you didn't either. But she assured everyone you did."

"You mean she said all this in front of our friends?"

"She did. And their reaction was more upsetting than anything Collette alleged. The others are taking her remarks seriously. They want to talk to her in detail about the whole matter."

"Did anyone say they'd like to talk to me?"

"That's what really bothers me. They're all behaving like you have no say in this whole matter. Even those right wing McKeons are sounding worse than the most liberal bleeding heart defense attorney around. I don't know what's gotten into everyone. It's almost like you are being put on trial."

"First and most importantly, I've never made eyes at Collette or anyone else since I met you. I hope you know that. Secondly, although I have no experience in such matters, if I were ever going to flirt with someone, do you know who is the last person on earth I would pick?"

"I hear you. And I'm not worried. It's almost like they're all playing some kind of sick joke on us. But they're acting way too serious for that to be the case. I don't really care to see any of them any time soon."

"So what happens now?"

"The others are going to meet with Collette. I told them I wanted no part of that. They apparently want to play police detective or psychologist and see what they come up with."

"Did anyone act like they cared what I might have to say about this?"

"No."

Two weeks passed. Neither Autry nor Edna saw anyone from their supposedly close knit group during that time.

One Wednesday morning after Autry had left for work, the doorbell rang. When Edna answered, she found Clarice, Delia, and Michaela standing there, all with serious looks on their faces. Standing behind them was Milt.

"May we come in, Edna?" Clarice asked.

Without saying a word, Edna held out her hand in a welcoming gesture and pointed to the living room. When all were seated, Edna stated in as friendly a manner as she could: "So, what's up?"

"We have all met three or four times with Collette," Clarice began. "Kent was there each time, too. Edna, we find everything she said to be quite convincing. She feels betrayed by the friendship and trust she has shown to Autry. He has really made her feel uncomfortable. She is not sure she wants to remain part of our group as long as Autry is present. She is very shaken by this whole thing."

"Any more specifics?" Edna asked calmly.

"No," Delia jumped in. "Just that he manages to do this in front of all of us when none of us is looking."

"Doesn't that strike you as just a bit unlikely?" Edna observed. "Has she claimed that Autry has ever seen her privately?"

"No," Milt replied. "Only when he drove her home that night. But she says he was way over the top on that occasion."

"Have any of you spoken to Autry about any of this and gotten his take on it?" Edna stated firmly.

"Well...no," Michaela responded with some hesitation. "But he would probably just deny the whole thing. What would you expect him to say?"

"The truth," said Edna. "My husband has never lied to me and I'm certain he's not lying about this. You people are pitiful! Do you have anything else to say?"

"Just that we are sorry to have to tell you all this," Delia answered. "We......."

"All what?" Edna interrupted. "You have told me nothing that you can substantiate. Who appointed you to this lynch mob? I don't know what Collette hopes to prove. She is the one who is way 'over the top'. And all of you are right there with her. Get out of my house!"

"May God bless you during this difficult time," Delia recited in a manner that attempted to be comforting but came off as condescending.

"Go to hell! All of you!" Edna replied.

Autry and Edna took a weeklong vacation in the U P to get their minds off of what had happened.

When they returned, there was a note in their mailbox. It read simply: "We all need to see you. Please call any of us."

After sharing the note with Autry, Edna crumbled it angrily and tossed it into the trash.

The following Saturday morning, the doorbell rang at 10 a. m. When Edna answered, all six members of the former gang of eight were there.

"May we come in?" Clarice stated, once again taking charge. "We have all made a terrible mistake."

"State your business right here," Edna replied forcefully. "Not a single one of you is welcome in our house."

She then turned to look inside.

"Autry," she called.

When he arrived, he stepped outside and closed the door behind him. He said nothing. It was Clarice who spoke first.

"Collette has something to say to both of you," she said.

Collette then stepped forward. After a brief pause, she spoke softly.

"I can't tell you how sorry I am," she said. "I made the whole thing up. Autry never did anything I said he did."

She stopped abruptly. Milt then added the following.

"We were wrong to accuse you of something you did not do," he said while looking directly at Autry. "May God forgive us all for our lack of trust in our friendship."

"Why, Collette?" Edna asked with a puzzled look on her face.

"I wanted to get back at you," Collette replied. "You have everything I don't. A loving husband, financial security, the respect of people all over town. I have none of those things and I just got tired of hearing from everyone how great you both are."

Autry finally spoke.

"Edna and I never want to see any of you again," was all he said.

Before anyone else could say a word, he and Edna walked into the house, closed the door, and pulled down the window shade that covered the small glass opening at the top.

His Name Was Dad

"I don't think I wanna do it. It'll be way too much extra work. I'm still getting used to the new school. Making friends. Harder classes. This would be on top of all the homework."

"I just feel it would be good for you. You'll gain a lot of confidence from the experience. Whatever you do some day, being able to speak in front of an audience can't help but make a difference."

Dylan Andrews had just told his father about the announcement in his freshman homeroom class that the local Optimist Club would be sponsoring a speech contest. Although most contestants would be sophomores, anyone who was not yet sixteen was eligible to enter.

Having been doubly promoted from fifth to seventh grade, Dylan was barely thirteen and was understandably often intimidated by students older than he was. At this point, that included everyone in the school.

"Dad, please don't make me do this," the young frosh pleaded. "I'm not ready for an extra project like this. How about if I wait until next year?"

"Imagine how much better you can do a year from now if you learn how the whole thing works this year," his father replied. "I'm not pressuring you to win. Just do the best you can and learn from the other boys. Some of them may do some things better than you. They'll be older. Others may make mistakes that you can avoid when it's your turn to speak."

"What if I forget my speech and totally embarrass myself? And you?" Dylan continued. "We have to memorize the whole thing.

No notes or anything. Just picture me walking away red faced and looking like a complete idiot."

"You have plenty of time to practice so that won't happen. One of your teachers will be your coach. He'll help you and give you some pointers."

"Yeah, Mrs. Wiefen said she would work with whoever is chosen to be in the contest. I'm not sure what I think of her. She seems a little tough and demanding. She'll probably push me hard. If I do a lousy job, she might even give me a bad grade in English class."

"She won't do that as long as you do all your work for that class. Sometimes we have to give a little extra effort for something worthwhile. This sounds like a real opportunity. I don't want to force you to do this or anything else. I want you to realize that this is a chance you shouldn't pass up. You have to want to do it yourself. I'm only encouraging you."

"Ohhh, don't put the burden of the decision on me," Dylan whined. "If I don't do it, you'll probably just remind me that it would have helped me in some class later on when I do have to make a speech."

"Now you're starting to think like a young man concerned about his future," his father said with a smile. "I've always wanted you to think that way. How about giving this a try?"

With a reluctant look on his face, Dylan said nothing. He just rose from his chair believing he had been outsmarted once again.

Ever since his mother had died five years ago, Dylan relied extensively, and at times exclusively, on his father's advice. While he did not always agree with what his father had to say, he knew the man had the best interests of his son in mind. His Dad always listened attentively and dispatched his best thoughts lovingly. He was never authoritarian or angry. That mattered a great deal to Dylan.

The next day he told Mrs. Wiefen he would be entering the speech contest.

Wesleyan Academy was the small private school in Bison Shores, a town of just over 30,000. The public high school was known for its superior athletic teams and greater percentage of students who did not graduate. Its mere size also meant that a few outstanding young men would seek to participate in the contest. Women were not prohibited from entering but Optimist Clubs during the 1950s were largely male organizations and traditional gender roles were still followed in most secondary schools.

Preliminary screening was necessary to establish who would be the three students to represent each school. Because he felt so uncomfortable standing before his own classmates, Dylan barely made the cut. Two sophomores with fairly smooth speaking skills were easy choices. In fact, had the school principal not decreed that one of the school's representatives had to be from the freshman class, Dylan would have gotten his wish to stay home on the night of the event.

Instead, he began writing his speech and practicing its delivery in front of the bathroom mirror. It *was* a great deal of additional work but, thanks largely to the encouragement he received at home, he persevered. Mrs. Wiefen corrected some of his grammar and suggested rewriting a sentence here and there.

Dylan's father worked for a small manufacturing company. Because he was unable to continue his own education beyond high school, he wanted more than anything else for his son to have that opportunity. Yet, he also knew not to put unnecessary pressure on Dylan who needed to have fun and enjoy friends, sports, and the outdoors while growing up. Clearly, his only child was the most important person in his life.

When the night of the contest arrived, father and son dressed in sport coats with neckties and rode to the Spaulding Hotel where dinner preceded the six presentations. Before going inside, his Dad reminded Dylan to just relax and do the best he could.

"Whatever happens, I'll be very proud of you," the man assured.

Dylan was surprised to hear words of support from the two older boys from his school. Before this evening, they had barely spoken to him. The three from Wesleyan also were introduced to the boys from Bison Shores High but little was said after handshakes occurred. The contestants drew numbers to determine the speaking order. Dylan was number 4.

It was nerve wracking sitting through three speeches while trying to remember the various parts of his own. One of the public school boys was pretty good. Another lost his train of thought half way through and had to sit down without finishing.

Dylan remembered that was his worst fear. He also recalled what his father had told him. He learned from all three of the speakers who preceded him. It was sort of like a "what to do" and "what not to do" set of lessons. It was now his turn.

As he stood in front of the fifty or so people in attendance, a surge of fear pierced his body. His first thought was to sit back down. He briefly glanced at Mrs. Wiefen whose stone-faced expression did not help at all. She even looked away, presumably so as not to distract him, but Dylan took this action as a concern on her part that he might disgrace his school.

Then he looked over at his Dad who only smiled, winked, and nodded his head. There was nothing but warmth and love in that brief meeting of their eyes.

Dylan decided to just let it fly. He remembered all the hard work he had put into this moment and decided it was not going to be for naught. He spoke with confidence and used hand gestures to provide emphasis when appropriate. He quickly felt that his audience was more of an ally than an adversary, even though he knew only a few who were present. The anonymity of the group actually became a positive factor since he knew he would never see most of the adults again.

At one point, he even forgot his next line but, without hesitating, he merely skipped over it. No one appeared to notice.

The applause was polite, as it had been for the previous three speakers. When Dylan sat down, he felt a huge sigh of relief. He looked over at his Dad who was aglow with pride.

Although he politely watched, Dylan paid little attention to the last two speeches. He instead recalled nearly every line he had just recited and concluded he did not do too badly. After much reflection and reevaluation, he decided to forget about the entire ordeal. The most important thing was that it was over.

After everyone applauded the final speaker, the four judges adjourned to discuss their verdict. Everyone now spoke quietly as a slight air of apprehension engulfed the room. After twenty minutes, all the contestants appeared outwardly calm although all but the boy who forgot his speech were becoming anxious to learn the results.

Finally, the judges returned. One of them, the president of the local Optimist Club, walked directly to the podium and adjusted the microphone. He briefly went through an expected ritual of commending all six speakers on their efforts and announced that three trophies would be given.

"The third place winner," he began, "is speaker number six: Gordon Marshall of Bison Shores High School."

The young man accepted his award and waved to the crowd before returning to his seat.

"The second place winner," the club president continued, "is speaker number one: Casper Finley of Wesleyan Academy."

Cas followed the same routine as the third place winner and, slightly embarrassed at the attention, quickly sat down.

At this moment, Dylan was more nervous than at any time during the evening. He thought his speech might have been good enough for third place but now realized he probably would come home empty handed. He quickly recalled the loving words from his father who had simply told him to do his best and not worry about anything else. He now knew his father would congratulate him on his effort regardless of the outcome. Dylan told himself that was all that mattered.

As he looked toward the podium, Dylan saw the club president reach for the last trophy, which was slightly larger than the first two.

"The first place winner of the 1959 Optimist Club Speech Contest," the president announced, "is speaker number four: Dylan Andrews of Wesleyan Academy."

Everyone in the room rose to their feet as Dylan momentarily remained seated. It took him two or three seconds to realize it was his name that had been called. Belatedly, he began the short walk to accept his award. The dozen or so steps seemed to take a very long time, not because he was purposely savoring the moment but because he could not believe this was happening.

"Congratulations, Dylan," the president stated while offering a friendly smile, a firm handshake, and the trophy itself.

"Thank you," was all Dylan, now in a mild state of shock, could say.

Before he had a chance to walk away, the president asked: "Could you maybe say a few words to everyone? In the ten year history of this contest, you are the youngest person ever to win it."

All eyes in the audience were once again fixated on the young speaker.

Dylan was unsure how to begin. His speech had been well rehearsed. He never imagined having to stand before everyone a second time to say something for which he was totally unprepared. After hesitating a moment to compose himself, the words came to him.

"I'd like to thank the Bison Shores Optimist Club for this opportunity and Mrs. Wiefen, my English teacher, for her help at school. But most of all, I want to thank my father for encouraging me to enter this contest when I didn't think I could do it. Thanks, Dad. This trophy is for you."

The other five contestants all offered congratulations as did a number of people Dylan had never met. Amidst all the confusion, he felt a bit overwhelmed at his momentary celebrity. The hug he received from his proud father as everyone looked on was the most rewarding moment of all.

"If your Mother could have seen you tonight," his Dad stated with a tear in his eye, "this would've been the happiest day of her life."

His father then paused to reflect upon the influence his late wife had had on their son. She loved to read novels as well as poetry and had chosen to name their son after her favorite author, Dylan Thomas. She had instilled in the young boy, even before he began

school, a love of learning that his father now hoped he c[...]
tinue to nourish. He then thought to himself how it was [...]
ficult and lonely being a single parent. Neither of those tribu[...]
mattered in the least this evening. At school the following d[...]
announcement of the contest winner was made over the pu[...]
address system. Many of his classmates and some older students [...]
did not even know patted Dylan on the back as he walked fron[...]
class to class. Others greeted him with either a "way to go!" or "hey,
nice going, man!" salutation.

His trophy rested atop the living room bookcase in his home.

Because of Dylan's tender age, he was eligible to enter the same
contest during his sophomore and junior years. A new speech was
required each time and the other contestants varied. Thanks to his
father's continuing support plus his own recently acquired self-
confidence, Dylan soon had two more first place trophies to add to
the living room bookcase.

Now sixteen and a senior, Dylan ran for class president and won
easily because he was likeable and eloquent when campaigning. He
was also able to participate in the local Rotary Club speech contest.
An experienced and polished speaking style again impressed an
entirely new team of judges. His father carefully noted how much
better and more relaxed his son's oratory had become in little more
than three years. First place awards in four consecutive annual
contests instilled much self-assurance in Dylan along with a lasting
respect for the wisdom of his father. The awards did not hurt his
college admissions applications either.

Years later as a young college professor, Dylan received his first
of five teaching awards in his lifelong career. Although his father
lived only to see this first plaque on his son's wall, Dylan never
forgot that his professional success was largely because of his being
gently encouraged to enter that first speech contest.

He often lamented that he never repaid the man who had set
the bar for outstanding fatherhood at such a high level. He did keep
those standards in mind, however, every time he offered support for
his own daughter and son.

233

uld con-
oth dif-
ations
y, an
blic
he

CPSIA information can be obtained at www.ICGtesting.com
Printed in the USA
LVOW082217191212

312347LV00001B/92/P